About the Author

LILY PRIOR is the author of six novels. She
lives in Oxford with her husband, son, and pug.

La Cucina

Seconda

Rosa's Recipes for Birth, Death, and
Eruptions of the Volcano

By Lily Prior

For my father, Mike

PROLOGUE

In spite of my protests, he pored on more and more of the precious olive oil, and smoothed it over me with the gestures of a pianist. He began massaging me with his whole body; the oil grew warm with the friction of his flesh against mine, and began to release its aroma of newly mown grass and wild flowers, sunshine and summer rain. The only sounds were the slapping of flesh on flesh, his breathing, heavy with exertion, and my groans of release, punctuated occasionally by the sound of a confused cock crowing, or the distant barking of a dog.

Menu

Antipasti

Appetizers

CHAPTER ONE

The figure of the man is standing at the gate. Leaning on it with his forearms, waiting for me. I feel his eyes on me. They're blue and sparkling as ever.

'Have I come to the right place, signorina?' he asks in an English accent, his rakish smile lighting up his face and my world.

'You have,' I answer, and my voice sounds from somewhere strangely far off.

He came back.

He had really come back to me and I wasn't dreaming it.

I threw myself into his arms with such force I nearly knocked him over. Tears streamed from my eyes so thick and fast he was a salty blur, and I buried my face in the soft warmth of his neck, yelping, gulping. The scent of him – the delicious scent I had so often tried to conjure up in my mind to console me through those long, empty nights – was all around me. It made me lurch, deep down, in that part of me that had lain dormant since he went away. His arms were around me, holding me tight, and I let myself merge into him. I let go of the pain of losing him, of missing him, of aching for him. I let go of everything that had divided us over those four wasted years, and without it I felt light, new–formed, weak.

'I thought you were dead', I blubbed into his neck, holding him in a wrestler's grip.

'I very nearly was', he said, 'God, I've missed you woman'.

I licked the place on his neck where my face was buried. To taste him. To make him real to me. Not a stranger.

We started kissing. Devouring one another with all the force of the passion trapped inside, destroying our separation, putting it behind us, making it again what it once was between us. We were together again. That was all that mattered now.

So many times I had tried to imagine this moment of seeing him again. And our coming together was a curious mixture of the mundane and the magical. He was a real person again, not some pale, imaginary being, but he was also a god; the one person on earth who was the personification of my every desire. How could he be all of this to me? I don't know, yet he was.

From far away came the sound of giggling and chattering, braying and barking. Rosario had loaded the triplets onto his mule, and was leading them through the gate, followed by the dogs.

'We'll be getting along', he said.

The baby Rosas were hiding their eyes behind their tiny fingers, peeping out through the gaps at the stranger who was cuddling in the yard with their aunt.

I noticed Inglese's face was smeared with something sticky. I wondered what it was, then realized it was the cheesy rice gloop from the *arancine* I had just been making with the girls; it must have rubbed off me onto him. Already that seemed so long ago, that normal life, that life before he came back.

Did he carry me up the steps into *la cucina*, or did I carry him? I can't quite remember how it happened. But we were there. And the feeling that I was bringing him home started me off crying again.

'It's just as you described', he said, looking around, stroking the sheen on the table with his fingertips, 'I feel as though I've been here before'.

I refused to feel shy about what would happen next. I pushed him backwards, gently, but firmly, onto the table among the snow of sprinkled flour, parmesan gratings, and zingy orange zest. I hitched up my skirt and leapt on top of him which was good going for a woman my size and age.

The legs of the table groaned in a human way, but held. I wasn't worried about it collapsing. The table that had always been at the center of the lives of the Fiores would withstand more than this.

'All right, I surrender!' he cried, throwing his hands up in the air and laughing, 'Do whatever you want to me'.

Our kisses melted me. I felt them in every part of my body. Nothing existed just then except the two of us on that kitchen table that had become the whole world. His lips, his tongue, plucked a string that resonated deep down in my loins. How I needed to have him inside me. I couldn't wait, really I couldn't. I wanted to roar, scream, shout, anything to let out the feeling of desperation and urgency shut up inside me.

Releasing his face which I had been holding between my hands so tight I left marks on it, I sought his shirt buttons. But I couldn't fiddle with them. That was out of the question. I just had to rip the shirt open, firing the buttons off like bullets, so they plinged onto the stone floor and rattled away into nooks where they wouldn't be found until many years had passed. I tore his shirt down his arms and off his chest. There was a scar, jagged and red, that hadn't been there before, but now wasn't the time to notice it, ask about it.

Beneath my fingers his flesh was warm, soft, hairy, lovely. I covered him with kisses, nibbles, little bites, not hard.

He nearly garroted me trying to get my apron off. He ripped open my dress. I wished I had on my better underwear, but how was I to know?

I had to clamber off to tackle his pants. As usual the belt was done up far too tight, making it hard to release the buckle. But my blood was up, and nothing could stop me. I ripped and pulled and heaved and tore and revealed him finally, magnificent, ready for me.

I shed the rest of my torn dress and we both attacked my corset, though not with a knife, like we had done back then. It was baggy and old and didn't put up much of a fight.

Then I leapt on top of him, wiggled into position, and impaled myself upon him, releasing a howl in which the whole story was bottled: my joy and my pain, my triumph, my ecstasy. This was my moment.

CHAPTER TWO

In Sicily we have a saying: *the price of happiness is death.* And it wasn't long before I was reminded how true that is. That wonderful night was also destined to be the most dreadful.

At the time I felt sad that l'Inglese and Guera never met. Or Pace, really. He was delirious by then, and the veil of death was fast descending upon him, as the blood pumped onto the pink satin vest, new on that morning, and which the boys were so proud of.

It was awful: Guera lying cold and dead and white and lifeless like wax, and poor, poor Pace, for whom nothing could be done, gradually slipping away from us.

Naturally, the death bed was hardly the best introduction to the rest of my family.

Those hotheads Nevio, Renzo and Audace, the eldest sons of my brother Giuseppe, were swearing a ritual vengeance just like you see in the movies.

All ten of Guiseppe's children take after Pervinca's side of the family. Wild, the lot of them. Mamma warned him not to marry into the

Rospo clan. But with Nevio already on the way, Giuseppe had no choice. Pervinca's father and brothers would have fed him to the pigs. They made a habit of it, apparently. Other wavering suitors to the many daughters had disappeared, never to be seen again. The eldest, Serenita, was so heartbroken when her sweetheart vanished that she threw herself down the well. They couldn't get her out. Took her a week to die. But old Nero Rospo maintained the human flesh imparted a succulent flavor to his pork.

Poor Biancamaria Ossobucco. She was literally out of her mind with torment. She was one minute collapsing, the next sobbing like a child, then running about tearing at her hair, beating the air with her fists, screaming:

'Is there nothing to be done? Save him! Somebody do something, for the love of the Madonna'.

But nothing could be done. The triplets, who had been asleep, woke up suddenly, and were trying to force spoonfuls of honey into Guera's lifeless mouth and Pace's barely alive one, lisping:

'Babbi. Eat! Eat! A little morsel of the honeycomb will make your hair grow curly'.

It reminded me of the time when Nonno Fiore died and I tried to resurrect him with a plate of freshly fried *panelle*.

O my poor little doves. My poor darling brothers.

L'Inglese stood at the back looking awkward, trying to disappear into the wall behind him. Every so often I caught a glimpse of him through the hordes that came and went like an ebbing tide: my five remaining brothers, plus my new brother, a selection of their many wives, and most of my sixty nephews and nieces, my twenty seven great nieces and nephews, not to mention other relatives, aunts, uncles, cousins, friends of the family, neighbors, business associates, onlookers, busy bodies, passers-by, beggars, and thieves. I saw him take frequent and surreptitious glances at his hair in the looking glass; it was thinner now, certainly, than it had been.

In the crowd nobody seemed to take any notice of him, but each time my eyes fell upon him I got a shock. It was like a dream where different parts of your life get mixed up together. He was there. He had come back. He was really here. With the whole of my family. And yet we were separated by a chasm. My dead and dying brothers were my preoccupation right now, as they should be. He, and I, would come later.

At each groan of poor Pace, the crowd responded with a scream, and although Dr Leobino was doing his best, it was clear there was no hope.

Padre Francesco, who was completely senile by this time, wandered about dribbling, making obscene gestures with his trembling hands, and although we are not a religious family, several of my sisters-in-law determined to write a letter of complaint about him to the bishop. Not that it would have done any good: the bishop and the priest were old friends, more than friends, according to the various rumors that regularly rumbled round the region. As it worked out, it wasn't necessary, but that part comes later.

At four, as it was beginning to grow light, my nieces Amoretta, Etna, and Maria Maddalena circulated with the refreshments: hot, strong coffee, almond cushions just out of the oven, and little sponge cakes topped off with a dollop of the new peach conserves.

Those who had been dozing woke up and started to eat, babies began wailing, and a pack of stray dogs that had got in through the open doors joined in with a horrible howling.

Many of the men and older boys had been drinking steadily since the tragedy began, and they became more and more rowdy, while poor Pace, whose skin had gone gray and greasy, was drawing farther and farther away from the tumult that surrounded him.

There was so much I wanted to say to him, to them both, but finally, when my turn came, and I was ushered to the bedside, my mind was a mush like bread soup. I bubbled away, and I don't know what I said, but I hope it was that I had loved them like a mother from the moment of their birth, and that I would love and look after the baby Rosas the same way, until I too closed my eyes for the last time.

At five, when the frustrated mule of Ippolito Brolese began braying and the caged songbirds on the balcony started twittering, Pace breathed his last, and everybody started wailing.

My poor dear boys had gone.

CHAPTER THREE

Dr Leobino snapped shut the clasp of his medical bag and I showed him to the door. As he was leaving he said:

'You should put some calamine lotion on that rash of yours, Rosa'.

I looked in the mirror and saw my face was as red and raw as minced beef. Still, I had no time for shame.

Finally, when the crowds were driven out, Biancamaria Ossobucco and I were able to prepare the bodies for burial. To be truthful they were already starting to reek, for it was the height of the summer, and the room was like an oven, and poor Guera had already been festering for some hours. We had to act fast.

To be truthful once again, Biancamaria Ossobucco was more of a hindrance than a help, for she kept fainting, and I had to keep breaking off in order to revive her, slapping at her pock-marked cheeks, and when that didn't work, wafting a bottle of evil-smelling salts under her broad nostrils.

When we peeled the blood encrusted shirt back from the black and gaping wound, we saw that the knife had gone clean through Guera from the front to the back, and even I broke down then. My boys. Butchered. And for what?

So we washed them and dried them, and their faces were sticky because of the honey, and we shaved them (already each had a bristly growth of beard; in our region whiskers, like every other crop, grow long and fast and strong) and we combed their hair and slicked it down with pomade the way they liked it. Then we dressed them in their wedding suit that they looked so handsome in that happy day not yet four years ago. It is true it was a little tight — there was a ripping sound as we pulled up the pants but we ignored it, and the buttons on the vest and the jacket didn't want to close, but by the time we had finished they looked very smart, I thought.

'My bridegrooms' sobbed Biancamaria Ossobucco, biting her fists in her grief until they bled.

We didn't have to wait long for the enormous coffin to arrive. Ernesto Tombi, the town's undertaker, had enlarged his business and was now a prosperous man.

The hard times following the War meant that many were going early to their graves, and although there may be no bread on the table, money is somehow scraped together for a funeral. Our people are strange that way; appearances must be kept up, and the dead honored, although the living must go hungry as a result.

Where there is want, there is often crime, and that, of course, leads to violence. The bandits in the hills had become more daring and dangerous, and as a result everybody armed themselves with weapons of one sort or another. It became common to see old women driving their flocks to market staggering under the weight of an antique harquebus or cudgel.

The turf wars between rival clans of Mafiosi became more murderous; disappearances were happening again — just like my poor dear Papa (I will always think of him as my papa, even though my real father, Rosario the half-wit, is still very much alive) — and, of course, this makes you fearful.

Everybody seemed to be getting 'warnings'; that was nothing unusual, and often you didn't know what you were being warned about. Just the previous week, Manlio Estivo, the man who sits under the palm tree near the public drinking fountain in the campo, received a human foot through the post, all wrapped up in birthday paper. He wrung his brain like a sponge but couldn't figure it out. After all, as he told anybody who would listen, he was born on the feast of *Ognisanti.* Then there was the time the Pinci family found the severed head of their mule, Vito, roasting in their bread oven. O yes, it was happening all the time, then.

The lack of hope for ordinary citizens makes rage bubble closer to the surface, like the fire under the crust of the volcano, and I think this, coupled with an awful coincidence and a terrible misunderstanding, led Bino Forbicina, a usually mild-mannered man, to do such an abominable thing.

Yet, in the midst of this misery, Ernesto Tombi was a man riding on the crest of a wave. It was said, when we were young, he was interested in courting me. But of course my heart was set on Bartolomeo, and after that particular tragedy I went away. Soon Ernesto Tombi married Piccarda Oleoso, who came with a motorcycle and sidecar combination, the first in the region, and the two of them raced around raising a cloud of dust in those carefree days before they began raising a crowd of daughters.

Although he had no sons, Ernesto took his daughters into the family firm, an unusual step in those days, but a wise one. Big Rita became an expert carpenter, and she had such a good eye that she never needed to get out a tape measure. As a favor to us, she hurried to the workshop as soon as news of the half-murder reached her ears, and, assisted by little Pina with the club foot (the receptionist and chief mourner), Marziana (the stone mason), and Rea Silvia (the bookkeeper), she was now struggling up the front steps with the results of her nights work.

Then the triplets were allowed in to scatter the flowers they had gathered in the courtyard: they were clutching squashed bougainvilleas, honeysuckles, daisies, marigolds and lavender. Rosina wanted to put a snail in, Rosita a handful of gravel and a dead baby bird fallen from its nest, and Little Rosa a ricotta pastry *little belly*, but Biancamaria Ossobucco drew the line at these things, and there was a lot of screaming and stamping of small feet which there always is when they don't get their way.

Of course they didn't realize that this was forever, and kept demanding that their *Babbi* wake up and play. For months, and even years afterward, they were asking me when *Babbi* were going to get up out of the pretty wooden box and play princesses or dollies or horses.

CHAPTER FOUR

Just as we were setting out from the house for the funeral, a man appeared from some institute or academy or other and tried to stop the procession. He actually wanted to buy the bodies and pickle them for exhibition in a travelling show of curiosities. He was joined by another fellow who wanted to use them for medical experimentation, and another still who represented some museum somewhere, or so he said. They started arguing with each other about who had the prior claim. Then it turned to fisticuffs.

As they rolled in the dust Audace appeared out of nowhere with an enormous meat cleaver and chased them away. Too much blood had been shed already. That boy would come to a bad end, I was convinced of it. As a result of this ugly episode, my brothers decided to mount a guard over the bodies, for even once they were buried, we knew the boys would not be safe.

So we proceeded through the streets, and the crowd of mourners grew and grew until it seemed that everyone in the region was there. There were people who I hadn't seen in years, some not since school, many I thought were already long dead. Shops were closed as a mark of respect. Newspapermen and photographers appeared, snapping their cameras in our faces. Reports subsequently appeared in all the newspapers and periodicals, even reaching as far away as Chicago, and this is how the news reached Aventina Valente, for nobody had thought to notify her. I still have the cuttings tucked away in my scrapbook. In one photograph you can make out l'Inglese, a little bit out of focus, yellow now, of course. It always surprises me to see photographs of him; to see that he was a real person, not just the phantom of my fevered dreams.

As is customary with a funeral, the bells had been ringing out since the early morning, but just as the procession was winding up the hill to the cemetery, there came a crash like a thunderbolt, a clang of bells in pain, and when the shock died away, there was an eerie silence that was like the end of the world.

Cows in the surrounding pastures started lowing, every mule in the region began to bray, dogs barked, and birds took flight in huge flocks that colored the sky black. People crossed themselves, and some of the more religious even fell on their knees in prayer. What was happening? Was the volcano about to erupt? Was there going to be another great landslide? An earthquake? Were we being bombed again? Had another war started?

When we reached the top of the hill, the sexton, old Porcu the Sardo, was sobbing in a thick cloud of white dust, and his tears traced lines down his earth-crusted face. He had warned the Padre, he said, years ago, that the beams in the campanile were being eaten away by the beetles, but the Padre maintained the beetles were doing God's work.

This morning, before going to dig the grave, Porcu had begged the priest not to ring the bells too enthusiastically, but of course Padre Francesco had taken no notice, and indeed had pulled on the ropes with more vigor than usual. The beams, their insides eaten away, could do nothing other than collapse, bringing the great bell and the little bell down right on top of the priest swinging below. Porcu's only consolation was that his death was instantaneous, and that he didn't suffer more than is usual when two bells weighing several tonnes land on your head.

'It's an omen', shrieked Vereconda, Leonardo's wife, who started to suffer an attack of her palpitations, and had to be sat down on the elaborate edifice of the proud Botti.

'It's a judgment, that much is certain', said Crispo Domani, the lottery ticket vendor.

'A judgment on who?' asked Bullo the wandering peddler, who, displaying his wares on the grave of the *fratelli* Farneti, was taking advantage of the climate of fear, selling lucky charms, religious relics, and amulets to the more superstitious of the villagers.

'What I don't understand is why the Good Lord waited so long to strike the bugger down,' said Dino Plotti the carter.

'Amen to that', said my niece Petronilla, fanning her mother with a wreath, 'Zia Rosa, whatever's happened to your face? And your neck, why I've never seen mosquito bites that big.'

I gave her one of my looks. I had no love of the priest, that's for sure, and I don't think anyone except poor old Porcu had any feeling other than contempt for him, but it did leave us with a sticky problem, because we had to bury Guera and Pace, and there was no other priest for miles around.

There was a pause as we wondered what to do. Postponement was out of the question. The full force of the midday sun was now streaming down and something was definitely beginning to ooze out of the joins in the coffin which lay on the gravel path. We all pretended not to notice, but those who were standing closest were clasping their handkerchiefs to their noses, and some were even vomiting. In retrospect, it would have been better if we had opted for a lead-lined one, but, as big Rita explained, she would have had to order the lead in specially from the mainland, and that would have taken at least a week.

Swarms of flies were buzzing and biting. Sunstroke and fainting were taking their toll. Some suggested we carry on without a priest and bury them ourselves. Others said the mayor, Don Cino Gusto, should step into the breach, but he was worried about exceeding his authority, and being excommunicated, and falling into eternal damnation, and besides it was lunchtime, and his wife, the fearsome Donna Rea Reparata, would fly into one of her rages if the pasta was left to cool, and, in short, he had to be getting along.

And so we were getting nowhere fast. By now the crowds of children were tired and hungry and had begun fighting and brawling and throwing stones and rolling in the dust.

Biancamaria Ossubucco, who had been holding herself together, was now having hysterics again because of the delay and everything seeming hopeless.

My niece Perpetua had gone into early labor on account of being squashed and trampled by the crowd, and she was carried away, shrieking in pain, to the house of her mother-in-law Concettina Capone, who has that lump the size and shape, not, as you might expect, of a walnut, but of an egg, on the back of her head.

There was chaos, and I was on the verge of conducting the service myself. Goodness knows I have been to enough funerals in my time; all around the photographs of my loved ones were staring at me from their gravestones; I was sure I could have done it without the Book.

But it was then that somebody remembered Ettore. I think it was Rosario who said 'Ettore' first, but of course nobody takes any notice of what he says. Then somebody else shouted above the din:

'Of course, Ettore should do it'.

'Where's Ettore?'

I should explain that Ettore, my nephew, son of my brother Salvatore and Ninfa, the first of his so-far four wives, is the only one in the history of our family to train for the priesthood, and is therefore regarded by many as a bit of an oddity; a saintly oddity, it is true. For the past two years he had been studying at the junior seminary in Catania, and after the summer recess was to leave for the Seminary of San Didimo della Pantofola in Palermo where he would prepare for Holy Orders.

Thereupon the poor stripling was found in the chapel, carried out bodily, and dressed in some antiquated vestments that Porcu found in a cupboard in the sacristy. Although he insisted he wasn't yet fit to administer the Sacraments, he was the nearest thing to a priest we had, and even if it wasn't absolutely right, I'm sure the Lord would see that we were doing our best in difficult circumstances.

So the funeral service went ahead, with little Ettore officiating, and I have to say he did it well and we were proud of him.

Finally, my poor dears were lowered into the grave.

But before anyone could take a handful of soil from the mound, Biancamaria Ossobucco threw herself down onto the coffin and lay on top of it screaming, hammering on it with her fists, demanding that we open it up to let her be put inside it also.

I wished she hadn't, on account of the triplets, for it was not right for them to see their mother so give way to her grief as this, and the next thing we saw was Rosario scrambling down into the grave with her, trying to give her what comfort he could, in his half-witted way, and it was heartbreaking.

I beseeched Biancamaria Ossobucco, for the love of her babies, to be strong, and come back up, and take her place amongst the living, for it was not yet her time to die. The little Rosas, who had been enjoying themselves sliding down the mound of earth on their bottoms so they were caked with muck and dust, now began to take notice of what the grown-ups were doing, and thought it was a game, and they too scrambled down into the grave, and started to hammer on the coffin with their tiny fists.

After that the dry ground around began to give way, and Zio Pietro Calzino, my mother's brother, who had just celebrated his one hundred and fourth birthday, and was making a special visit from his home in Adrano, was quickly swallowed up to his crêpey neck. This led to more panic and confusion because some of the bystanders began to fear landslides like the catastrophic one of 1941 that had claimed the life of many in the region, and they stampeded from the cemetery like a herd.

Those of us that remained set to work, clawing at the soil with our fingers to release Zio Pietro, and although Mauro finally managed to haul him out, he had lost the will to live.

'The grave is claiming me', he remarked weakly, 'My time has come', and with that, he lay himself down on the ground, crossed his arms over his puny chest, and promptly died.

It was then that the herd of goats burst in, and they began nibble Zio Pietro, and others of the seniors who weren't fast on their feet, and before long they had destroyed the floral tributes, and the shepherd boy, Simple Fogna, who has a lot to answer for, was nowhere to be found.

CHAPTER FIVE

It was certainly a funeral everybody would remember.

That night, back at the *fattoria*, my mind felt like it had been put through the mincer. As well as my mental anguish, I felt my body was broken. Every bit of me hurt. My teeth, my earlobes, my hair, even my fingernails. My funeral shoes, where I had kicked them off, reminded me of every coffin I had ever followed.

L'Inglese stripped off my mud-caked clothes, lay me down on the bed, and poured most of a bottle of our best olive oil over my back. The shock of it, the coolness and wetness, jolted me out of the daze I had fallen into.

'What are you doing?' I cried in dismay, 'The best oil! The first pressing!' Then, as an afterthought, 'The sheets!'

'Don't be so practical, *signorina*', he replied, 'Don't fret about your oil. Never mind the sheets. Try to relax a little. What you need is a massage'.

Slowly, gently, his fingertips went to work on my scalp, soothing my poor wounded brain with their rhythmic pressure. Then those fingertips caressed my ears coaxing them to release their pain, before proceeding down my neck and into my shoulders where my muscles were knotted like old hanks of rope. He probed and wheedled there, kneading those sinews like dough with his fingers and the heels of his hands, until the knots were smoothed out and the place began to hum with a glow of warmth.

Then he worked on down my back, pummeling me this time with the sides of his hands, up and down, up and down, a thousand times. The only sounds were the slapping of flesh on flesh, his breathing heavy with exertion, and my groans of release, punctuated occasionally by the sound of a confused cock crowing, or the distant barking of a dog.

Then it was the turn of my buttocks, my thighs – thick slabs of dimpled flesh – and as he tackled my sturdy calves where the muscles are stringy and tough, I couldn't help but wince as he pinched and pounded, chafed and chopped.

Finally he reached my feet. I don't think anybody had ever touched my feet before this. As he rubbed the soles of them in a circular motion with his thumbs, easing out every last bit of tension, and manipulated my toes, pinched painfully by those too-tight shoes, I felt I could quite like having my feet fiddled with from now on.

Then he turned me over so he could work on my front, while he sat astride me, naked. In spite of my protests, he pored on more and more of the precious oil, and smoothed it over me with the gestures of a pianist. Then he began massaging me with his whole body; the oil grew warm with the friction of his flesh against mine, and began to release its aroma of newly mown grass and wild flowers, sunshine and summer rain.

In spite of my grief, I couldn't help laughing at the craziness of this whole thing, at him, and me, middle-aged and flabby and coated in oil like an anchovy. He was laughing too. His lovely silky hair tickled my breasts, my belly. Then he was licking me, probing me deeply with his tongue, sucking me hard, and I was mewing, curling up, and kicking my legs in the air. Yes, I was yowling and lurching and thumping the greasy bed on either side with my arms like a giant bird flapping, and at last he thrust himself into me, spearing me, filling me, and my screams of rapture sliced through the silence of the sleeping world, rousing the cats that began to screech, the pigs to snort, and the mules to bray.

Afterwards I drifted in and out of consciousness. I was floating on my own private cloud. I was vaguely aware of l'Inglese saying he was going to make us something to eat, and I was basking in the sunlight of my love, listening to the music of the flowers coming from somewhere far, far away, when l'Inglese reappeared with a plate of his famous eggs and a bottle of wine.

He fed me the sumptuous buttery egg dish with his fingers. O it was good. Silky, rich, and delicious.

And now that we had had something to eat I began to feel warm and glowing like a flower opening its petals and I began to want more.

Now it was l'Inglese's turn for a massage. Quickly I climbed on top of him.

'You really are insatiable, woman', he said, laughing.

So I poured the dregs of the bottle of olive oil onto him. Then, with my breasts, I smeared it over him, smoothing it into his skin, every part of him. And we loved each other some more.

I was right about the sheets though. Come laundry day, it was the devil's own work to get the oil out of them, and still some stains remain, as a reminder of that crazy, greasy night.

CHAPTER SIX

It may have been that night, or it may have been the next, when we had *that conversation*. I think I'm right in saying it was soon after he came back. When we had been making love again and again throughout the night, and of course, during the day, when we could, in the larder, in the barn, on the mound of newly mown hay that smelled of sunshine, but was very prickly, anywhere and everywhere.

But I digress. I know the time I'm thinking of was night time because we were in bed. It was toward the end of the night, but not yet dawn, because the ray of sunlight that burns like a brand across the ceiling when it comes through the place in the shutter where there is a tiny hole was not yet there. Yes, it was still cool, and browny mauve, and I know this because my eyes opened suddenly, and I was awake, and I heard my voice asking:

'Why did you leave?'

I remember groaning, inside, then. I didn't want my voice to ask questions like this, but it was acting on its own initiative, and continued:

'In Palermo, I mean, then, before...' It sounded flustered, now, my voice.

He stirred, and his voice, still thickly sleepy, answered:

'I had to'.

He turned toward me, reaching his arm under my neck, pulling us together, until my head was nestling in the crook of his arm, and went on:

'Go, I mean. It was sudden. I couldn't get word to you. I wanted to. But there wasn't time'.

'I looked for you. I went back there. To that house. Three times. The last time it was all shut up'. There was a pause, 'I thought you were dead'.

'I nearly was'.

'How? Why?'

'It was, well, it was a stupid thing, really. It was just about money. I owed a man some money. And he wanted me to pay him. But I didn't have it. I would have got it. But he grew impatient. So he sent some of his heavies round. To the house. So I had to leave. Lie low, for a while, you understand?'

'For four years?'

'Well, yes. It wasn't just that. There were other, er, complications'.

'Complications'.

'Yes, exactly. But I never stopped thinking about you. Ever. As soon as I could, I came looking for you. I went to your apartment. It wasn't there. The fire...'

'Yes, I nearly died. I was in hospital for weeks. Damaged my lungs. Then Guera and Pace came and got me, and brought me home'.

'Nobody knew where you'd gone. I went into the grocer's down the street. That interfering busybody, your landlady...'

'Poor Nonna Frolla. She died, you know, because of the fire. It was my fault. I started it...'

Tears swam in my eyes as I regarded myself in the light of a murderess.

'Come on, sweetheart', he said, leaning close, wiping my tears away with his fingers, stroking my face, 'It was an accident. They said it was...'

'Who said?'

'That's the funny thing. The old man, her husband, he's married that tart from the library. What's her name? Concetta?'

'Costanza'.

'That's it. Sitting on his lap behind the counter. Billing and cooing'.

'No!'

'Yes!'

'But he must be a hundred and fifteen by now!'

'Well, you know the old cliché: 'You're only as old as the woman you feel'. So, on that basis he's only about twenty three. Anyway, I asked them where you'd gone, and none of them knew, but that didn't stop them making things up, and they were about to send me off on a wild goose chase to Lipari, when that peeping tom came in..'

'Signor Rivoli!'

'That's him. Nasty little peeping creep. Got very excited at the mention of you, he did. Said you'd received two letters while you lived in the Via Vicolo Brugno, one in the summer of '58 had the postmark smudged, but the previous one, which you received in the spring of '38 was postmarked Castiglione di Sicilia, Catania Province. So instead of punching him on the nose, I shook him warmly by the hand, and came straight here'.

While he was talking I shuddered at the thought of Signor Rivoli keeping me under such scrutiny all that time. He probably had dossiers on me, in which his observations were carefully recorded in his spidery handwriting. It was sinister.

There was a pause. Then l'Inglese added,

'I'm not too late, am I?'

'No. I just had to know, that's all',

I said it quietly, but I still wasn't convinced that I did know. There were those 'complications', which I knew would stick their needles into my mind when I was lying awake at night. But I didn't want to make a lot of it. He had thought about me. Come back, when he could, to find me. He was here, now. That was all that mattered really. The past was the past, and couldn't be changed.

It was good to have got that conversation out of the way. It had been lurking there like a hurdle in a race, and had to be got over.

So we snuggled up together and dozed a little, sweetly, sleepily, like kittens. Before I knew it, it was light, and time to get up and feed the pigs.

CHAPTER SEVEN

As the steaming slops splattered out of my pail into the trough, splashing my bare legs with sticky scraps, I felt sorry for myself, it is true. Why couldn't I enjoy my happiness a little longer? A day, or two, a little week, even. Why did it have to happen that very night?

'Answer me that', I said to big Priscilla, our old breeding sow, as she nudged me smartly out of the way. But Priscilla was too interested in her breakfast to bother with me. Soon the cool, young air was filled with the sound of happy grunting as Priscilla and the bristly tribe of her offspring savored their meal.

There were tomato skins and artichoke peelings, some left over *pennette* and summer squash, lots of *tenerumi* leaves, whey and wheat berries and all sorts of other good things. I take a pride in feeding my pigs well, and I know that they enjoy better food than many humans in the region. It's a little pleasure, but I do like to see the animals feeding heartily. For a moment I felt a simple joy. Then I remembered my heartache, and a knife sliced through my chest.

At that same moment, I felt eyes on my back. I turned around, expecting l'Inglese to be standing there behind me, but it was brother Mauro, leaning against the wall, inhaling deeply on a cigarette, looking at me as though I had no clothes on. I did a quick check. Yes, I was decent. I pulled my skirt down a bit, over my knees. Adjusted the neck of my housedress to make sure it wasn't gaping open. Lurking at the back of my mind was the feeling of awkwardness that he had already seen me naked, and he was probably remembering it now.

Mauro nodded his head towards the house.

'Is he staying long?' He blew out a plume of smoke, 'Your friend?'

'What's it to you?' I asked, making myself busy scraping out the last traces from my pail with my big wooden spoon, then clanging it on the side of the trough like beating a drum.

He shrugged.

'I'll be here when he's gone', he replied.

Now it was my turn to shrug.

'Suit yourself', I said, and came back inside to prepare breakfast.

When he's gone. Those words stung me like a hornet. He had only just come. I had had him only for a very few hours, and that in the midst of murder. I hadn't been able to enjoy him yet. Then to be confronted already with his going. I wouldn't think about. Not yet. Not for a long time. Although I knew in my heart he would leave again, I suppressed it. Like forcing the lid onto a bubbling saucepan of *maccu* I wouldn't let that thought boil over into my conscious mind for a long time.

La cucina was still brown with shadows. It takes a while for the morning to penetrate that part of the house. But it was high time I was getting on with my work. I tipped a quantity of flour onto the table for the morning's bread, but I'd forgotten the yeast, and when I came back with it from the pantry, I found Mamma sitting at the table, drawing patterns in the scattered flour with her fingertip.

I wasn't surprised. It seemed quite normal for her to be there. After all, the ghosts of us Fiores are everywhere. Just because my relatives are dead, it doesn't mean they move out of the house.

'I always said they would come to a bad end, those two', she said with a grim kind of satisfaction. 'And I was right'.

Her voice was the same as it always was. And she looked just as she always looked: face brown and wrinkled like a walnut, white hair sticking up, black dress and cardigan. You wouldn't have thought that she was dead at all really, if you didn't know it for sure.

'But Mamma', I said, adding the water to the flour, as though it was the most normal thing to be having a conversation with your dead mother while you made your morning bread, 'it wasn't because of anything they'd done. It wasn't their fault'.

'You plant trouble, you harvest trouble, that's what I say', she said.

Uove

Eggs

CHAPTER EIGHT

It had come about like this.

Ombretta Gengiva, who had assumed the position of midwife following the death of her mother Margarita in the devastating landslide of
1941, had been called out to the Forbicina farm to assist at the birth of
the first child to the newly married couple Bino and Angela, his bride,
who had come all the way from the spring of Femmina Morta in the
Nebrodi mountains far to the west.

Although their wedding was barely seven months since, Angela had
swelled so much it seemed she was carrying at least twins and very
likely triplets or even quads. Of course, this is not unusual in our region. Multiple births are common, and only last wintertime my
brother Salvatore and his current wife Consuelo were delivered of
quads: two boys, Nord and Sud, and two girls Est and Ovest, which
everybody at first thought was a joke, and indeed it may have started
out as a joke, but then we got used to it and couldn't think of them
being called anything else, so the names stuck.

But I am digressing from the story of the Forbicina birth and its dreadful ripple of consequences. For some reason (some said Angela had been poisoned by the quince preserves of her mother–in–law, others said that eating excessive quantities of sardines had induced an early labor), Ombretta Gengiva was called out before the expected time, and when she arrived at the farm she quickly realized there was something wrong.

Angela had clearly been in labor for some days already and hadn't liked to tell anyone on account of it not being enough time since the wedding. The babies weren't lying as they should: there was a jumble of arms, legs, and other parts which she couldn't clearly identify, and they were in odd places. It was obvious they weren't going to come out without a terrible struggle.

As Ombretta Gengiva explained afterward, in the twenty one years since her mother's death, God rest her soul, she had delivered exactly five thousand six hundred and forty seven babies throughout the length and breadth of the region, and yet none other had been like this one.

In her confusion, she applied to the spirit of her dead mother for guidance, and almost immediately Margarita Gengiva appeared in a visitation in the birthing room. With her toothless gums spraying a burst of saliva, just as they had done when she was in her prime, she delivered the chilling news:

''Tis like it were with Isabella Fiore, identical'.

Poor Angela, being a foreigner, didn't know the local legend, but Ombretta Gengiva fell on her knees uttering an urgent prayer to Santa Margarita, her mother's namesake, the patron saint of childbirth.

'It'll be a monster all right', shrieked Margarita Gengiva as her ectoplasm began to vanish, 'a thing joined together with the wrong number of heads and parts and hideously deformed, and it'll be the work of the Devil that's for sure'.

Angela passed out at this, as many women would, and had to be brought round with smelling salts.

Somehow word had already spread, and villagers were tramping toward the farm, determined to be there when the monster was born. Of course, times had moved on, it was 1962 after all, and some came on *motorini* and even in the tiny three wheeler trucks, called *Api*, that were beginning to arrive from the mainland.

Old mother Forbicina, who, as often happens, was the last to know about the goings-on in her own house, appeared on her steps with a shotgun.

'Bugger off', she shouted at the crowd, spraying a burst of shot into the air. The albino cat, Tocco, who happened to be lying on the roof of the pigsty toying with a mouse, was the first casualty of that terrible night.

When she heard why there was a gathering in her yard, Madre Forbicina blanched, and her face was as white as the dead cat, and she strode into the birthing room to demand an explanation from her daughter-in-law. Angela, who was lapsing in and out of consciousness, hid under the covers, and Ombretta Gengiva, bravely, with no thought for her own safety, prized the gun away, and banished the mother-in-law from the room.

Thwarted, Madre Forbicina attacked her son Bino for bringing disgrace on the family. She scratched him and bit him and pulled out clumps of his already meager hair, while Old Man Forbicina stood feebly by, feeling sorry for his son, but not prepared to divert the flow of his wife's wrath onto himself by intervening. After all, his hair was long gone, and his lone remaining tooth was a source of comfort he was reluctant to relinquish.

The screams from the upstairs grew ever more anguished. It was a sultry night, and the air was still, and sounds carried far through the open windows. The braying of the mules in the garden of Piramo Brina, the gentle creaking of the melons growing, and, across the valley, my own cries of rapture mingled with the cooing of the doves, and caused Simple Fogna, who had once again sneaked his goats into our apple orchard, to wonder why Rosa Fiore was making such a rumpus. O that night. The night of my life.

In the distance the volcano was quiet, although a tongue of bright lava was licking around the top, illuminating the dark night, and giving off a sulfury smell that you could taste on your lips.

In the Forbicina farmyard, Dante Brodo was selling lemon *granita* from the back of his truck and was doing a roaring trade as those gathered waited for what would happen, and the cries of poor Angela made everybody's throat hoarse.

Finally, just after midnight, it must have been, the screaming sound of more than one newborn rent the air, causing those who had been dozing to wake up and rush toward the house.

Ombretta Gengiva threw open the shutters and announced:

'Tis a creature joined, it's true, like Guera and Pace Fiore, but girls, not boys, with one great big head between 'em, and two scrawny bodies'.

The crowd gasped at the realization that history was repeating itself.

'I were there on that night too', said Mafalda Pruneto who was now an old woman, and an old woman anxious to get in the first word, 'And it did turn my ricotta rancid as I feared. Whole week's production had to be turned out and fed to the pigs. And nobody would pay me nothing for the waste. I said to Isabella Fiore, I said to her, 'it's all down to you, you should make it right'. Fetched me a punch on the nose she did. Swelled to the size of an eggplant. She were a wild cat, that one. Oh yes, it's glad I am I'm retired from cheese making now. There'll be ricotta going off throughout the region. I don't know that the pecorino won't be going bad also..'.

'I remember now, I was worried about my wine', said Fuscolo Bancale, rubbing his hoary chin, 'but as it turns out twenty–three was a good year. I've still got a few bottles tucked away. Happen sixty-two will turn out alright, who knows...'

Donatello Mancini, who had been a pimpled altar boy at the time of Guera and Pace's birth, and was now fat and fifty, chipped in:

'I myself saw with my own eyes Isabella Fiore mating with a water buffalo. She only had herself to blame'.

'You were a liar then, and you're a liar now', said Sesto Fissaggi.

'Bino Forbicina, now, he's been made to look a fool'.

'That particular pot of stew was bubbling before he married her, I'll be bound'.

'That's what they're like, those mountain bandits'.

'That's what comes of marrying with foreigners'.

'Speaking of foreigners, have you heard there's one over at the Fiore place right now? Up to all sorts with the spinster Rosa. Been asking for her all over the region, apparently, hunting her down like a dog'.

'What is the world coming to?'

Everyone was so busy reminiscing about the past, and speculating about the immoral goings-on of Angela Forbicina and the people of Nebrodi, that it came as a surprise when Bino burst out of the house brandishing the enormous dagger that had been hanging above the fireplace since the time of the Spaniards.

The crowd cowered, expecting who knew what? He looked wild, certainly. What man wouldn't in his circumstances? Indeed, he stood on the front steps and let out a bellow like a bull, and those that heard it said it made their blood run cold in their veins.

Just at that moment, who should hobble up but Padre Francesco? He was holding a cross in his hand, but instead of uttering the benediction the crowd expected, he started to sing lewd songs.

It was then that he raised his cassock revealing what he had under-neath, which, to be truthful, wasn't very much, and it was at this point that Bino stuck the dagger through his belt, took hold of the priest, and threw him bodily down the steps.

As the priest writhed in the dust there came the sound of galloping horses, the thunder of wheels, the jangling of harness and a wagon hurtled into the yard scattering the onlookers. Responding to the roar released by the driver, a mountainous woman, the heavy horses in the shafts, which were foaming a green foam, skidded to a halt, just in the nick of time, with the result that Padre Francesco was only buffeted rather than trampled.

'What have you done to my Angela?' Demanded the mountainous woman, in a voice as deep as a well shaft.

'Me? It's she that's made a fool of me', replied Bino bitterly, 'And there's two who are guilty, and will pay the price'.

With that he leapt off the steps, vaulted the priest, seized the motor scooter of Probo Basso, started it up, and sped off out of the yard leaving everybody gawping.

Then the mountainous woman, who was his mother-in-law, jumped down from the wagon, strode manfully round to the other side and

lifted down a tiny man from the passenger's seat (a man whom nobody had noticed at all until that point). She carried him up the steps
like a dolly, and they disappeared into the house.

The crowd was divided: whether to follow Bino and see what he did,
or stay and watch the battle of the mothers-in-law, which offered the
prospect of good entertainment, but would be best if it were staged
outdoors. It came about that those who had some mode of transport
other than their legs took off after Bino, and those that didn't stayed,
on the basis that they thus had a chance of still seeing something.

CHAPTER NINE

In the evenings, Guera and Pace used to conduct their business meet-
ings at the bar of Nestore with the limp (this was to distinguish him
from the other Nestore who didn't have a limp, but he didn't have a
bar either – he was a blacksmith). They had their own table in a little
alcove at the back and Nestore would look after them. As well as
serving the drinks, he acted as their receptionist, organized the people
who wanted to see them, and did any odd jobs that needed doing and
so on. They had come a long way since the days when they sat in the
old pigsty at the *fattoria* and the locals used to form a line to ask them
about a missing goose or an auspicious time to harvest wheat.

What I have never been able to understand, and I've thought about it
a lot since the night of the tragedy, is why they couldn't predict what
was going to happen – and somehow stop it? But then, they didn't
predict the night of the triplets birth either. Perhaps they could only see
things that happened to other people, not themselves. Or perhaps they
were too busy making money to pay any attention to their second
sight. Who knows?

From what Nestore said afterwards, they had had a busy evening,
with lots of people coming in and out as usual. Nestore was cleaning
up and getting ready to close, and Guera and Pace were drinking a
final cup of coffee, when Bino Forbicina tore in. He was like a

madman, definitely. His hair was an upstanding bush. His eyes were red and staring. He was the volcano ready to erupt.

He pushed past Nestore and said simply:

'The time of the pomegranates'.

Then there was the flash of the blade in the light of the bare bulb, and before anyone could do anything, a gush of blood surged out of Guera's chest, and he was dead, and Pace immediately started to die, and Nestore tried in vain to stem the flow of blood with the cloth he had just been using to wipe down the tables.

And Bino Forbicina was gone.

CHAPTER TEN

In my mind, I often turn back to that night before the tragedy happened, and it seems to me now, after the passage of the years, like a
dream. And yet I know it did really happen. It wasn't one of my
fantasies. Yes, before all the other things happened, before life, or
more precisely death, got in the way of it, my l'Inglese and I were in
the bubble of our own private world where there was only us and
nothing else.

We made love again and again, for although we were no longer
young, love makes everybody a teenager. We were in my bed, where
I had lain so many solitary nights dreaming about him, or trying to
dream about him, and trying to imagine what it would be like if he
came back, and here he was.

In one way it seemed so normal that he should be here, and in another
way it really was a dream come true, and there was still a part of me
that couldn't really believe it. You read in romantic stories that the
heroine has to pinch herself to make sure she's not dreaming, and I
felt like that myself.

So we lay in that hot night and we couldn't keep our hands and other
parts off each other, and that feeling of urgency would well up again,
like a pot boiling, and had to be satisfied. I remember sitting astride

66

him, gripping him with my muscles, yodeling with all my might, and I felt I could burst like a big bubble of joy, and there be nothing left.

Then, during the lulls, when we would flop down side by side in the little bed like sardines in a can, we just couldn't help laughing, like children. I couldn't stop touching him, just to reassure myself that he was really there. I've never felt such dizziness. I wanted to get up and dance and sing at the top of my lungs. O the smell of him was like heaven bottled. I couldn't stop burying my face in him and breathing him in. Our lips were sore from the thousands of kisses we had made, and I could feel my face burning from the friction of his whiskers, and I couldn't help but nibble him and nuzzle him and suck him and bite him.

From time to time, one of us, usually him, would drift off to sleep, and I looked at him when he was sleeping and I felt such love for him that I had to cover him once more with kisses, every little bit of him, and somewhere inside I felt the pain of knowing I could never love him enough, that we had been robbed of so much time we would never get back.

I don't know what time it was, but we both woke up and were hungry, ravenously hungry; it had been hours since we last ate anything. So we went down to *la cucina* naked, just as we were. There was nobody else around, and the night was so steamy, and we were ourselves giving off heat. L'Inglese said I was so hot he could fry an egg on my skin and he was keen to try it as an experiment.

As it was, though, we didn't fry eggs. I got out from the larder a dish of *caponata*, our delicious plump eggplants simmered in a rich tomato sauce along with olives, capers, a little sugar, and my own little twist, some prickly pears, which I had bottled last fall. I also set out some of my rustic bread, a fresh, salted ricotta, and some lovely *prosciutto crudo*, all that remained of Daniele, the last pig I had slaughtered.

We sat at the ancient table feeding each other, with our fingers, the way we used to before, drinking a jug of our homemade wine, and laughing. For pudding there was a platter of fruit from the farm: wonderful peaches, strawberries, raspberries, luscious figs, and a juicy melon whose perfume filled the room. Before long, I was part of a fruit salad, with the cut up fruits arranged over my body, and l'Inglese was licking up the trickles of juice that ran in rivulets down my skin, and I was squealing and laughing and crying with the joy of it all.

It was then that there were shouts out in the yard, and I knew that tragedy had struck, although I didn't know in what way. The spell was broken, I scrambled up, and the fruits fell and splattered onto the floor. My brother Mauro, my new brother, that is, leapt up the steps and into *la cucina*, and I could only find an oven cloth to cover myself with, which wasn't enough, for it was small and punctured with burns. Mauro's eyes feasted on me, and I said:

'Who's dead?'

And he said:

'Guera'.

And it was then that something inside me died also, and thinking back on it now causes a gaping wound to open up inside me. I had, of course, a thousand questions, the first of which was:

'And Pace?'

And he said,

'Not good',

And the second blow was struck. Although I had no way of knowing at that point the twins had been stabbed, I was feeling their pain, and I swear, a terrible, burning sensation was searing through my chest.

Of course it was a ridiculous situation, but when there's death nothing else matters. I ran up the stairs to get some clothes on and l'Inglese followed me.

'Shall I come?' he asked.

I said 'Of course, you're family'.

Having thrown on some clothes, we ran back downstairs. Mauro was waiting for us and we set off at a run. Rosario was in the yard, and he had heard the rumpus, and when we told him, Rosario collapsed. His face turned turquoise and he frothed at the mouth. Nobody knew he was so devoted to the twins. It was only after the subsequent turn of events that we discovered he wasn't. So Mauro picked him up like a sack and threw him over his shoulder, for Mauro is as wide as he is tall, and is stronger than any other man in the region, and even now wins the laurel crown of Ercole at the *festa* of San Giacomo di Prugno.

All of us scrambled onto the tractor, with Mauro driving, and me and l'Inglese clinging onto Rosario, trying not to be flung off, and in this way we trundled into town, to the house where my beloved twins lay dead and dying.

It was only later when I asked myself why we didn't take the truck, instead of all balancing on the tractor, but in the panic of that horrible time, I, for one, wasn't thinking straight.

Minestre

Soup

CHAPTER ELEVEN

The time of the wild asparagus.

I have been trying to remember when my brother Mauro first came amongst us. I know it was the time of the wild asparagus because I had spent many hours hunting for it amongst the prickles and had only a small basket of spears for my efforts, and because I had been for some hours in the wild places where it grows, I had not heard the news that a stranger had come. When I arrived back at the *fattoria,* disheveled and scratched, my hair full of foliage like a thicket, I found him waiting in *la cucina*, taking a thorough look at everything, examining my cookware, and testing the sharpness of my knives.

Giuseppe, who was with him, explained that he was the son of Papa, and we should welcome him into our home and our hearts, and this left a lot of questions unasked and unanswered.

I have to say from the start he did not act toward me like a brother should, and, naturally, I knew that being the son of Filippo, he was not exactly my brother, but did he know that? Familiar, that's what he was. He looked like Filippo, it's true, but better. With better teeth, certainly. Filippo mistrusted dentists, and had never in his life visited one. His was a nice face. A kind, square, solid sort of face. His age seemed more or less like the rest of us. A little younger, maybe. His hair was dark, and thick, and glossy. There was no trace of a mountain cap like that which Filippo always wore, and which I still had in my little trunk of special treasures. A little moth eaten it is true, after all this time, but I would not part with it for the world. Where had he come from? Where had he grown up? Who was his mother? In short, what was his story? But I felt awkward about asking these questions.

Yes familiar that's what he was. While I was preparing my *frittata* he came up very close behind me, so that I could feel the warmth of his body, and his smell, the smell of melted butter, surrounded me, and I have to say it was a good smell, (goodness knows, our men are not known for the beauty of their aroma, particularly in the height of summer) and I could feel his breath on my neck, and in spite of what I thought, in my mind, my body felt alive to these things.

As well as this, he tried to interfere with my whisking of the eggs, the amount of salt, the quantity of oil to be warmed in the pan, and so on. And he kept touching me. Whether it was by accident or not. The way he looked at me with his black eyes made me feel not a little bit uncomfortable. And it seemed that his eyes were often on me, like a fly on a dollop of jam.

Of course, I insisted on doing things my own way; I pride myself on the perfection of my *frittate*, and moreover I had been the one creep- ing on my belly in the undergrowth seeking out the tender spears, I had been the one to be prickled and scratched, in short, they were my asparagus, and I asked him politely, but firmly, to keep his suggestions to himself.

By the time it was ready, the succulent scent filled the air, and news that the first *frittata* of the new asparagus was ready in *la cucina* spread like a swarm around the *fattoria.* A line of farmhands were already on the steps, and when I finally opened the door there was a rampage to the table. Mauro managed to seat himself beside me and his excitement bubbled up like a schoolboy's when I served him with a generous slice. Of course, I noticed, when he took that first sumptuous bite, his eyes close in appreciation, and he savored every sensation of taste and texture. He turned to me with a broad smile, revealing even, white teeth, and said,
'Sister', (that word had a faint ring of mockery about it), 'You were right, and I was wrong; this frittata is perfect; it couldn't be better'.

I removed his hand from my thigh, where it had crept under the table, and smiled back.

'Thank you, *brother*, I'm glad you like it'.

Somehow, I can't remember quite how it came about, it was decided that he should move his stuff into the old grain store that we had rebuilt, next to where Rosario lived, and that he would take his place amongst us as a farmhand. I have to say that in spite of his cheek, and his love of gossip, he was a good worker. He was stronger and more hardworking than any of my real brothers, who welcomed him as one of their own. It was as though he belonged there, like a missing piece of a jigsaw puzzle that you have given up looking for, and are later surprised to find in a dark corner, when you least expect it. Seeing them all together made me realize my separateness, for they are all very much alike, part of a club to which I would never belong, being, as I was, the image of Rosario the half-wit.

CHAPTER TWELVE

Shortly after this I was harvesting peas. I had it in mind to make a gorgeous *frittella* of peas, artichokes, of which there were many beauties, and the baby broad beans. I was in my kitchen garden, of which I am rather proud, for I keep it well ordered, and I had raked out a bed ready to sow more of the beans, which grow fast at this time of year in our rich and fertile volcanic soil.

Yes, I was harvesting peas, and filling my basket with them, and occasionally, often, in fact, I couldn't help popping open a pod, and with my lips plucking the tender peas from their fuzzy nests.

All around me was the delicious scent of fresh, zingy growth, and the peaty smell of the black earth. From time to time the little breeze carried the whispered fragrance of mint or basil or peach blossom. The bees worked away with the utmost seriousness, and as I looked around me I thought how good it was. Solid and good. The sky was the bluest of blues. The spring sunshine was shining on my face. I was glad to be alive.

Here was my new brother, Mauro, having a look round, and full of praise he was, too, for my arrangements and my produce. I invited him to share some of the peas, and he looked at me with those brown as black eyes, and they are the sort of eyes that can read your thoughts, and those always make me feel a bit flustered.

He sat down next to me in the sunshine, and he didn't say very much except make 'mmmmmm' noises as he relished the peas. Together we popped open the pods, and sucked up the peas, and chewed them, and savored them, and smacked our lips, and the whole time he had a look of enquiry on his face, a sort of half–smile, as though he was waiting for something.

Then he did something astonishing.

He leant towards me with his lips. I noticed his lips were rather nice lips: they were soft and dry, pale and flexing, reaching and open. His breath was minty with the smell of the peas we had just been eating, of the green, the spring and the new growth and sweetness. Those lips, his lips, brushed against mine, and that brush was really like an elec–tric shock that jolted through my whole body. Then his lips fastened on, and they were kissing. Kissing mine. Me.

Of course, I was about to pull away. For a moment I resisted, and was going to push him away, and deliver him a slap, too, for his cheek. But then, and I don't understand it, that kiss was a moment of bliss. It was as though I'd never done kissing before. It was all new: quiveringly beautiful, erotic and tender.

I liked what those kisses were doing to me. The person making the kisses and I were joined together in a way that my body understood, and although my mind was whirling away on all sorts of things, I didn't want it to stop. I wanted to go on and on feeling like this. I kissed back. And he kissed back. It was amazing. Magical. Incredible.

It didn't stop there. I started to feel a flexing and a curling up in that part of my body deep inside, so I dropped the peas I was holding in my hands, and took hold of his face instead. I held on to it and pulled it toward me. Taking his cue from me I felt his hands take hold of me, of my body, and his hands were strong and gentle and felt lovely when they were on my body, touching it, caressing it just the way it likes, and it was as though his body knew my body.

Somehow it came about that we were lying down in the plot I had just raked, in the bed of soft black soil that smelled so sweet, where the naked worms were wriggling. I lay back and closed my eyes and felt the sun warm my eyelids and felt the spring all around me, and he was kissing my neck as he undid my buttons gently, one by one. He was opening me, like a pea pod, and I was open to the cool fresh air.

There came the twittering of the birds and the buzzing of the bees and the gentle grunting of the pigs beyond the fence, and the scent of green, and I was naked and could feel spring with my body like an animal. Then he was close, over me, on top of me, heavy, and inside me heavy, and where I so wanted and needed him to be that I couldn't help but shout out:

'Yes, that's it. Right there. Yes. O yes. Yes. Yes. Like that. Don't stop. I beg you. Don't stop doing that'.

It must have come out rather loud.

'Don't stop doing what, Rosa?'

Mauro's voice came from somewhere far, far away. He had stopped. Abruptly. The world had stopped turning. I opened my eyes. We were still sitting by the pea vines, fully clothed. I fell back down to earth, a long fall. I had imagined the whole thing. The worst part of it was he had clearly been listening to me moaning and crying out. I could feel my face flushing hot. I scrambled up without looking at him.

'Must get the loaves out before they burn',

I muttered, trying to sound business-like, and picking up my basket of peas I hurried back to *la cucina*, feeling a fool.

Luckily the loaves weren't burnt, but they were a darker shade of umber than usual. I ripped the tough, outer leaves from my artichokes with a fury. The shame of it, Rosa Fiore, I scolded myself, cutting out the chokes and slicing fiercely. It was ridiculous. I was ridiculous. I dropped the slices into lemon water to stop them going brown. It didn't mean that I wanted it to happen. I chopped my onion finely and it was very soon done. Didn't mean I found my brother attractive. Of course not. I podded a whole heap of broad beans, running my thumb from one end to the other inside, pushing out the beans into a pale yellow-green mound on the table. This repetitive job began to soothe me. It was only because I had been starved of love for so long that it had come about. Next I shucked the big basket of peas, and that calmed me some more. I love shelling legumes. I could do it all day. And I knew from experience that if I cooked in a rage my *frittella* wouldn't taste as good as it could. There would be a taint of bitterness that would spoil it. I hadn't had one of my fantasies for a long time. I would have to keep a careful check on myself, so that bad habit didn't creep up on me again.

Next I heated some oil with a knob of butter, drained and dried my artichoke slices, and sautéed them gently with the onion for a few minutes. Then it was time to add my peas and my beans, a splash of water, some sea salt, and some black pepper, and allow the whole to bubble away merrily filling *la cucina* with an enticing aroma. By now I felt almost calm. When the broad beans and peas are just tender, not soft, you must remove the pan from the heat, add a good sprinkling of chopped parsley, a slug of the best oil, and allow it to cool so that the flavors blend together into a perfect harmony of spring tastes, when it will make a delicious lunch, served with some thick slices of bread, and a mild, fresh ricotta.

Of course, amongst the first into *la cucina* for lunch was brother Mauro, and although I could not bring myself to look at him, I could feel his eyes upon me, and my cheeks flushed at the recollection of how silly I had been.

Pane

Bread

CHAPTER THIRTEEN

Anyway, now my Inglese was here, and naturally I had absolutely no interest in my brother. However, my brothers, my original brothers, that is, were very much interested in him.

One morning l'Inglese was lying late in bed. He wasn't an early riser, and he said, since I allowed him very little sleep at night, he had to catch up, when he could, during the day.

I, on the other hand, have never been one for lying in bed when the sun is up. I have to feed the farmhands and the animals, and they keep early hours. For us, the best part of the day is the cool, rose–pink time, before the white of the heat makes us sluggish. In addition I have never liked to get behind in my work, so I was only too pleased to leave him dozing upstairs, while I set out my ledgers on the ancient table, perched my spectacles on my nose, and lost myself in my ac-counts, taxes, and the essential management of the farm.

I wasn't left undisturbed for long, however. I had barely started when Leonardo, Mario, Giuliano, Giuseppe and Salvatore shuffled into *la cucina* in single file just as I was adding up a long column of figures. I held up my hand to silence them so I didn't lose count, and they stood looking awkward: sniffing, coughing, rubbing their faces with their grubby fingers, waiting for me to finish.

I wrote down the total and then looked over the top of my glasses at them, feeling like a schoolmistress:

'Now what's all this about?'

Mario, Giuliano, Giuseppe and Salvatore all turned to look at Leonardo. He, in turn, looked to his right, but there was nobody there. As the eldest, the buck stopped with him. He took a deep breath, nervously rubbed his big hands on the seat of his pants and plunged in:

'It's about the foreigner',

I knew it would be. But I said nothing. I wasn't going to make this easy for them.

Leonardo, having made a start, looked at the others for moral support, and now the genie was out of the bottle, they variously chipped in with:

'What's going on?'

'You're bringing shame on the family'.

'You're acting like a *puttana*'.

'No good will come of it'.
'It's just like when Mamma took up with Antonino Calabrese. He was a foreigner. Look what happened there. She had to shoot him up the arse, in the end'.

'He don't belong here, Rosa'.

'Foreigners. They're no good, I tell you'.

'You had a man before; look how that ended'.

'That's right, Rosa. It don't work out for you'.

'We're only saying this for your own good'.

'Because we care about you'.

By now they had just about run out of steam, and lapsed once more into the embarrassed silence.

'Has anyone anything else to say?' I asked, my pencil still poised, looking from one to the other.

They shook their heads, and wriggled and shuffled some more. Only Giuseppe, whose stomach was never far from his thoughts, added:

'What's for lunch?'
'Ricotta pie. Now, if you're quite sure everyone's had their say', I said, 'You can go'.

With relief they filed out of la *cucina* once more, and went down the steps into the yard, leaving me to get on with my accounts in peace. After that they never returned to the subject of l'Inglese, not to me anyway. They were not friendly toward him; although he tried to get on with them, they largely ignored him. Sometimes they played tricks on him. Once they positioned a bucket of water above a door so that it soaked him when he walked through. Another time they filled his seductive shoes with pig droppings, and the stench could never be got rid of. But later, when they discovered a mutual love of playing cards, they got on much better.

CHAPTER FOURTEEN

In the aftermath of the tragedy, everything seemed colored by blood, and yet life must, and will, go on.

One of the next things to happen was the arrival of the new priest, Padre Bonaventura. What was surprising was that he came so soon. We thought we would be without a priest for some weeks, at least, if not months, for the Bishop does not act fast. But within a week of the tragedy Padre Buonaventura was seen riding into town on a threadbare mule, with his few possessions strapped onto his back: a banjo, a set of golf clubs, and a gilded cage (empty), the residence of the fat white rat that was clinging to his hat. He was young(ish) with a full head of hair and a dazzling set of teeth which he was not slow to reveal in a film star's smile that led to a sudden surge of religious fervor amongst our women. He had barely brushed the dust from his cassock before a line was forming outside the confessional.

There was no shortage of work for him to do. One of his first tasks was to bury his predecessor, and although Porcu the Sardo was the only genuine mourner, he was elbowed out of the way at the grave that he himself had dug by the crowd of girls and matrons (many of them old enough to know better) making eyes at the new priest.

It was no surprise to anybody when the tufted head of Bino Forbicina was found in the fountain in the Campo di Santa Marta. His body (at least it was thought to be his body) was not found until many years later, when an earthquake destroyed the new road on stilts to nowhere outside the town, and it was wedged there, inside one of the supports, perfectly preserved. Of course there was gossip. Bino's own mother was a popular choice. As was his mother-in-law, the mountainous mountain woman of Nebrodi. I don't pay any attention to what people say, but I remember thinking it more than a coincidence that my nephew Nevio chose that same time to go off and seek his fortune in America. Nevertheless, Padre Buonaventura buried the head with all due rites in a doll-sized coffin prepared with care by Rita Tombi.

On that same afternoon he conducted the baptism of the Siamese babies, and they were named Wanda and Wilma. Biancamaria Ossobucco had befriended Angela Forbicina, and stood as godmother. Although there was no truth whatsoever in the rumor that Guera and Pace had fathered them, Biancamaria Ossobucco could not have been fonder of these poor little souls, and I suppose having them around made her feel some connection with the husbands she had lost.

At this time, when the tragedy was still a gaping wound, I filled myself with l'Inglese, not allowing any room for my heartbreak to fester. He was like a life raft to me at that time, and I don't know what I would have done without him.

I showed him with pride all over our land: the olive groves and the groves of lemons, oranges and citrons; the plantations of almond, walnut, chestnut and pistachio trees; the vineyards; the orchards of ripening peaches, nectarines, cherries, apples, pears, and figs; and the melon plot where you can hear the creaking of the melons growing. Together we walked through the meadows where the golden wheat was a beautiful sight to see. I showed him also the improvements I had made since my return from the city: the cottages I had repaired and the new olive press, the barn with its new roof. I showed off our flock of sheep and our chubby pigs, the dairy where we make our ricotta, the cantina where we make and store our wine, and last of all, my kitchen garden, where I grow much of what we cook and eat.

Together we prepared wonderful meals based on our flavor-filled produce. Simple things, like *tortiglioni* with raw tomatoes and fragrant basil, fresh summer greens soup, or *spaghetti* with rich tomato sauce, ricotta, and eggplant slices.

In those moments when we cooked together, it was like it was then, in Palermo, when we were alone. In those moments I could almost forget my responsibilities. But outside of those times, it was different. Then it was like a game. Now it was real life. I didn't know whether what we had would blossom and flower, or whether the tender bud would swell but then wither, buffeted by the harsh breezes of reality.

CHAPTER FIFTEEN

One night when the moon was full and bright I remember thinking it was just the right night to harvest jasmine for syrup, to be used in squash preserves, and to flavor the wonderful watermelon pudding for which our region is justly famous.

So we set out with baskets along the overgrown cart track on the far side of the olive grove which winds up the hill to a little copse of prickly pears. Beyond that, you must cut through the underbrush, where cardoons grow thick and thistly, and where a wild cat sometimes makes her nest, to the secret place where the old *cisterna* fills with the crystal waters of the spring.

It was still very hot. Fat, salty drops were tickling the nape of my neck before trickling down my spine inside my clothes. There was no breeze at all, and what air there was was stuffed with buzzing insects. Biting flies were attracted to my bare legs and arms, and I had to keep swiping at them to beat them off.

The sweet, heavy scent guided us to the place where the jasmine blossoms were plentiful, and as a nightingale sang somewhere, hidden in the branches, we plucked the flowers by the light of the moon. This is important, for they say that the moonlight intensifies the perfume, and makes a more fragrant infusion. We worked away for a time, for you need a great many flowers to give sufficient strength to your syrup, but it wasn't long before my lazy apprentice had tired of his task and was wondering off, lighting a cigarette, and exploring the *cisterna*, which was below the level of the surrounding ground, reached by a flight of steps, and circled by a crumbling stone wall.

Finally I had filled both baskets, and that was enough; there was no way to carry more. In the still, black water of the *cisterna*, the moon was reflected like a huge, silver circle.

'Fancy a dip, *amore*?' L'Inglese asked, beginning to unbutton his shirt.

'In there?'

'Why not?'

I could think of lots of reasons why not. The need to get the jasmine blossoms into water quickly before they lost some of their intensity. That we had no towels. That somebody might see. That it had never been done before. That it wasn't the sort of thing we did, as a general rule.

Then I thought, simply, 'Why not, indeed?'

And then it was a race to see who could rip their clothes off and rush into the water first. He beat me, but only just, by leaping into the water from the top of the steps, while I was more cautious and went on down to the bottom step before plunging. We both screamed. O it was cold. I wasn't prepared for how icy it was. It didn't seem to have been warmed by the summer sun at all. And it was deep. We couldn't touch the bottom, certainly, and had to keep paddling with arms and legs to stay afloat. It was definitely refreshing.

Then a voice said:

'You're not drowning are you?'

It was Mauro, sitting on the wall above.

'I heard screams', he explained.

'Just cooling off', I said.

I wanted to get out by now, but didn't want to, with him looking on. And he didn't seem to be in any hurry to leave. In fact, he lit a cigarette, and went on watching. Being watched certainly seemed to take the fun out of it. In fact, I wished then that I hadn't done it. I felt somehow foolish.

'I'm getting out now', I said, 'so if you wouldn't mind turning your back..'

'Want me to pass you a towel?'

'It's okay, thanks'.

L'Inglese splashed over to the steps and got out. At the same time I noticed something swimming in the water. A big furry thing with sharp teeth and a thick tail. A nutria.

I screamed and my scream echoed around the round walls. If there's a creature that makes the hairs on the back of my neck rise up it's a nutria. I can't stand the things: a cross between an enormous water rat and a beaver with a thick and horrible tail and razor–sharp teeth. Swimming in the *cisterna* with one was the stuff of nightmares that was sure to haunt me for the rest of my life.

I swam like an Olympic athlete toward the steps and vaulted up them. I didn't care that Mauro was watching. My only concern was getting out of there.

I rushed past l'Inglese, hurrying to the place where we had left our clothes, trying to cover up as much of myself as I could with my fold-ed arms. I had had dreams like this. Often.

I could no longer see Mauro; he had wandered off, but I still felt as though his eyes were on me. When you're wet, your clothes stick to you, and mine seemed to be fighting me. In my haste I ripped off one of my sleeves. All my clothes were in shreds these days. I would have to think about buying some more. We were almost dressed when l'Inglese screamed out and fell down backwards on the ground clutching his foot, howling like a wolf.

At the same time, I'm sure I could hear laughter coming from the copse on the hill.

'Something's bitten me', l'Inglese groaned through clenched teeth. 'Must be a snake'.

But it wasn't a snake. There was something in his shoe. By the light of the moon, I could just make it out: a squashed scorpion.

'Is it fatal?' he moaned, white as the moon.

'No', I said, 'No worse than a hornet. You'll live'.

CHAPTER SIXTEEN

I practically had to carry l'Inglese back to the *fattoria*, and the two baskets of blossoms which I was too stubborn to leave behind. Quickly, as the moths flapped against the window panes, and while the perfume and the moonlight were still strong, I got the flowers into pitchers of water, sealing the tops with weights to keep the blooms submerged, and the air out.

That night it was pain not passion that kept us awake. L'Inglese's foot swelled up like a melon, the lips of the wound went violet, and the following morning, after I had filtered the jasmine water, I had to harvest the squash alone.

They do say the uglier the squash, the better the preserves will taste, and fortunately there were some hideous looking brutes lurking in the squash patch. They were long and thin like eels, with warts and strange swellings and discolorations. Some were even growing hair.

Back in *la cucina*, while l'Inglese moaned and felt sorry for himself, I boiled the peeled and chopped chunks of squash in water until *al dente*, then drained them, and set them outside on trays in the yard, in the full sun, for them to dehydrate and shrivel and intensify in flavor. I love to include the sun as one of the ingredients in my dishes. It makes the flavors so vivid and brightly colored. It reminded me of the time we made 'strattu, in the garden of the villa, before he went away. He would go away again, I knew it in my heart.

'What do we do while it's shriveling up?' he asked.

'The thousand other jobs that are waiting to be done', I answered.

'First, I need a lie down', he said, slyly, 'I'm feeling rather weak', and he hauled himself onto the table and lay back amongst the squash peel and seeds and discarded jasmine flowers fomented by now, and releasing a musky odor. With his head propped up on a sack of sugar, he beckoned me to climb on top of him. I fought a quick battle with my conscience. I am usually a very conscientious and orderly person, but then I reasoned I had the rest of my life to do the laundry and scrub floors and knead dough and peel peppers and pick peaches and feed chickens. After he'd gone I would do those things. After he'd gone. Now I would grasp happiness with both hands. So I let go of my resistance and took off my clothes − that way would save another good dress from being ripped. I hadn't noticed how many mosquito bites I had until that point. Looked like I had the measles. That would teach me to run about naked outside after dark. As he watched me I felt a warm wet feeling filling up my body. Finally I climbed up on to the table and it groaned. Then we were laughing as a solitary blue bottle buzzed, and out in the yard the hungry chickens were clucking. Soon I was sitting astride his face and he was sucking me so hard I was shrieking with the great, glorious unbearableness of it all.

I don't really understand it, but when I was with him time just disappeared. I would imagine ten minutes had passed when it was, in fact, two hours. This way the morning vanished, and the sun was at its highest already, and the brightness outside was dazzling, and it was almost lunchtime. I had to race to get a meal ready for the farmhands, and it wasn't what I'd planned, but something much quicker to prepare, *pasta fritta*, yesterday's leftover pasta, which I was going to give to the pigs, fried with a cheesy crust. It was delicious enough, but I hadn't had time to harvest and prepare any vegetables, and we ran out of bread, and there were low-pitched grumbles about standards slipping which made me determined that this shouldn't happen again. I take a pride that our farmhands are the best fed in the region, and I didn't want to disappoint them. But at the same time I couldn't help glowing and basking in the joyous hum of my body, and I couldn't stop smiling as I thought of each great big glossy orgasm that felt like an eruption of the volcano.

After lunch was cleared away, and the farmhands had gone away to have an hour's sleep in the shade of the orange trees or in the barn, I brought in the squash and they were perfect: just dried out enough to be chewy but still slightly sticky. I showed l'Inglese how to chop the squash pieces into small dice, put them into a cauldron with an equal weight of sugar to squash, and just the right amount of water. You must stir the mixture frequently until it is almost boiling, but not quite, and then add your fragrant jasmine water, again not too much, and not too little. The mixture will release a wonderful fragrance and thicken until the syrup is ready to coat the back of your spoon and the squash chunks are tender. Then is the time to carefully fill your sterilized jars, right up to the top, so no air remains, and quickly cap them shut.

As they cooled I made l'Inglese write out the labels in his beautiful handwriting, and when I pasted the labels on I felt extremely pleased with these lovely pale-green jars of preserves. I've still got one left, a souvenir, which I keep as a little secret in my trunk. It's true that the color of the preserve has faded over time from green to gray, and the label is brown with age. I'll never eat it, but whenever I find it again it whispers to me of that night picking jasmine, swimming in the *cisterna* with the nutria, the scorpion bite, and that naughty morning making love on the kitchen table.

CHAPTER SEVENTEEN

Because of his wounded foot, l'Inglese was the only one on the farm who couldn't help with the cherry harvest. He had to lie in bed, with a new novel he was keen to read, and his cold *pranzo* ready on a tray, for this is one of the few days in the year of the farm when I do not cook at midday. We have to work fast to pick them at the peak of ripeness, and get them packed off to the wholesalers at Catania before they spoil, and even the dilapidated farmhands come out of retirement to help, and it really is all hands to the pump.

It was in the afternoon, and we were taking a little break from our work, and of our group at the top of the orchard, old Aulo was lying like a log, snoring loudly, and Mauro and I were sitting in the shade eating fruits from the baskets we had just filled. The cherries were wonderful that year: big, black, plump, sweet, and bursting with juice, so that we had purple hands and purple-smeared faces like small children.

'How old are you, Mauro?' I asked him idly, as the cherry I was eating burst on my tongue, filling my mouth with succulent sweetness.

'I'll be thirty six come Santa Lucia. Why?'

I ignored the question, and did some quick mental arithmetic.

'But how can you be thirty five when Papa died in 1927?'

'He didn't. He died last year'.

'Last year? No. How could he? I was twelve at the time and I remember it very well. His grave is in the cemetery, you can see it for yourself..'

'I already have. He has another one in Saluci. It's very similar. Except he looks older in the photograph. And the dates are different, of course'.

I felt my forehead wrinkling up, which it does when I am trying to work something out. Another grave. Saluci. It didn't make any sense.

'You know, Rosa', Mauro continued, 'Papa's last thoughts were of you. I think he felt bad about it all the rest of his life. On his deathbed he said to me, 'Mauro, I want you to find Rosa. Tell her I'm sorry. Ask her to forgive me', and then he died'.

I didn't say anything. Far in the distance I could hear the faint tinkling of clockwork music. I was about to hear something that would change one of the certainties of my life. Again.

'I feel a bit awkward having to break this to you. Me being a newcomer and all. But it seems Papa and your Mamma weren't getting
along so well..'

'They never got on well. I don't think they ever liked each other'.

'And she told him you weren't... She told him...'

'That I wasn't his child? It's all right, I know that'.

Mauro breathed a sigh of relief, and then continued:

'Well, he was devastated because you were always his favorite, he
said. Daddy's little girl. But by then he had fallen in love with my
mother, and I was about to be born. So he did something that would
smite his conscience for the rest of his life: he faked his own death,
and started a new life with us over in Saluci'.

'But I believed it', I said, 'All this time I thought he was dead'.

I felt that familiar going mad feeling that I had had several times before in my life.

'I know it must come as a terrible shock', said Mauro, his black eyes
fixed on me kindly. 'I asked him why he did such a desperate thing.
If he had to go, why not explain, and pay visits and so on, but just to

abandon his family that way, have them think he was dead, I can't understand it'.

'It was because of Mamma', I said, 'she wouldn't agree to that'.

'That's just what he said,' Mauro agreed, 'he said she would have killed him'.

'She would have, definitely. She shot her second husband, you know. He's buried just over there'.

I looked over to the unmarked spot where the remains of Antonino Calabrese lay.

'He, Papa, I mean, tried to leave once before, he said. And she shot him. He still had the bullet lodged in the back of his neck. The wound never healed'.

'I thought it was a boil', I said, bewildered, 'under that mustard plaster. When I think of Papa, I always see him with that plaster on his neck. I didn't know it was a bullet, under there. I didn't know he had tried to leave'.

I continued, talking to myself, just as much as him:

'It's strange, when you have believed things for so long, and then it turns out they're wrong things. It makes me feel dizzy, sort of, like I don't know what to think, any more. Still, I suppose it doesn't make any difference now'.

'Not now, no', he said, gently, 'but I suppose it shows how he was thinking, at the time, that he believed there was no other way'.

I felt my eyes burning. I crumpled up and started sobbing. I felt angry. I felt cheated. I felt a fool.

'I'm really sorry'.

Mauro leaned over, put his arm around my shoulder, and was almost giving me a hug. His smell, the scent of melting butter, combined with the juicy aroma of the cherries he had been eating and harvesting, and together they were like the ingredients of a cake.

'I feel bad being the one to tell you'.

'It's all right', I sniffed, 'It's not your fault. I just have to get over it, that's all'.

I shrugged him off, scrambled up, and picking up an empty basket, climbed back up my ladder. I began picking again, and that's the thing about the work on the farm, the slow, quiet work in the fields, or in the yard, or in the dairy, or in *la cucina*, yes, the slow, quiet work I find helps to untangle my thoughts and calm my nerves like nothing else can.

There were still a lot of questions to ask, but I didn't want to ask them now. My poor brain had enough to process as it was.

As I picked, carefully, gently, I began to try and put things in order. When I was twelve my beloved father disappeared. I found his mountain cap in the yard. It was lying there like a dead animal. It was so much a part of him, indeed I had never seen him without it on, that it was just like finding a body part lying there. I can still remember the shock of it, the feeling of certainty that he was dead, an effect he must have planned. I would feel differently about the cap from now on. It would seem like an imposter.

Anyway, so, we thought he was dead, but he lived on in Saluci, only about thirty kilometers away, on the far side of the volcano, with his new family, up until last year. Meanwhile we buried him (of course, what we buried was an empty coffin, like all families devastated by *lupara bianca*, the white death, or disappearance). It seems only yesterday when the twins were done out in knickerbockers and tricorn hats, and I carried the mountain cap and wouldn't let it go. Then, shortly afterwards, Mamma interviewed all those suitors, and Antonino Calabrese came and I watched with the twins through the window, as they writhed in the parlor, and it seemed to us, in our innocence, that they were fighting. So then Mamma married Antonino Calabrese, becoming in the process a bigamist, and subsequently a murderess.

'There's something else I have to tell you'.

It was Mauro. He was standing at the foot of my ladder. I held onto my basket of cherries with one hand, and with the other I patted my skirt close to my legs in case he could see up it.

'It's time for the truth to come out'.

My heart sank. What other revelations were waiting to uproot me? I looked down at his purple face through a halo of leaves.

'I love you'.

Was this one of his jokes?

'I fell in love with you the moment I saw you. The day I came. When you had been hunting the asparagus and looked wild'.

I didn't know what to say. I kept peering down at him through the leaves, waiting for the right thing to say to occur to me.

'At first I thought I shouldn't feel like this. I tried to fight it. But it's no good. You're not my sister, and it's all right for us to love each other'.

He was looking at me, clearly waiting for me to say something.

'I don't love you'.

It had to be said. I've never been once for mincing my words.

'You don't think you do', he said, 'But that's just because you're caught up in a fantasy with that foreigner. But it's not real. And you can't see it yet. He doesn't belong here. Where is he now? Lying abed, when everybody else is working. He'll go back to his life. And when the time comes, you'll want him to go. They say that love conquers all, but that's a fairy tale. All that hearts and flowers stuff. It's just nonsense'.

He fell silent for a moment, then went on:

'Love needs solid foundations for it to work. You'll see I'm right. You'll learn to let him go. And I'll be waiting. I'll win you over in the end'.

'You're very confident aren't you?'

'Yes', he said, 'and do you want to know something else?'

'No', I said, 'I don't'.

'*Va bene*', he conceded, 'I'll save the other thing'.

Then he went back to his ladder and got on with his picking.

My head was so stuffed full I felt it could burst. All I had done was ask him how old he was. That would be a lesson to me not to ask personal questions in future.

That night I pushed the mountain cap into the stove and watched it crackle and burn. It gave off a smell like a long-dead dog. I let go of the beliefs that went with it, and imagined that my sadness was the smoke, and once it had disappeared up the chimney, it was gone.

Merende

Snacks

CHAPTER SEVENTEEN

The time of the cherry harvest was followed closely by the *festa*. Normally this is one of the most thrilling times for us, because apart from the natural disasters which we have plenty of in the region, there isn't a lot of what you would call excitement in our lives.

Naturally it was colored by our grief for the twins, as was everything, and now I had the strange news about Papa weighing on my mind too. I kept thinking about him living on close by. All those years when it would have been possible to go over there and see him, and now it was too late. It just didn't make any sense.

For days past there had been the getting ready of the fairground, which was on that scrubby piece of land behind the old Bourbon prison, where, every year, on the 17th February, there falls a rain of toads, and later, something dreadful happened there, but now is not the time to mention it.

There was always a great flurry of activity before the *festa*. The gypsies arrived with their carts, and their caravans, and there were, of course, in these modern times, some trucks, and tents were pitched, and there was a lot of dust and the setting up of the stalls, and side-shows, and the chorals for the animals, and the main ring for the contests.

The children would hang around there watching, and getting into mischief. Inevitably a bit of pilfering went on: missing eggs, chickens, sometimes even a goat. Given the villagers were fiercely competitive about the vegetable contests at the *festa* there was an ever present fear that their prize produce would be plundered for the gypsies' stock-pots. In addition there was sometimes drunkenness, and rowdy behavior, and the fear of being bewitched, and on the day, the excitement sometimes led people to foolishness, that could end in murder, revenge and vendettas.

We all thought about not going, on account of the tragedy, but would good would it serve, not to enjoy ourselves? Guera and Pace were always in the thick of the *festa*, and they wouldn't have wanted us to miss it on their account. I thought it would be good for Biancamaria Ossobucco, for she had shut herself up in the house since the murders, refusing to come out. It would distract her, albeit for a few brief hours, from the devastating grief that was eating away at her like a moth in an old coat.

So the day dawned and we set off, l'Inglese and I, and the swelling of his foot had gone down so that he was now able to get on his seductive shoes, and I have to say I was proud to be on his arm, and we strolled into town. It was already fiercely hot, and of course the black does intensify the heat, and before we were even half-way there I could feel the beads of sweat pinking at my hair line, and tracing a path down my spine, and dampening my underwear, making it stick.

Droves of people were heading in, and amongst them Rosario caught my eye. He had got himself spruced up, with a necktie on, and a rose in the buttonhole of his jacket, and unless I am mistaken, he had even had a wash, for there was a pinkishness about him that we didn't usually see. Some of the farmhands were laughing at him, and ribbing him about going to the *festa* to find a wife. I had begun to worry about him recently. He had been acting stranger than normal, that's for sure.

When we arrived at the fairground the whole of the region had turned out. The volcano itself was in celebratory mood, puffing plumes of rose pink smoke into the bright blue sky. The din was terrific, with the chattering of expectant villagers, laughing children giddy with excitement, and the hawkers and peddlers shouting their wares:

'Lemonade',

'*Granita*',

'Fortunes — all true',

'Wooden legs, low prices',
'Vanishing cream',

'False teeth'.

Beggars with hideous deformities were lying on the ground being trodden on by the crowd, and their cries blended with the voices of the animals: the braying of the mules tied up in rows, the squawking of exotic birds in the bird seller's tent, and the bleating of the goats of Simple Fogna who were huddled around him, releasing their odor of dust and dung.

Of course, there was no escaping my relatives. My nieces and nephews, in particular, were everywhere at once. Popping up and making sport of Zia Rosa and her 'honeysuckle' as they called l'Inglese.

Inside the fence we headed first toward the magnificent vegetable displays: I love those, and I knew l'Inglese would too. Here all the bounty and beauty of our fertile region is displayed, and it is best to come early, before the heat makes everything wilt, as it inevitably does.

Sempronio Baldacucci always wins the prize for his eggplants, and this year would be no different I was sure; they were the biggest I had ever seen, almost the size of melons, glossy and sleek, and the deepest purple gets before it reaches black.

As usual Innocente Capone, whose sons and daughters have married to my nieces and nephews, our two families growing together like the tendrils of a beanstalk, had his magnificent pink onions on display. So strong were they, a pungent cloud rising from them was making everybody cry. The judges holding their clipboards were howling, and Innocente, secure of his gold medal, was weeping fat tears of onion juice.

There were of course, the peppers grown into amazing shapes, and the zucchini, summer squash – the rudest ones usually win the prizes – and garlic bulbs plaited into sculptures: the winner was a life–size traditional cart and a mule to draw it, made by the Dragotto family who had carried it on their backs all the way from Belpasso. It was impressive, certainly, but as usual the tomatoes got my vote. There were many glorious ones, of countless varieties, from the most enormous beefy ones the size of footballs, to tiny darling ones the size of marbles, their sweet fragrance filling the air, and their brilliant color forming a bright splash of red like paint on the dusty brown of the fairground.

The summer fruits were lovely: wonderful peaches, apricots, strawberries, raspberries, and melons, arranged in huge displays. O the perfume was incredible, the very essence of the summer.

The marzipan models were displayed under an awning, but in spite of the meager shade it was clear that some of the exhibits were already beginning to melt. Betta Brina was quick to claim her Madonna was shedding real tears, that it was a miracle, and she should win first prize, but it was obvious to me it was only the almond oil seeping out of the marzipan. It had been my intention to enter myself this year, in the Astonished Madonna class, and also the possibly the animal class, for people do compliment me on my Easter lambs, and also on my piglets. But I hadn't been able to, what with l'Inglese coming back and taking up all my time, and the murder, and everything else, and I wouldn't want to enter if I didn't think I would win. But I do pride myself on my *pasta reale*, and one year, I promised myself, I would take the first prize.

In the pork tent there were sausages of every shape and size, from the tiny ones the size of a baby's thumb, through to ones of the most incredible size, long and narrow, short and fat, and every color: pink, red, purple, black, brown, even green. It was no surprise that the first prize went to Old Man Rospo, with his uniquely flavored pork.

There were the hams also, cooked and uncooked, smoked, and un-smoked. We must have sampled everything. L'Inglese was delighted with it all, feeding me ribbons of this and slices of that, congratulating everybody on their produce.

As we were leaving the tent I guessed the name of Samuele Contaggi's piglet, although goodness knows we have enough of our own to fatten. I looked her in the eye, and I knew with a certainty that her name was Nerissa.

Then we went on to the other big tent where the local cheeses were being tasted, and we tried the fresh pecorino and the aged, the salted ones and the ones with the peppercorns. We tasted the ricotta, fresh and salted and baked and there were those with the candied fruits inside, the lemon peel and orange peel and angelica, sultanas and even chocolate, and all of them excellent. All the local cheese makers were gathered there, and somebody who was everywhere was Mafalda Pruneto, who, though retired, can't help but interfere. Although it was only a short time since she had been forecasting disasters in cheese making throughout the region, she seemed to have forgotten all that, and was proclaiming loudly that it was a good year for cheese, and none of it had gone rancid at all.

There were jams and chutneys, pickles, bottled vegetables, olives, and olive oils, honeycombs in their frames, runny honey in jars, wines, liqueurs, and at the far end were the loaves made into the Madonna, life-size, and the angel Gabriel with wings and everything, ever so well done they were.

As we wandered around I remembered that other time when we had strolled through the Viruccia market in Palermo, when we were just getting to know one another, and what a long time ago that seemed. Then we were tentative, well I was, certainly, not yet lovers, poised on the brink of becoming lovers, and now, we could laugh together, like people who had been a couple a long time. But we hadn't really. We hardly knew each other. Our bodies knew each other very well, but our minds? Weren't they still relative strangers? I was starting to analyze things, and I didn't want to do that. I just wanted to live in the moment. I could think it all out later. After he'd gone. That thought slipped into my mind. The evil seed that Mauro had planted there.

CHAPTER EIGHTEEN

I could see people looking at us and nudging one another and gossiping. The word *straniero* seemed to be on everyone's lips. I didn't care. I felt proud. Let them look. We had got to the market place, where things were for sale rather than being in a competition, and we wandered slowly around every stall in the place.

L'Inglese was out to charm, chatting with the stallholders, and buying all sorts of things he couldn't need like a mop and bucket, a butterfly net, a magnifying glass, and a bottle of invisible ink. He insisted on buying a parrot from the scraggy old birdman. I had known that birdman all my life. Every year he came. I had no taste for caged birds after I lost my dear old friend Celeste in the fire that destroyed my little home in Palermo. In fact, I suddenly realized that Celeste must have come from this very birdman, thirty odd years ago.

When I remonstrated with l'Inglese, he said,

'You'll just have to trust me on this one, *signorina*. This parrot is ours',

So he added the gilded cage and its inhabitant, a little green parrot with a red cockade and yellow beard, to his armload of goods, and we continued shopping.

L'Inglese got very excited when he came upon the stall of Merlo the apothecary. He drew the old charlatan aside and began to whisper earnestly in his ear:

'I'm extremely worried about it...seven of them last night...five the night before...if this continues... none left....do you think it could be the water?... Nasty brown stuff....'

From the look of delight on his face, Old Merlo must have thought his name day had come early. He quickly selected half a dozen bottles of different colored potions and various flagons of pills and began to scribble out a schedule for their use. It looked very complicated. And expensive.

'Guaranteed results, you say?' said l'Inglese, 'Jolly good'.

I didn't like to pry. If he had a medical condition and didn't want me to know about it, I felt I shouldn't eavesdrop, so I wandered on to the next stall along the avenue, Ballotta's Intimo, where giant under-pants hung like ships sails from the awning and there were trusses and surgical supports and voluminous nightgowns suitable for nuns, and rubbery corsets, just like the one l'Inglese had sliced off me with a knife that time so long ago. He laughed when he saw it.

'I remember you, beastly thing', he said to it, giving it a friendly twang, then turning to the toothless gypsy woman behind the counter:

'Haven't you got anything lighter weight?' he asked, 'More suitable for this heat?'

'Not much', she lisped, and even I could barely understand her, 'It don't sell, see, the flimsy'.

But she rummaged around in a box and then in triumph pulled out a frothy, lacey confection, the sort of thing a bride would have in her trousseau. Definitely flimsy.

'The very thing', he cried, joyfully, holding it up.

Immediately it was paid for and wrapped up in paper and wedged under his arm.

My gifts for him were more practical: I chose a straw hat with a smart blue ribbon round the crown, a fly swatter, and a bottle of Albo Bonazinga's lemon cologne.

It was a good thing we had reached the last of the stalls, for we could scarcely carry everything, and certainly couldn't have managed any more.

CHAPTER NINETEEN

In the next section were the curiosities; the tents where you had to pay to see poor souls being exhibited. I've never liked those. If I hadn't been alert that day when those men tried to steal Guera and Pace away, they could have spent their lives in a side-show being stared at and poked by the paying public. I hoped poor Angela Forbicina had her babies safely hidden away. So we avoided the bearded lady, the cat woman with a genuine tail, the giant man, the snake boy, who had no legs, and was covered all over with silver scales, and the duck-girl with what was advertised as a real bill.

Next to those were the clairvoyants, the palm-readers, and the crystal ball gazers, and there were crowds clustered around there waiting their turns in the tents, mostly young girls and lads. I was surprised to see Rosario coming out of one of the tents. I hoped his head hadn't been filled with nonsense. It contains enough of that already.

In the main ring the strength trials were being held. There were the usual tug-of-war contests between local teams, arm-wrestling, pig-lifting, and after this was the big event, the contest to see who, if anyone, could lift Santina Maccarrone, the carnival queen.

Now Santina Maccarrone is a famous singer, and she has travelled the whole world on cruise liners and she has seen everything there is to see, and she has been shipwrecked many times, and seized by pirates, and nothing surprises her any more. She is famous also, throughout our region, for her enormous size and weight. She is the biggest woman we have got, and for this reason, when her singing schedule permits, she becomes the carnival queen.

It was rumored that Santina had been eating more than usual recently in an attempt to outdo the competitors. For if nobody could lift her, she would herself pocket the prize money of a thousand lire and a year's supply of pasta donated by Pasta Fresca Morabito.

It was rumored also that Silvia and Basilio Morabito were worried sick in case Santina won, because the business was struggling to survive anyway in those times of poverty and uncertainty, and Santina's mighty appetite could only mean ruin.

Anyway, there had already been a lot of entrants, and several of our men who prided themselves on their strength had gone away nursing hernias, and l'Inglese and I arrived just in time to see my brother Mauro rubbing his hands together in the basin of corn flour, preparing to take his turn.

Santina Maccarone was seated in the special throne on tall legs, beneath which the contestant had to position himself, and the judges were standing around waiting. Santina was enjoying her moment of glory, offering insults to the competitors, casting doubt on the manhood of many, and Mauro was ready now and the countdown began.

I hoped that he wouldn't injure himself, for he is a good worker, and we would need him at harvest time which would soon be upon us. Silence fell over the fairground as Mauro crossed himself and offered up a silent prayer to the Madonna. The tension was mounting as he began the attempt and for a moment or two it looked hopeless. He strained. His face went the color of eggplant. The veins stood out on his neck. His eyes bulged and looked bloodshot, and I thought he was about to burst open with the exertion like Salvo Musolino did in last year's contest.

But then, the legs of the throne tottered and cleared the ground and Santina Maccarone was aloft. She was actually up in the air on Mauro's back. The crowd went wild with applause and cheering, Mauro lifted her higher still, took a few steps, and then began to parade around the enclosure carrying Santina Maccarone. Nobody had ever seen anything like it.

Finally, after what seemed like ages, he set her down and was mobbed by the crowd of admiring supporters. He was himself lifted up onto their shoulders in a lap of honor, before being presented with his medal by Donna Rea Reparata Gusto, the mayor's wife, who was pictured for the local paper feeling his mighty biceps. I've got that clipping, too, pasted in my scrapbook. Then Mauro announced in a generous gesture that he would split his prize with Santina Maccarone: he would keep the money, but she could have the year's supply of pasta. At this Santina Maccarone clapped her fat, little hands together with a child's delight, and her piggy eyes shone with greed, but poor Silvia and Basilio Morabito were left weeping.

Next into the ring were the mules and their drivers for the owner who looks most like his mule contest. Although it is supposed to be a light-hearted competition, the entrants take it incredibly seriously, and this year was going to be a difficult one to decide because there were some very strong contenders. I was surprised to see that Rosario was not in the enclosure, for he makes a habit of entering every year with his mule, Carciofo, although, of course, he never wins. After Donna Rea Reparata Gusto had examined all the entrants' teeth and whiskers and knees, the prize finally went to old Licurgo Pastone and Dolores.

CHAPTER TWENTY

The highlight, indeed the whole purpose of the *festa*, is the procession, when our local girls and unmarried women dress up as the Madonna, and parade through the streets of the town, finally arriving at the fairground for a display of folk dancing, and a blessing by the priest. But I have to say every year it is becoming more of a beauty pageant.

As usual many of my nieces were taking part: I spotted Rea Silvia, Pupa, Tranquilla, Biancofiore, Modeste, Amoretta, Etna, Carita, Belcolore, Anna Monica, Maria Maddalena, Frugolina, Occhibella, my great nieces Magnolia and Mimosa, Stella and Luna, Ginevra, Franca, Ambra, Teresa, Floria, Gardenia, Perla, Camelia, Anna Daria, Anna Carla, Anna Marta, Antonina, Roberta, and bringing up the rear were the baby Rosas, chaperoned by Biancamaria Ossobucco in the heaviest of mourning. Behind her, like a shadow, was Rosario, which I wasn't pleased about, because the procession is strictly for women only, and he was asking for trouble with the fathers and the brothers by being where he wasn't wanted.

Looking at some of my bolder nieces, and some of the other girls, I have to say that in my opinion the Madonna would never have appeared looking like that. The bigger girls were smeared in greasy make-up, and some of their costumes were very revealing, causing lots of irreligious comments from the local boys who were, of course, ogling.

When the girls took their positions for the dancing, it became obvious to all that something had happened to Etna's skirt. Most of it was missing. And all that remained was barely decent. L'Inglese said it was a 'miniskirt', and that they were all the rage in the rest of the world, apparently. Well I have to say here, in the region, we had never seen anything like it.

Before the band could strike up, my sister-in-law Pervinca, feeling the shame to her family and the slurs that the bystanders must be heaping on her, burst through the ranks of spectators, breached the barriers, and ran for all she was worth towards the formation where Etna was waiting for her cue. The girl saw trouble approaching, and took to her heels, but she was no match for her mother whose rage had given her wings. Pervinca lost no time in tackling her wayward daughter to the ground, then dragging her off by the hair, with muttered curses about what would happen when she got her home.

Then the dancing got underway in earnest, and my eyes were glued to the baby Rosas. Tears of pride streamed down my cheeks as they pranced about, flourishing their crucifixes and marching in step with the other, much bigger girls. O how proud the boys would have been. My poor boys. Now tears of sorrow blended with the tears of pride and l'Inglese understood. He folded me in his arms and gave me a good squeeze.

Then there was the blessing, and afterward Padre Buonaventura was carried off by a crowd of the bigger girls to the refreshment tent. It is certainly the case that since he has come amongst us, many of my nieces seem much more interested in going to church than they were before.

CHAPTER TWENTY ONE

The main part of the *festa* was now over. After the procession the men tend to start drinking, and the women tend to return to their work, for the children get tired out, the animals must be fed, and all the work done, *festa* or no.

'What goes on in that tent over there?' l'Inglese asked me.

'O nothing much, just the men playing card games', I replied, needing a sit down after being on my feet all of the afternoon in the hot sun. Typically, vanity had got the better of me, and my newish shoes had given me blisters.

'Card games?' He said, his interest aroused, 'let's just have a look shall we?'

So we went over, and as I suspected there was nothing much going on at all, just tables with men sitting at them playing cards. Nothing worth looking at certainly.

'That's all', I said, 'Shall we go and find Biancamaria Ossobuco and the girls and eat *granita*?'

'I might just try my luck for a bit', he said, 'that is, if you don't mind?'

'No', I said, a bit surprised.

I didn't mind. But what could there be interesting about playing cards?

'I'll go and find the girls, and I'll meet you back here later'.

I took most of the packages (he kept hold of the medicines himself), and went in search of Biancamaria Ossobucco and the girls. It took me a while to discover them, for the crowds were still thick. I felt like abandoning the mop and bucket, and several of the other things, for we had many just like them already at home. But then I thought he would be sad if I did. The poor parrot clearly needed a drink, but how to give him one? I rearranged the things in a way which I hoped would be easier to carry and went on. Eventually I found them marveling at the act of a fire eater who was swallowing great burning torches and it made me thirstier than ever.

So we went on together, and after squeezing through the sweaty hordes, we reached the refreshment tent. There, tackling an ice cream sundae that was almost as big as himself, was the doll-sized Old Man Patti, father of poor Angela.

We made our selections, and I chose coffee, of course, and then, when Rosario went to take a bite of his, pistachio, it was, I remember, I noticed straight away that he had developed teeth. Teeth!

'Heavens above!' I couldn't help but cry out at the astonishing sight,

'What in the name of the Madonna have you got in your mouth?'

The baby Rosas burst into laughter which is so infectious I wish I could preserve it in a bottle, and at the same time began wiggling about so much that they had to be frog-marched to the latrine tent by Biancamaria Ossobucco who shouted back over her shoulder:

'He bought them from Bullo. Supplies all the movie stars, he says. Don't you think they look nice, Rosa?'

I wasn't so sure. With them in he reminded me of the shark they once exhibited in a tank at the *festa* of Santa Albina. After the girls had gone there was a bit of an embarrassed silence. As I licked my ice, I saw Rosario prize out the teeth and slip them into his pocket.

'Just really for looking at, see', I heard him mutter.

At that point Samuele Contaggi rushed up to me and thrust his piglet into my arms.

'Been looking for you everywhere', he said, running off in the direction of the card-players tent,

'I say, that foreigner of yours, some poker player, he is, there's Vincenze Scalabrino, losing his shirt, but won't give up. Old Innocente Capone, every scent of his prize money gone, weeping, he is, and not because of the vapor of his onions...'

Intent on his words I didn't notice Nerissa, whom I held in one hand, gobbling up the *granita* I had in the other. Poker playing. It was not something I knew anything about. But I didn't like the idea of Vincenzo, the husband of my niece Penelope, and the father of three tiny children, wasting his hard-earned money in this way. Or of l'Inglese taking it. At this point the triplets raced back followed by Biancamaria Ossobucco. They were delighted with the piglet and were soon squabbling over who should have the next turn at feeding her *granita* which the piglet gobbled greedily. Then they remembered the parrot, and so more *granita* was poked through the bars of his cage, until his feathers were plastered down and he was sitting in a slick of melted pink ice mixed with seeds, bruised fruit, and droppings.

A dance floor had been put down over the scrubby grass and Privato's band was playing. My nephew, Privato. Plays the violin. Guido Maccarone (the brother of Santina the fat woman, and he is not fat, as you would expect, but lean and thin), he plays the piano accordion and sings in a deep baritone those sentimental numbers, and the other one, Sesto Vinci, plays the trumpet.

The local youth were dancing, and amongst them was strutting Padre Buonaventura with his film star smile, and Rosario said,

'Not like a priest, that one',

But of course, nobody takes any notice of what he says. The baby Rosas were soon dancing too, and we stood and watched. Mauro whirled past with Donna Rea Reparata Gusto. Santina Maccarone, a fine dancer, like most fat people are, was twirling in the arms of the birdman. Although it was crowded, it seemed to me that Noe Randone the husband of my niece Brunetta was dancing with Consuelo Ingrassia, Salvatore's latest wife. Ludo Capone, the husband of Brunetta's twin sister Brunella was dancing with Raffaela Capone, the wife of my nephew Gentile. Paolo Scafidi, who is married to Petronilla, was dancing with Giuliano's wife Galatea Mocambo. Everybody seemed mixed up, and I hoped it wouldn't end in a fight as these things so often do.

We wandered on from there to watch the tightrope walker, the puppet show, the jugglers, and the people who stand very still on plinths and pretend to be statues and then startle you when you're least expecting it by moving. Finally the triplets were overtired and fractious and started arguing and biting each other and pulling hair, and it was time for them to be getting home to bed. For some reason Rosario wanted to see Biancamaria Ossobucco and the girls home, for he said there were bandits about, so he loaded all of my shopping onto the back of Carciofo and they went away, leaving me with only the parrot and the piglet to carry.

CHAPTER TWENTY TWO

By now the attractions of the *festa* were worn down like a heel, and it was time for us too to be heading home. I felt reluctant to enter the gambling tent. It is not a place for women, and I didn't want to embarrass l'Inglese. I didn't want the other men to think that he was tied to my apron strings, but eventually, after hanging around for while more, in the end I forced myself through the flap.

Inside it was hot as an oven, crowded, and thick with the fog of tobacco smoke. I pushed my way through the crush of onlookers. There were now only two players at the big table: l'Inglese, with a huge mound of coins and notes before him, and, opposite him, was Don Umberto Sogno, the father and murderer of my first love, Bartolomeo.

The sight of him felt like a slap across my face; I had not seen him close to since that night, the night of the murder, when he had thrown me bodily out of his house, twenty nine years ago. He had aged, of course. His hair was no longer black, but the color of steel. Yet he still had that air of pride and power, as though he owned the region, and everyone and everything in it. This scene was like one of my nightmares: my lover and the murderer of my first lover facing one another in combat.

There was silence, and a tension that was prickly, then Don Umberto pushed back his chair and stood up. He looked at l'Inglese as he had once looked at me, with venom and with hatred, and with a controlled gesture he flicked his cards across the table.

The crowd on that side parted to make way for him and his henchmen and it was only after they had left the tent that someone turned the volume up and there was a hubbub of chattering and gasping and coughing.

I watched as l'Inglese gathered the notes into wads that he stuffed with difficulty into the pockets of his too-tight pants, and scooped the coins into the apothecary's bag, and when that was full, he tipped them into his hat. Although it was a big hat, they still spilled over.

I made my way round the table to him. His eyes danced when they saw me and he gave me a big smile, but I was caught up in the vortex of the past. Yet, in spite of my preoccupation, still I noticed something strange about him: he was pale and sweaty and twitchy.

We made our way outside with the piglet and the parrot and the hat of money and there were muttered voices saying that Don Umberto wouldn't look kindly on his defeat, his loss of face.

'Let's get a drink', he said, and we went to the place where Taddeo Brutto had set up his bar behind some rows of trestle tables and chairs where only the men were idling and drinking and arm—wrestling at this hour.

L'Inglese clinked his glass against mine, and then swallowed the wine in one gulp.

'We're a winning team, signorina', he said, taking Nerissa from me and tickling her soft, sticky, pink belly, 'Lady Luck has been smiling on us both'.

I wasn't so sure.

'Do you know who that was?' I asked him quietly.

'No'.

'Do you remember what I told you about why I left here and went to Palermo, all those years ago?'

'Of course I do. How could I forget something like that? Your first love had been murdered'.

'By him. That man you were playing cards with. That man is, was, his father'.

L'Inglese blanched. He reached for my hand and squeezed it hard.

'You poor darling', he said, looking into my eyes. His were full of sympathy, 'That must have given you such a shock, coming face to face with him, like that. The bastard! If I'd known I'd have knocked him down, as well as relieving him of his money'.

'He won't like losing. It's not the money. It's the loss of face. With everybody watching, like that...'

'Well, if he's not prepared to lose, he shouldn't play', he interrupted.

'You don't understand the way things are here', I said, 'There are people you don't want to make enemies of. No good will come of it, I tell you.'

'That's not my Rosa talking. She's not afraid of anybody'.

'That's true', I said, 'I'm not afraid of anything for myself. But for you, I am. I know what that man is capable of'.

'Does that mean you love me?'

'Of course I love you. Do you need to ask?'

'She loves me', he shouted out loud, throwing his arms up into the air.

'Ssshhhh', I hissed, embarrassed because people were looking. He was acting drunk, but I didn't think he had drunk very much.

It was time to go. As we walked towards the gate, we passed Mauro and a bunch of his cronies arm-wrestling.

'Come on, Stranger', Mauro said to l'Inglese, 'Come and try your luck against me'.

'No thanks, Strongman', he replied, 'I don't need a broken arm'.

'Better a broken arm, than a broken neck'.

'Hopefully, I'll avoid both'.

'I wouldn't put money on it'.

I pulled l'Inglese away. I didn't want the evening to end in a fight.

There were so many coins in the hat, they kept spilling out onto the ground, leaving a trail of gold behind us like in a fairy tale.

'All that money', I said, 'It isn't right'.

'What isn't right?'

'Samuele Contaggi said that Vincenzo Scalabrino, he's married to Penelope, Giuseppe's Penelope, not Penelope Muscatello, he said that he, Vincenzo, I mean, lost all his money, and you took it, but he can't afford to lose it'.

'In that case, *signorina*, he shouldn't play cards either. It's quite simple'.

'But can't you give it back? You've got so much of it'.

'That's not the way it works'.

On the way home the stars came out one by one. It was still hot, without a breeze. The perfume of wallflowers was sweet and strong. The hedges along the way were filled with the giggles and squeals of young lovers, and, if I recognized some voices, those not so young, and not so single. L'Inglese sang snatches of love songs in English and the parrot, though dehydrated and tired out, joined in with a few squawks here and there. Charmed, Nerissa fell asleep in my arms and snored tenderly. I'm not usually sentimental about animals, but I knew then that Nerissa would be a pet, and that I would never slaughter her and salt her and make her into hams.

I was so tired after such a day I would have happily gone straight to sleep. L'Inglese offered to cook, while I had a soak in the bath, and I was lying there wallowing in the fragrant bubbles thinking through all the things that had happened, and it seemed like a week had taken place in a day. Then l'Inglese came in with a glass of wine for me, and he began to look at me in that way he has, and now he was climbing into the tub too, with all his clothes on, causing the water to cascade over the edge. So he was climbing on top of me and I was screaming with laughter, and he was laughing too, and we were half-drowned and there was water everywhere. The floor was flooded, and afterward some of the tiles came up, and never did lie flat down again. Often, when I'm lying there in the tub, all this time later, after so much has happened, I still remember it, and it still makes me smile, even now.

Pizza

CHAPTER TWENTY THREE

It wasn't long before Don Umberto took his revenge. That same night, in the middle of the night, for of course, we had been making love again and again, and it seemed that I had only just closed my eyes when a bright light made me open them again. It couldn't be day already. But it wasn't the sun that was shining in my face, it was a flashlight. Bleary in the glare, I made out men, standing around the bed, three of them. My heart lurched inside my chest. I couldn't breathe. What should I do? L'Inglese still seemed to be asleep.

'What do you want?' I whispered.

They had guns.

'The stranger', said one.

'Wakey, wakey', said another.

'Come on, Sleeping Beauty, time to get up', said the third.

I was trying to think. What could I use as a weapon? In these lawless times I knew many of our people concealed axes, swords and cudgels beneath their pillows in case of attack by bandits in the night. I had always pooh-poohed such measures, refusing to live in fear, but, clearly, I was wrong. If only I had a hatchet to hand, I would give these assassins what for.

I had only a small vase of bell flowers, and a pot of hand cream (gardenia scented) within reach. I couldn't launch an assault with those.

One of the men reached out and pulled the covers off roughly, revealing our naked bodies to the public view. Incensed, I snatched the covers back to shield myself. L'Inglese stirred.

'Rosa, please, let me get some sleep', he muttered, sleepily, 'We'll do it again in the morning'.

'Come on, get up', the man said sharply. His gun made a clicking sound and this succeeded in waking l'Inglese finally.

'They've got guns', I said to l'Inglese, and to the men I said:

'At least let us get dressed before you shoot us'.

We hunted around for our clothes while the men watched. I was always having dreams like this, being watched, while I had no clothes on. I suppose it started with Signor Rivoli, the Peeping Tom, who lived across the way from my little apartment in Palermo, and who often used to spy on me while I was undressing. I picked up the blouse I had been wearing, but it had been torn in half by l'Inglese in his impatience to get it off.

'I'll have to get something out of the closet', I said to the men.

'All right, but no funny business', said the tallest of the men, who seemed to be in charge, and he motioned with his gun to the guard robe in the corner. I backed toward it, trying to shield myself with my hands and arms in front. It was impossible. My overflowing body defied any attempt at modesty.

After a hundred mile journey I got to the closet door and opened it. When I moved one of the hangers aside I nearly burst with shock. Mauro was in there, hiding amongst the clothes. Frantically he gestured me to be silent, and I smothered my loud gasp with a fit of coughing. It was then that I noticed Mauro was wearing one of my dresses, the blue spotted shirtwaist, the one I was looking for. He also had on a smear of pink lipstick.

'Come on, sister, this ain't no fashion parade', said one of the assassins, losing patience. He was the one with the quivering wart dangling from the end of his nose.

I reached into the closet and grabbed another dress, it was red, and it was strange because I never remembered seeing it before. I don't think it was mine, but in the circumstances it would have to do. I pulled it on and it was a bit tight, and I heard the now-familiar sound of ripping at the back as I thrust my body into it.

At the same time Mauro managed to slip me one of my big kitchen knives. He had a gun. He nodded at me, and together we launched an attack. Screaming with fear and panic, terror and rage, I charged across the room brandishing the knife. Gunfire blasted out. Mauro was shooting. The baddies were shooting. My own screams were deafening me. I was in such a frenzy I didn't know what I did. I thrust at the tall baddy with the knife; I don't know how it was possible but l'Inglese got in the way. I watched in helpless slow motion as the knife went into him instead. The big thrust with all my weight behind it went right into him. Horrified I wrenched the blade out, but there was a big, round hole in his chest, and out of it gushed blood, such red blood, and so much of it, it was pumping out and squirting onto me, and where it splashed on my dress, the dress stained white, not red.

L'Inglese collapsed onto the ground and his naked body looked so white and the blood was so red. Nerissa the piglet was there, running

through the pool of blood, leaving a trail of tiny red trotter prints behind her on the floor. I was still screaming and the third assassin, the
one with the teeth of a horse said:

'We came here to kill him, but you've saved us a job, sister'.

The assassin was right. L'Inglese was dead. My beloved, my own
true darling, was dead.

I roared like a mother when her baby is in the path of a speeding train:

'NO',

Now, somehow, Don Umberto himself was there in the room, the man
who had killed both my darlings, both of them. I grabbed him by the
throat, and held on, and I was certainly going to throttle all the life
out of him.

He was fighting back but I wouldn't give up. I was fighting, and
would die fighting. It was then that I realized it wasn't Don Umberto, I was fighting, it was l'Inglese. He wasn't dead after all. He was
alive. He was alive. I had him by the throat, and I was strangling
him. He was trying to pull my hands off his throat, and he was
screaming:

'Rosa, stop it. Get off. Wake up. You're killing me'.

I was sobbing:

'You're alive. You're not dead. You're alive'.

We were in bed. It was a dream. Only a dream. I had been dreaming. I stopped strangling him. He was making hoarse, choking, dying noises. Finally he rasped:

'Good God Rosa, you nearly did for me then'.

His face was blue, and his neck was black.

'I'm sorry', I gasped. I was exhausted. I wanted to cry.

'I had a bad dream. I dreamt that Don Umberto had sent assassins
to kill you. It was awful'.

My heart was beating at double speed for a long time, and I was so
sweaty it looked like I'd been swimming. It took me ages to calm
down, while l'Inglese's neck swelled and puffed up like a bullfrog. I
felt terribly guilty. Suppose I had killed him?

It was only later that we were able to laugh about it.

'I'd rather take my chances with the assassins,' he said, but I think he was joking. I hope he was. 'I've always thought you were a danger-ous woman. I shall be afraid every time I go to bed with you from now on'.

'You're right to be afraid', I said, 'Now lie down and do exactly as I tell you', and with that I leapt on top of him.

CHAPTER TWENTY FOUR

The following morning l'Inglese began a new regime. First he carried out a thorough investigation of the bed, paying particular attention to the pillows, the sheets, and even the surrounding floor, crawl-
ing around it on his hands and knees.

'Have you lost something?' I asked, intrigued, but he gave me a look
which encouraged me to say no more, and come down to *la cucina* to
start preparing breakfast.

He then spent ages in the bathroom, and when he emerged he was a
glossy pink in the face and smelt medicinal, which was odd, because
his own natural smell, the smell I loved, was gone. To my shame his
neck was still black, but the swelling had gone down slightly.

It was also at this time that he began to take pills and liquid medicines
at set and frequent hours, and he began to carry about a portable mirror, in which I caught him often taking long and surreptitious glances
at the reflection of his head.

'You do realize that Old Merlo is no more an apothecary than I am',
I said to him, but my warnings fell on deaf ears.

That same morning it was time for the parrot to undergo a course of instruction. L'Inglese sat himself on the steps leading up to *la cucina*, with the parrot perching on his hand. He was teaching it to speak English. Nerissa, the piglet, had quickly grown used to her new home, and her status as a pet, and followed me everywhere like a dog.

I had been harvesting watermelons, having a craving for a pudding to use some of the jasmine syrup, and so big and juicy were they, I had to bring them back in my barrow, for I could scarcely carry one in my arms, but not more.

It appeared that the parrot was called Betty, and was a willing and able student. Already he could say 'Hello Betty', 'cheese', 'volcano', and 'too hot'.

And it was too hot already. By the time I had carried the watermelons up the steps and into *la cucina* my hair was plastered to my scalp with sweat and my dress was clinging to me. I was only too glad to sit down with a cooling glass of lemonade, but when I heard the sound of distant shouting, I knew there was more bad news to come.

'Who's dead this time?' Was the first thought that passed through my mind.

I almost didn't want to know. I hurried down the steps, past l'Inglese
and the parrot, as Leonardo, Mario, Giuliano, Salvatore and Mauro
raced into the yard.

'Who's dead this time?' I asked, squinting into the sun.

'They've gone', Giuliano cried out.

'Who've gone?'

'The twins',

and

'Amoretta's missing' came the jumbled replies.

'The twins?' I cried.

'Bodies dug up' they said together.

I slumped down on the bottom step: 'No!'

'But we'll find them'.

'If we're quick'.

'Amoretta's bed's not been slept in'.

'Pervinca's got an axe'.

'She'll murder somebody for sure'.

'She may have gone with the gypsies'.

'Giuseppe's gone after them'

My brothers charged off to get the tractor and the truck to join in the search. My first fear was for Biancamaria Ossobucco. How would she bear this terrible blow?

Reluctantly l'Inglese returned Betty to his cage, and we hurried on foot to the cemetery. Biancamaria Ossobucco was sure to be there.

Since the day of the burial, a watch had been kept on the grave over-night by my surviving brothers, their many sons, sons-in-law, friends of the family, and some of the farm hands. But last night everybody had been at the *festa*, and the grave had been neglected. It was then that the body snatchers had seized their opportunity.

When we arrived, sure enough Biancamaria Ossobucco was on her knees in the gaping hole in the ground, looking as forlorn as it was possible to look. The triplets were digging for worms in the earth that had been hastily scattered all around. Rosario was there too. And the goats of Simple Fogna were, as usual, eating the wreaths and flowers on the freshest graves.

'It's a judgment upon me Rosa', she said weakly, when she saw me.

'Nonsense, dear'. I said, 'What makes you say that?'

She looked at Rosario, 'I'm too ashamed to tell you', she said.

'Now', I said, in a firm voice, 'I want you to put nonsense like that out of your head. You were the best of wives to the boys. They couldn't have wished for a better one. There are greedy and unscrupulous people in this world who will make money any way they can. That is no fault of yours. And yes, it is a terrible thing that has happened, but the boys, our beloved boys, weren't in there any more, in that box, underground. They're gone, to a better place, where no one can harm them. Now I want you to get up, for the sake of those baby girls, you can't do any good here, and come on home with me'.

So once again we hauled Biancamaria Ossobucco up, out of the grave, loaded the baby Rosas onto Carciofo's back, and went back to their house in town.

'Have you eaten?' I asked, and, of course, I could tell by the look of her, that Biancamaria Ossobucco hadn't eaten for days, so I went into the kitchen and rolled up my sleeves.

I washed the baby Rosas' hands and got them to help me, one to harvest basil from the courtyard, one to sprinkle salt on the eggplant, one to crumble the ricotta and so on. L'Inglese was standing in front of the big looking glass trying to view the back of his head.

'Why has that funny man come here?' Asked Rosita, with the bluntness typical of small children.

'Shall we give him a job too?' I asked them.

They nodded.

'You seem to have more than enough helpers', he said, 'As I'm surplus to requirements I might just go down to the *Due Ladrone* and see what's going on. If that's all right..?'

'Of course', I said, 'I'm sorry....'

For all of this, I wanted to say. For having to comfort Biancamaria Ossobucco. For my murdered brothers bodies being snatched. For all the things that got in the way of us just being alone together, and loving each other, without responsibility for anything else, like it was then, for those few days, before you went away. Before you go away again.

'No, no, it's fine', he said, 'I won't be long'.

And so he went. And later I sat Biancamaria Ossobucco down with a plate of spaghetti with eggplant and tomato sauce. She couldn't eat very much, on account of having lost her appetite, but she did eat some to please me. Rosario was fussing about her, and I don't know how she stands it. I would have to speak to him when I got the opportunity. The baby Rosas soon had red faces and were smeared all over with sauce, and I didn't have time to notice l'Inglese wasn't there. It was past three when I had put the triplets down to have a nap, washed the dishes, and tidied everything away.

I left the house and almost immediately I passed a priest. He raised his hat to me, and introduced himself as Padre Goffredo, the new priest to the town, and could I direct him to the Via San Angelo? which I did. It was only after he had walked away carrying a small valise and a violin case that I thought it was strange because we already had Padre Buonaventura.

I went to look for l'Inglese at the *Due Ladrone*, but it was closed by now, and there was nobody there. My legs walked me on, into the *campo*, but it too was deserted. Even Manlio Estivo, the man who never moves from his spot on the wall under the palm tree near the public drinking fountain was missing. I began to climb the narrow streets toward the citadel. The sun beat down relentlessly. I felt my body grow hot and moist and pungent. There were piles of stray cats lying still, looking dead. My ears strained for any sound other than the pulse beating in my head. Only later did it come: footsteps, behind me. I didn't want to turn around. Momentarily I braced myself to feel the impact of the knife slicing into the back of my neck. So this is what it feels like: the moment before you die.

But the blow didn't come. A voice, a woman's voice called my name. I spun round. It was a woman in black. It was Sophia Bacci.

Now Sophia Bacci is the girl whom Bartolomeo's father had wanted him to marry. It was his refusal to become betrothed to her that had led to the argument that made Don Umberto murder his own son. In spite of this, Sophia Bacci has always behaved kindly to me. She has never had another love, and has remained faithful to Bartolomeo's memory all these years.

I tottered. She reached out and clutched me, steadying me.

'Are you all right, Rosa?'

Only then did I start breathing again. Together we went and sat on the low wall that divides the street from the sheer drop beyond.

'It was strange', I said, feeling odd, but ridiculous, 'I had a premonition of death'.

'Whose?' she asked, alarmed.

'Mine'.

She shuddered. She still looked like a girl although we are the same age. She is thin, of course, which makes a difference, but her face is lined, and without vitality, I suppose because she hasn't really lived; all these years she has been in mourning. Now we were in matching black.

'I'm so sorry about your brothers', she said.

I thanked her with a sad smile.

Then she lowered her voice, as if she were afraid of being overheard, although of course there was nobody there except the two of us and the cats, and the words fell out of her mouth in a hurry.

'Rosa, I came here specially to find you. I heard some talk. I think your *straniero* is in danger. I think he should go away..'

'But he's only just come'. I said.

'But you know the way things are. Suppose something were to happen to him? How would you bear it, if it happened..*again*?'

I knew what she meant. I couldn't bear it.

'I better get home', I said, getting up. I felt an urgent need to be back at the *fattoria*. I think it's important to follow those sorts of impulses. 'Thank you for coming to warn me. It was good of you'.

We walked back down the hill together without talking.

'Be careful, Rosa, won't you?' She said, giving me a hug, at the place where our ways parted.

'I will', I said.

As I walked home I tried to think. What to do for the best. I wished l'Inglese hadn't got involved with Don Umberto. Of all the people he could have beaten at cards, why did it have to be that murdering *Mafioso*? Still, what's done is done. You can't change the past. Only the future. Why couldn't we just be left in peace? I didn't want to live in fear. I didn't want to send him away. I didn't want him to be murdered. Although I didn't want to worry, I began to feel very worried indeed. Common sense told me I couldn't keep watch over him all the time. It wasn't realistic. I couldn't keep him like Betty, a caged bird.

I was home before I knew it. My troubled thoughts had given speed to my legs, and I was very hot and dusty by the time I arrived back at the *fattoria*. When I got there everything seemed wrong.

'*Amore?*' I called out, hurrying up the steps to *la cucina*. Was he there? Inside there was definitely something amiss. The old place could speak to me without words. My heart began to beat irregularly. What was I going to find? I had felt like this the time I found poor Crocifisso's body in the glass case at the Library. I didn't want to find a body now. I didn't want to see l'Inglese's murdered body on the floor. I wanted to close my eyes so that I wouldn't see whatever it was that was waiting there.

And then, on the table, I found her. Nerissa. Cold and hard, with a bullet through her head, and a playing card, the Ace of Hearts, pinned through her side with one of my sharp knives. I must have screamed. My nerves were so overwrought. It was horrible. Poor little mite. Although I am, by nature, a butcher, I felt sick. That they should come in, and do this to her, in my kitchen. Then there were footfalls running up the steps.

'*Amore?*' I called, but it wasn't my love, it was Mauro. I was so disappointed.

'Look', I said, pointing with a shaking finger.

He grimaced in disgust.

'Bastards', he muttered.

I think he was trying to get hold of me, to give me a hug, but I shrugged him off. It was an awkward moment.

'Have you seen him?' I asked.

'No', he said, in a way that seemed not very interested, 'He's one of the few people I haven't been looking for. I've been over to Antillo looking for the twins, but it turned out to be a wild goose chase, and I've just got back from Linguaglossa on the trail of Amoretta. It turns out she has run off with the priest, and not only that, he isn't a priest at all, but a conman who just pretends to be a priest'.

'A conman?' I said, struggling to take in yet more bad news. 'So that explains it: there's a new priest in town. I saw him'.

'I know. Pervinca has already attacked him with an axe'.

'No!'

'Yes. He'll never play the violin again'.

'She chopped off his hands?'

'No. It was all he had to defend himself. Now it's only fit for fire-wood'.

Mauro picked up the little stiff body of Nerissa, and went off with her to bury her.

Then I heard l'Inglese's voice:

'Very hot, very, very, very hot'.

'*Amore?*'

I couldn't see him. Then I realized it was the parrot, Betty. It sounded uncannily like l'Ingese's voice. At least the assassins hadn't murdered the parrot as well as the piglet.

I cleared everything off the table, filled the new pail with water, took soap and a scrubbing brush, and set about giving the ancient table a very good scrub, as if by doing that I could erase my anguished feelings. Back and forth I scrubbed, thousands and thousands of times, and soon I was wet with sweat and soapy water. By the time I was finished the table was lighter in color than it had ever been. But still he didn't come. Would he come? Please let him come.

I then felt the urge for a cheesecake. The complicated recipe was just what I needed to slow down the whirling of my brain; and once it was cooked, the eating of it could only soothe me some more.

I roasted some almonds in a big tray in the oven and *la cucina* was filled with their toasty, nutty scent, and once they had cooled a little I ground them finely in my pestle and mortar, a handful at a time, crushing them with the action of my wrist and forearm and upper arm and shoulder and back, putting my whole body into the crushing as though I could in this way crush my fears. My hand grew hot and tired and I ground away and soon the almonds were a powdery heap upon the spotless table.

Then I beat together butter and sugar. My wooden spoon and my hand and arm flew round and round so fast they were a blur, and soon the mixture was light and fluffy and it was time to add the egg yolks, beating each one in hard until the gloop was yellow and shiny and thick.

To my powdered almonds I added a handful of flour, a pinch of baking powder and a pinch of salt, and the finely grated zest of lemons, and the lemons were zingy and fresh and their sharp scent burst in the air, and I folded these dry ingredients into my buttery-egg gloop, until the mixture was thick and pale in color and my spoon left a trail like a ribbon across the surface.

Next I took my lovely fresh ricotta and whisked into it the juice of my lemons until it was light and runny, and then folded this too into my cake batter.

Finally it was time to whip the egg whites. This is the perfect job for when you are upset. For about half an hour I just whisked. I whisked and I whisked and I whisked. And as I whisked, I wished. I wished l'Inglese would soon come trotting up the steps with a big smile on his face. And I wished Don Umberto would get his just deserts. Yes, those egg whites were his body and I was whipping him. Perhaps I should murder him myself? Free the region finally from his grip of fear. And I wished ill on his henchmen, the piglet murderers, and the body snatchers. And I whipped up good wishes for Amoretta and her bogus priest. I know how it is to be young and in love. I hoped they would be happy. And I felt for poor Pervinca, in her fury. Once the cheesecake was cooked I would take her a large slice. There is nothing like it for calming the nerves.

After all of this my arm was aching, and my hand was hot and metal-smelling from the whisk, and the egg whites were a thick and fluffy cloud that didn't move when I turned the bowl upside down. Then it was time to fold, ever so lightly and deftly, the egg whites into my cheesy gloop, retaining the light as airness of the whites as much as possible. This done, I gently pored the whole of the mixture into a buttered pan, scraped out the last traces from the bowl, and put it in the oven the cook.

After a few moments *la cucina* was filled with the wonderful aroma which carried on the air far and wide and led the passers-by and the farmhands to raise their noses, inhale, and say:

'Aaahhhh, Rosa's preparing a cheesecake, unless I'm much mistaken.'

'One flavored with lemon, by the scent of it'.

Down in the valley everybody began to feel the pangs of hunger. Children abandoned their games and ran home to demand snacks. Dogs howled. And in the asylum several of the maniacs were later found to have devoured their own pillows.

I licked the spoon and thought about l'Inglese. I hoped he was all right. Where could he be all this time? Should I tell him to go, like Sophia Bacci said? But I didn't want him to go. I wanted to keep him. But if he stayed how would I keep him safe?

CHAPTER TWENTY FIVE

Finally the cheesecake was ready, when the skewer I stuck into it came out clean, with no traces of gloop on it. I waited a little while for it to cool, but I couldn't wait too long. I cut into it with a knife and a fragrant steam rose in a succulent cloud. I lifted one half onto a plate, and ran down the track to Giuseppe's house. I didn't want to be out long, in case l'Inglese came back. Their house is only about a ten minute walk, but I managed to run it in five, although I am not built for running, and I was taking care not to drop the cheesecake.

Inside the house, it was dismal. Guiseppe wasn't there; he had gone with Renzo and Audace to Riposto because Manlio Estivo's brother's cousin's neighbor, Old Pipito, said that he had been there early in the morning and had seen a priest and a young girl waiting to board a ship bound for Crete, and they had hurried away to find out if it was true. Old Man Rospo, with various of his sons, had gone east, to Timpone, on the far side of the volcano, following a reported sighting of the lovers at the Gattopardo Pizzeria in the piazza. Rumors were rife. Such is our peoples' love of gossip, that everybody wanted a moment in the limelight, and made all sorts of preposterous claims that weren't true at all.

Old Mamma Rospo was at the house, sharpening an enormous meat cleaver with a ruthless look upon her face. Pervinca, as it turned out, couldn't eat the cheesecake because she had been sedated by Dr

Leobino after the attack on the new priest. He had told her the things that she hadn't wanted to hear: that he had only just been appointed by the bishop, there hadn't been a temporary priest: Padre Buonaventura hadn't been appointed at all, and as far as the new priest knew he, Buonaventura, was an imposter.

The final straw came when Padre Goffreddo revealed that the only relic of Padre Buonaventura left in the presbytery, apart from a quantity of rat droppings, was a glossy brown wig abandoned in the back of a cupboard. It seems it wasn't only Buonaventura's credentials that were false. At least his teeth were real, or so we thought. Any hint of their being really dentures would surely have sent poor Pervinca over the edge.

This episode wasn't a good start for the priest. Besides the strain on his nerves, the violin had been in his family for some two hundred years. He must have been wondering just what sort of a town it was he had come to.

The children hadn't been fed the whole day. Carita, Navale, Belcolore, Anna Monica, and little Roberta (who had been left behind by Nevio and his wife Vinca when they embarked on the *Marco Polo* bound for America), left off their game of murder the priest and fell upon the cheesecake with delighted cries. Etna I didn't like the look of. She was lying in a corner like a discarded puppet, not seeming to see or hear what was going on around her, and she kept repeating something that nobody could make out. It was certainly a family blighted by tragedy. I urged Doda Rospo to put down the cleaver and cook something for the children's supper instead, but she only muttered:

'Feed him to the pigs, we will, when we catch up with him. And her, too, the strumpet'.

I could see she wasn't to be relied upon, so in spite of my impatience to get home again, once more I rolled up my sleeves and set to work preparing supper for the children.

I had no illusions about the housekeeping of my sister-in-law Pervinca, but one glance into her pantry confirmed my views, and also showed why my brother Giuseppe had always continued to eat at the *fattoria*, rather than here with his own family.

I would be proud to show anybody into my store cupboards, but here there were no lovingly labeled jars and bottles prepared in times of plenty. Instead there were cans of cheap commercial salsa from the Pronto Pomodoro factory, whose proprietor, Probo Pronto, had, at the time of Bartolomeo's death, sent me a *Mafioso*'s warning when I was myself brewing industrial quantities of tomato sauce. There were sacks of flour that had been devoured by rats, and old rinds of cheese and bacon which displayed the tooth marks of larger animals: a porcupine, maybe, or a nutria. Possibly the very beast that had taken up residence in the cisterna. I shivered at the memory. In addition there were heaps of hairy mould growing on things that I could no longer recognize. It was a disgrace. How those children had not starved before now I did not know. In the morning I would bring over supplies to replenish the larder, and once the furor was over, and Pervinca was more herself again, I would teach her the basics of housekeeping.

I take a pride in being able to make a good meal out of anything, and within half an hour I set upon the table a steaming mound of *lasagneddi* with tomato sauce topped with toasted breadcrumbs, and, despite my fears for l'Inglese, I watched those little faces devouring it with relish, and felt glad. Only Etna refused to eat. She would not get up from the floor where she lay and would not answer me. Mamma would say it was the wild Rospo blood coursing through her veins. I felt deeply troubled, but I didn't know what else to do.

CHAPTER TWENTY SIX

After the smaller ones had been fed, washed, and put to bed, I hurried away, hoping I would find l'Inglese waiting for me at home. As I turned into the yard I smelled the unmistakable aroma of *Formaggio all'Argentiera*, the delicious dish of melted cheese flavored with garlic and oregano. It was this dish I cooked that time in the middle of the night, when I had just met l'Inglese, and the thought of him was keeping me awake. The scent had roused the whole neighborhood. And Nonna Frolla had come knocking on my door to pry and to complain. Was it possible that l'Inglese was preparing it for me right now? My taste buds burst into life and already I could feel the soft squidgy cheesiness oozing onto my tongue. Lower down, I felt a surge of warmth and wetness. In spite of my weariness I burst up the steps. But it wasn't l'Inglese. To my disappointment, again, I found only Mauro standing by the stove.

'No, he's not here', he said, reading my look, 'Come and have something to eat'.

Where could he be all this time?

Mauro handed me a plate with a large chunk of warm bread on it, and, as I watched, he pored over the thick, oozy melted cheese. There was also a dish of braised radicchio.

'This is good', I said, taking a bite.

'You seem surprised'.

'No, it's just that I usually do the cooking around here'.

'I know. I guessed you had been feeding everybody else, but hadn't eaten yourself'.

He was right. I hadn't eaten. But I hadn't felt hungry until that moment. Now I was starving. His food was good. Very good. And it was a change to have someone prepare something for me. But on the other hand it is my kitchen after all, and I couldn't help feeling a bit put out.

After this, we began eating the cheesecake. I have always found cheese very comforting in times of trouble. We were eating a third slice when a voice said:

'Hello, that looks good', and it wasn't the parrot this time, it was l'Inglese.

He was back. I ran and flung myself into his arms nearly knocking him over. I was sobbing as I told him what Sophia Bacci had heard about him being in danger, and how he didn't come for so long, and I was worried about him. I garbled on about the murder of the innocent piglet, about Amoretta running off with the priest, except he wasn't really a priest at all, and his hair wasn't real either, and how Pervinca had chopped up the Priest's heirloom violin, had been sedated, and had porcupines in her pantry. Finally I ran out of breath like a clockwork toy run down, and holding on to him I felt completely exhausted.

Then he held me really tight and kissed me and soothed me with:

'It's all right. Everything's all right', which is a simple thing, but it's what my poor nervous ears really wanted to hear.

It was only much later that I remembered Mauro. But he was no longer there. He had gone. And it was later still that I realized Mauro had not made a big mess when he had been cooking, the way most men do in a kitchen. Everything was tidied up and put back in its place.

Later I had to wait for l'Inglese to complete his rituals in the bathroom before he came, and that was a change, because before he couldn't wait to get me into bed. Then, later, as we lay there, l'Inglese said I wasn't to worry about Don Umberto; he certainly wasn't worried about him. He said that he, l'Inglese, had to go away on business for a week or so which was unavoidable, and that while he was away any trouble with Don Umberto would blow over, and he

would come back again and everything would be all right, he promised.

I wanted to believe him. I didn't want to live in fear. I didn't want
to cling onto him like a desperate woman either. He had his life to
live, and I had mine. I didn't want to smother him like a vine, and
make it hard for him to breathe. So, as he covered my body in kisses,
I finally began to calm down after what had been another difficult
day.

Pasta

CHAPTER TWENTY SEVEN

The next morning l'Inglese went away. To the mainland. On business. He would be back in a week. I knew I would miss him, but strangely enough, I also felt a sense of relief. If he was away, Don Umberto couldn't murder him. I could look forward to seeing him when he returned because I believed him when he said he would come back. I didn't want to add the worry that he would disappear again to my long list of other worries, although I knew, in the night, I would feel that fear poking at me with a sharp finger.

Also, a part of me wanted a normal life, where we didn't have to be together all the time, where he could do his things and I could do mine. My kitchen garden was constantly on my mind. At this time of excessive growth I could barely harvest everything before it was attacked by wasps or decay, and I wanted to do a lot of preserving and bottling of my produce in preparation for the winter months. In addition to my regular workload, I needed to look after Biancamaria Ossobucco and the triplets, and Giuseppe's family also.

The search for the lovers continued, but I kept to myself my hopes that they wouldn't be found. It was plain to see that no good could come to them if they were discovered. At best they would be forced apart, and at worst they would both be killed and fed to Old Man Rospo's pigs.

The search for the twins' bodies continued for some weeks, and although the various search parties did all they could, they were never recovered. Naturally there were all sorts of sightings and rumors: a giant coffin had been seen on the back of a truck in Gela; a travelling show in Enna had exhibited a skeleton which could only have been theirs; their remains were submersed in a tank like a monster from the deep; and so it went on, but although hopes were raised, they were just as soon dashed again.

After a while the grave was covered over. To make herself feel better, Biancamaria Ossobucco commissioned a life-size statue of Guera and Pace from a stone mason in Randazzo, and had it set up so that they seemed to be in command of the cemetery. This did cause some jealousy, because we now had the biggest monument, bigger even than that of the Botti, and it became famous, so tourists posed to have their pictures taken with it. That was later, though. Much later. At the time I mean there weren't any tourists.

It was only years later that we found out the twins' skeleton was on permanent exhibition in the Pitt Rivers Museum in Oxford, England, and it is still there, even now, displayed between the shrunken heads from Peru and the mummified crocodile.

Anyway, as usual, I am rushing ahead. I spent that day very busily indeed. So much so that I really didn't have time to pine for l'Inglese; in fact, I hardly even thought about him, although I was a little bit ashamed of my hysterical behavior of yesterday. I don't know what had got into me.

The first thing I wanted to tackle was Pervinca's pantry. When I opened the door of my own store cupboard I was filled with a simple joy and pride at the sight of my produce, which I had grown and harvested myself, all of it lovingly preserved, neatly labeled, and arranged according to category, in alphabetical order. Not for nothing had I been a librarian for twenty five years. Yes, although we had never been close, on her recovery I would show Pervinca what she should aim for, in terms of her larder.

So I selected brightly colored jars of salsa, pickled artichokes, egg-plants in brine, courgettes flavored with mint sprigs, fennel slices interspersed with the fronds of their feathery tops, mushrooms I had hunted last fall, red and yellow peppers, and a few larger jars of mixed vegetables: pearl onions, cauliflower florets, celery, baby carrots, green beans and garlic. I also gathered some bottled fruits in sugar syrup: peaches, apricots, pears and plums, greengages and gooseberries.

I loaded the heavy carton into my wheelbarrow, and added some fresh foods too: loaves of bread, a large smoked blood sausage which I had made from Mimi last winter (I always remembered which of the pigs provided particular hams or sausages), a jar of pine-nut cookies, and a tub of fresh ricotta, one of a batch which Rosario had just brought in from the dairy. Finally I added a roll of oilcloth which I had in stock, my sharp scissors, a scrubbing brush and bucket, and set off along the rutted track to my brother's house.

When I arrived at Guiseppe's, Pervinca was still asleep. Apparently Dr Leobino had given her enough sleeping draught to sedate a horse. I suppose it was for the best; if she were up she would be rampaging around in a warlike rage, and who knew who her next victim would be? Giuseppe was still on the trail of the lovers, Etna was still catatonic, and the younger children were still running wild.

Immediately I tackled the pantry. I scooped all of the disgusting and decaying stuff into the trash. Then I set about a most thorough cleaning. I have to say I do not think those shelves had been scrubbed in many years. The dust and cobwebs were thick and hairy. I blocked up a large hole where it seemed to me the rodents were getting in. Then I cut off strips of oil cloth and lined the shelves. Finally I arranged the jars and bottles neatly in rows, and I was extremely pleased with the result. I gave clear instructions to Doda Rospo about what she was to give to the children for lunch, and told her that I would return with a cooked meal for their supper. It was difficult to distract her attention away from the sharpening of knives, and I cautioned her not to leave them lying around within the children's reach. The last thing we needed right now was another tragedy.

I then returned to the *fattoria*, where my tomatoes were an urgent concern. There were so many of them at the peak of ripeness that I couldn't delay, and I had to get my *'strattu* started if I was to have enough to see us through the winter. As I harvested the many hundreds of tomatoes that were perfectly ripe I definitely heard the explosion and looked up at the volcano wondering if it was about to erupt. Yet it didn't look particularly angry. I didn't think any more about it then, but got on with my harvesting. The scent of a ripe tomato is one of my favorite smells and I sniffed each one lovingly as I plucked it.

By lunchtime my chopped, salted tomatoes were spread out on wooden boards in the sun. As I turned them over from time to time with a big wooden spoon, I felt an overwhelming sense of satisfaction. There would be a great many bottles of paste to last us through the winter, and each would contain a measure of this day's sunshine.

Of course, you must pay a lot of attention to your *'strattu*, you can't neglect it, and must move it about often with your spoon so that the juices evaporate evenly. In the afternoon I was still stirring, busy with my thoughts, when the lizards scattered at some sudden movement. I

looked up and was surprised by Sophia Bacci being there, a black figure against the vivid red blur of the tomatoes, in the bright of the sun.

'Rosa', she said, 'I wanted to tell you myself. He's dead. Don Um-
berto. There was an explosion. In the barber's shop of Bruno
Fissaggi. It was a bomb. He's dead. Bruno Fissaggi and Selmo
Archangelo are in hospital'

She took hold of me and hugged me.

'All these years I've hated him', she added, 'and now I feel free'.

I was surprised. It's not usually good when someone dies. But in this
case, it was. I didn't have to worry about him murdering l'Inglese
any more. And it was the end of the tragedy of Bartolomeo. His
murderer would finally be brought to justice. I had no doubt he would
pay the price. I had put a curse on him yesterday, and today he was
dead. Perhaps like Guera and Pace, I, too, had magic powers? I
didn't know. But I did feel lighthearted.

Later that same afternoon, I came back to the '*strattu* after I had been
harvesting peaches, and I found Mauro wandering around with a
spoon, stirring. I did wish he wouldn't interfere.

'Has he gone?' he asked with hope in his voice.

'He's coming back', I replied, taking the spoon from him.

'I had a holiday romance once', he said. 'It can't last'.

'Who's on holiday?'

'He is', he replied.

I didn't want to have this conversation so I turned my back on him and carried on stirring.

Before long he piped up again:

'Have you heard about Festo Pustolino?'

'No', I replied, without enthusiasm.

'Apparently he was in the Via Molino when the bomb went off. Almost immediately he felt something land on the brim of his hat. And what do you think it was?'

'I don't know', I said, turning around, 'What was it?'

He looked at me with his black eyes sparkling, waiting for my curiosity to mount, before he announced with a flourish:

'A thumb!'

'How awful!'

'Anyway, he handed it in, and it was packed in ice and rushed to the hospital, and they're going to see if they can re-attach it. To Bruno Fissaggi'.

Mauro always seemed to hear the gossip first. He's got that sort of a face that encourages people to tell him things. And although he's a newcomer, he seems to fit right in, as though he's been here all his life instead of only a few months.

'New hat, it was too', he added, 'he'd only just got it at the *festa*. Benedetta bought it for him for his birthday. She's done her best to clean the bloodstain off it, but Festo says he can't feel happy with it on his head any more'.

Whenever I used a jar of that *'strattu*, I remembered the day I made it, the day Don Umberto died. And it tasted delicious, I can tell you.

CHAPTER TWENTY EIGHT

The day after this, I remember it quite clearly, because it was the day when the volcano was puffing a great quantity of orange smoke that filled the sky with peculiarly–shaped clouds, and we were eating the watermelon pudding. Don Umberto was dead. L'Inglese would be safe when he came back. And I was getting on with my work, doing all the things I needed to do. The jars of *'strattu* were lined up in the larder, along with a good many of bottled peaches in syrup. Brilliant white laundry was drying out on the grass. A neat pile of typewritten letters were ready for the post. I had sharpened my pencils. Fed the pigs. Collected the eggs. Scrubbed the steps. And made a mound of *causunedda* for supper, which we would eat with a sauce of anchovies, and braised escarole.

To make the watermelon pudding you need a good few melons, for it is quite delicious, and one helping is never enough. First you must remove the rind and the seeds, and squeeze the pulp through a fine sieve, which takes a long time. Put your juice in a saucepan with some sugar and some cornstarch and mix to make sure there are no lumps. Then you heat it on the stove, stirring constantly to make sure it doesn't stick to the bottom of the pan and taste burnt. As soon as tiny bubbles begin to form around the outside of the pan take it off the heat, and stir in some powdered cinnamon stick and a good cupful of your jasmine water. Allow this to cool, then add some chunks of chocolate, and, if you like, add a spoonful or two of your squash preserves which you have chopped very finely. Moisten your little glass bowls with a splash of cold water to prevent the pudding from sticking, and fill them with your mixture. Put them in a cool place to set, and then you may decorate them with grated chocolate, jasmine blossoms and a few crushed pistachios if you like.

I do remember the pudding clearly, and I have to say it was succulent and so refreshing, too, in the heat. As I scraped the inside of the dish with the spoon to release the last little traces of cinnamon and chocolate I became aware that Rosario, on the other side of the table, had taken up the hand of Biancamaria Ossobucco in his own and was stroking it lovingly. I sucked the spoon and the chopped chocolate morsels melted into my tongue and I thought that finally he had lost what was left of his limited reason and I began to wonder what I should do about it. Should I have him shut up in the Santa Pasqua rest home for lunatics before he began causing trouble in the region? For our men are a jealous lot, and jealousy had already been the cause of the death of my beloved brothers.

My mind was running on like this when a glance passed between the two of them which stopped me in my tracks. Then, without any of his usual mumbling and slobbering and stuttering, Rosario said, as clear as anything:

'Rosa, I want your permission to marry Biancamaria'.

My mouth must have fallen open, and a wasp was buzzing around trying to get inside, so I waved it away, and acting according to its own instructions my hand reached for another dish of pudding and started to spoon it in. Looking back on it, I'm glad I didn't laugh, but to be truthful I didn't find it funny. My tongue savored the pudding, and I didn't say anything, because it's a habit of mine, when I don't know what to say, to say nothing, and after a few more spoonfuls of the pudding had gone in, Rosario said:

'You're not angry, are you, Rosa?'

'No', I replied, licking my lips. I wasn't angry.

'Only', he continued 'I love her and she loves me'.

I was skeptical to say the least. I looked at Biancamaria Ossobucco, and she was blushing like an apricot.

'And what do you say Biancamaria Ossobucco?' I asked her.

'It's true', she whispered, 'I know it's not long since the boys were taken from me', here her eyes began to fill with tears and Rosario squeezed her hand tighter, and she was right, it wasn't long, for the period of mourning was not yet over.

'But he's always been kind to me Rosa'.

Here Rosario butted in 'I've always loved her, see, always'.

'I'm not the kind of woman who's good to be alone. He's a good man, and he wants me, and you don't blame me, do you Rosa, for you've always been so good to me, and if I thought it was going to grieve you I wouldn't agree. That's why I wanted him to ask you before I said yes or no'.

I found myself eating a third pudding, and when it was gone I answered:

'Well, if you do love each other, and you're sure this is what you really want, then I'll not stand in your way, of course I won't. Life is short, and I believe we must follow our hearts. If you believe you'll be happy together than let me be the first to wish you joy'.

At this Rosario leapt up like a boy of twenty with tears in his eyes and a look of rapture on his face. He scooped Biancamaria Ossobucco up into his arms, and she's no lightweight, believe me, and kissed her, and laughed, and kissed her again, and threw her up into the air and caught her again, and she was laughing and screaming and crying and I have to say this is one sight it never occurred to me I should see.

After Rosario had carried his bride away, I noticed the smoke in the sky had turned to gold. Very pretty, it was, too. I needed to unwind my mind, and so, of course, I reached for a sack of flour, and soon had a mound of dough under my arms. As I pounded away I thought the following, in no particular order: that my father would become my brother-in-law also, my nieces would also be my sisters, and my sister-in-law would become my step-mother.

The change in Rosario was something which I no amount of thumping could hammer out. He was like a normal person. What had happened to the half-wit we knew and loved? Is it possible that happiness had wrought such changes in him? I wouldn't have believed it. Of course, even if he had somehow recovered his wits, he still had to be a good few years older than Biancamaria Ossobucco, but from what I had just seen, love had turned him into a carefree youth.

It turned out that I was the only one shocked by the announcement. Everyone knew what I alone did not: that he had loved her ever since she had first come to the brothel in Adrano, and he used to save up all his wages and spend them just to talk to her. Although she had married the twins he had never given up hope that she would eventually be his. Yes, everybody else in the region had predicted the marriage, even on the night the twins were murdered. I remember thinking it was strange at the time that Rosario had collapsed at the news. I thought it was because he was devastated, but it seems now it was because his dream of Biancamaria Ossobucco was at last a possibility.

I'm sure I didn't imagine it: I heard laughter. It was Mamma laughing. Although I couldn't see her. Then she said, 'Lining up, they
are, to marry that pockmarked whore. Who'd have believed it, eh?'

Salsa

Sauce

CHAPTER TWENTY NINE

Strange as it is for me to admit, Biancamaria Ossobucco was not the only one to attract a suitor at this time. It was while l'Inglese was away on that business trip that another stranger came amongst us, the third one since the spring.

That morning Mauro had appeared with an enormous octopus which he had bought from the fish vendor, Old Zumbo. It was a beauty, fresh as anything, sea–scented, and reddish brown and rubbery, and they do say that a man who brings octopus in his arms brings love in his heart, but I don't pay attention to those old wives' tales. While I was holding it in my hands, I happened to look out into the yard over the half–door, and squinting into the bright sun I saw a figure approaching the gate. I knew it wasn't l'Inglese, for he was not due to return until Monday, and besides, this was a different figure entirely. Small, thin. A stranger, certainly. He was wearing an enormous hat like a sombrero, which made it impossible to see his head, and his figure I did not recognize either in his brightly colored smock, but he leant his arms on the gate in the same way that l'Inglese had done when he first arrived, and it was strange.

I filled my largest basin with cold water, carefully lowered the octopus in, covered him with a cloth, and went out to take a look at the stranger. I was wondering who it could be, and when I got close enough I felt it was someone I knew, but still I could not put a name to him.

'Signorina Fiore', he said.

I looked hard at him. I had heard that voice somewhere before.

'You don't remember me', he said sadly, squinting at me, 'Gerberto Rivoli. We were neighbors in the Via Vicolo Brugno'.

'Signor Rivoli', I said, aghast, 'Is it really you? You look different. Are you ill?'

'My spectacles', he replied, 'I look better without them, but in truth I do not see too well'.

I watched as he rummaged in a swollen knapsack, found the spectacles, and put them on. The lenses, thick as the bottom of bottles, made his face look familiar in an instant.

'Ah, it is you', I said, 'I recognize you now'.

After we had cleared up that little mystery I wasn't sure there was anything else to say.

'I see the Mount Etna is puffing', he said, gesturing towards the volcano where the thick smoke was swirling in a circular motion, 'will there be an eruption?'

'O I shouldn't think so', I replied, 'She's always smoking. It's quite normal'.

Immediately word was circulating among the farmhands that another stranger had come seeking Rosa.

'I took a week's leave of absence from the bank', he said, 'my subordinate, Crotto, is holding the fort'.

'Why?'

'I came to see you'.

'Whatever for?' I could not think of one single, solitary reason.

'To give you this...'

He rummaged again in his knapsack. He pulled out graying winter underwear, a pair of striped pajamas, a tube of *Emo* ointment for the treatment of piles, and threw them down in the dust in disgust.

'Where is it?' he cried, 'Don't say I have left it behind'.

The rummaging went on for so long it grew awkward. The heap at his feet grew to contain a rope ladder, a pair of roller skates, and a stuffed rabbit. I began to wonder just what he was going to get out next. Finally, with a triumphant look upon his face, he drew out something wrapped up in newspaper and handed it to me through the bars of the gate.

I unwrapped it. It was a silver plate. My commemorative plate from the library. It was engraved with the words:

Rosa Evangelina Fiore
Awarded for 25 Years Service at the Biblioteca Nationale
1933–1958

'It's a pretty name, Evangelina. I didn't know that was your middle name. Suits you'.

He was looking with pride at the plate in my hands. He went on:

'That foreigner came looking for you. Belligerent fellow. Big *pancia*. Little moustache. It gave me the idea of finding you myself. I've been keeping this for you, in case you came back. I give it a good polish every now and again — you can see it's not tarnished'.

'Thanks'.

I didn't want to invite him in, but I felt I had at least to offer him a drink. He'd come all that way. I opened the gate to admit him, and there was a flurry of fur and teeth and dust as every sheep dog in the valley rushed to attack him. I beat them off with the plate but nevertheless he sustained several nasty bites.

'Dogs do not like me', he said, sucking his bleeding hand, 'it is regrettable, but true'.

Inside *la cucina* his weak eyes were everywhere at once. The farmhands kept coming in to take a look at the second foreigner that had come to find me. They spoke about him openly:

'Runty little fellow, this one', said Luciano.

'She bigger'n him, 'tis true', agreed Gaddo, 'but I do like a bigger woman, myself'.

'What's happened to the other suitor, the chubby one?' asked old Aulo.

'Happen he'll tweak this one's nose for him when he comes back'.

'Like eruptions of the volcano, so it is. Nothing for years, then two at once'.

'Like wasps to a pot of jam, they are'.

I waved them away like wasps: 'Haven't any of you got any work to do?'

'Nice place you have here', said Signor Rivoli.

I gave him a weak smile by way of reply. I really wanted him to go now. I remembered those times when he came to visit me in the hospital after the fire. I feigned sleep while he sat in the vinyl armchair that made embarrassing squeaks every time he moved. I had nothing to say to him then, and I had nothing to say to him now.

'I went to the infirmary one day', said Signor Rivoli, strange that we were thinking the same thing, 'and you had gone. The nuns said you had been taken by the agents of Lucifer'.

'O no', I said, 'they weren't the agents of anybody. They were my brothers'.

Once again we lapsed into silence. I could see he was willing himself to say something.

'I have some news of your old friends', he said, 'Signor Frolla has married the little girl from the library'.

'Costanza. I know'.

He deflated like a pricked balloon. Then he had another idea.

'They have a puppy dog. One with a little, squashy, wrinkly face, the same make as other one, the one that got trampled in the burning building'.

'A pug'.

'A pug, yes. He bit me also'.

I nodded.

'Signora Bandiera has a new and huge arrangement of the hair. The hive of the bee is how it is described.'

I nodded again.

'Have you any questions?'

'No', I answered truthfully, 'all of that seems a different life to me now'.

I stood up.

'Well, it was very kind of you to bring the plate', I said, 'but if you'll excuse me, I've got an octopus salad to prepare, I don't want it going off, and I've got to feed the pigs. They get hungry about this time....'

'Do you think you'll come back?'

'To Palermo? O no. My life is here now'.

'I was hoping you'd come back'.

There was a pause, and then he added:

'With me'.

'With you?' I was incredulous.

'As my wife'.

Now I was more than incredulous. What is more than incredulous? Flabbergasted? Yes, I was flabbergasted.

'I've got a ring and everything', he said, hurriedly. 'It's in my knapsack. Where is my knapsack? Please, just let me find it'.

Once again he started to rummage. Out came the tube of ointment. By now it had lost its lid and a thick worm of salmon-colored paste squeezed out onto the flagstone floor.

'No. Please', I cried. I was aware of the desperation in my voice. 'Please don't get it out. I can't marry you. It's very kind of you, but I can't'.

'Please can I just show it to you before you say no?'

'No'.

'It won't take me long to find it'.

'I'm sorry. It won't make any difference to my decision'.

I really couldn't bear for this interview to go on any longer. I wanted to take hold of him bodily and push him to the door. But I didn't want to touch him. Time seemed to have stopped still. He wasn't moving.

'I'm sorry', I said again, and I meant it, I was sorry. 'Thank you. Good bye'.

'You don't want time to think it over?'

'No. Thank you. No. Goodbye'.

And with that I was finally able to close the half door behind him. I felt drained. Weak. If anyone had told me that morning Signor

Rivoli would appear and propose marriage to me, I would not have believed them.

Finally, I was able to return to the octopus. I filled my largest cauldron with water, added a handful of sea salt, and brought it to the boil. Once it was boiling merrily I added a good slug of white wine, maybe half a bottle, and, in truth, I took a few gulps of the wine myself also, and taking hold of the octopus by the head I dipped its tentacles into the boiling water, in and out three times. As it was such a big and heavy one, this was not as easy as it sounds. Then I put the whole of the octopus into the pot, covered it with a lid, and left it to cook for about half an hour.

While it was bubbling, I tried to wipe the hemorrhoid cream off the floor. It was extremely sticky, and would not come off completely. There always remained that slightly sticky spot, so that in passing your shoe tended to adhere there for a moment, and every time it reminded me of that embarrassing occasion with the pervert Signor Rivoli.

Of course, I did not forget to take the octopus off the heat at the right time, and then left it in the water for another half hour to soften it. Once it was softened I removed it from the pot, and taking a sharp knife sliced off the head. The head is the tastiest part of the octopus, and I guessed Mauro should have it, as in truth he was the owner of the octopus, and he must have had to pay a lot for it. So I emptied out the inky insides of the head, and put it onto a large serving platter. Next I chopped each of the eight chubby tentacled legs into bite-sized chunks, and added them to the platter along with quantities of chopped celery and several handfuls of black olives. I seasoned the dish liberally with salt and freshly ground black pepper, before adding the best olive oil, tossing everything together with my hands to cover and coat. Finally I added some finely chopped parsley and left it in a cool place for the flavors to mingle.

Yes, you must leave it for at least an hour. Just before serving you may add some fresh green salad leaves, and, if you wish, some chopped, boiled new potatoes, as well as a good squeeze of lemon juice. Wonderful.

At supper that night the farmhands clustered around my silver plate which I had displayed with pride on the dresser. They had never seen such a splendid thing, and were mightily impressed by it, and for those of them that could not read, I had to read out several times the words of the engraving. They enjoyed the joke about the numbers of suitors tramping towards the *fattoria,* but they enjoyed the wonderful *insalata di polpi* more. Despite my protests, Mauro insisted that I should have the head of the octopus myself, and it was absolutely succulent, like a chewy dream of the sea. Something about that dish that night made us happy and glowing, and afterward, as the farmhands began to wend their way home in the dusk, they joined together in singing the old folk songs that Filippo used to sing, and as I listened to their voices diminishing I had the feeling they were the best farm-hands in the world.

That night, as I lay alone in my little bed, where the seductive scent of l'Ingese lingered on the pillows, overlaid though, by the menthol of his medications, I couldn't help but think how strange it was. I had never thought of myself as being attractive to the opposite sex. I know I am somewhat fat, and my thighs flap against each other when I walk, and do not have a beautiful face, and my hair is growing grayer by the day, and my feet have bunions because of wearing unsuitable shoes, and yet not only do I have my lover, the experienced, debonair, man of the world l'Inglese, but my brother Mauro, who says he loves me, although of course I take what he says with a pinch of salt, and suddenly, although he does not seem right in the head, and I know he is a pervert, Signor Rivoli has proposed marriage to me. I confess I did feel somewhat conceited. I almost wished that Costanza, the library assistant who always used to laugh at me, and who had now married Nonno Frolla, could know that I had the wherewithal to attract not one, not two, but three whole men, and they were none of them aged more than fifty.

CHAPTER THIRTY

But Signor Rivoli had not returned to Palermo as I thought. That night he got into my room. It happened like this. I was asleep but felt someone climbing carefully into bed beside me. I was still heavy with sleep in the thickly perfumed heat of the night. Through the windows, open behind the shutters, came no breath of air, only the singing of the cicadas, the contented bleating of the goats of Simple Fogna (who had, I discovered the following morning, got into my vegetable garden with disastrous consequences), and the mewing of amorous cats.

Through this thick veil of sleep I assumed it was l'Inglese, and I reached out and touched him. He was wearing his clothes which was strange because he always came to bed naked. In my sleep I began to undress him. I undid the shirt buttons, fought with the sleeves, struggled with the belt buckle, my old adversary. Underneath he was wearing flannel underwear which he had never done before. Why, in July, had he chosen to put it on? I fought to get it off. It was twangy and tough. I was still asleep, but less so, probably only a quarter asleep, but soft and warm and deliciously dozy.

He had lost weight. As I ran my fingers over him his whole body was smaller than I remembered. And he smelled different. His usual seductive aroma of cologne, brandy and tobacco, the scent that never failed to strike a note that quivered deep inside my body: it wasn't there. Instead there was an alien scent of something rancid, something gone off and unpleasant. In the morning I would ask him why.

But not now. Now was the time to enjoy his body joined with my body.

I reached out for his willy, and with one touch of my hand it sprang up like a spring. It, too, was smaller than I remembered. Thinner, certainly. Like a pencil. I didn't like it. I dropped it, but it twanged back up.

'Don't stop, Signorina Fiore, I beg you', said a voice, a thin, high-pitched voice. And it was not the voice of l'Inglese.

Suddenly I was wide and startlingly awake. I had a suspicion of whom that voice belonged to. I fumbled for the lamp at the bedside and switched it on. It was Signor Rivoli and I screamed at the shocking realization that it was so.

'I like also the light on', he said, his eyes screwed up into wrinkled spiders behind the bottle bottom glasses.

'No', I shouted in horror and disbelief, 'There's been a mistake. I thought it was someone else'.

'No', he said, 'There is no mistake. I know really you desire me. You ladies like the little joke. The playing of the hard to get, no? Is it not so?'

With that he lunged on top of me and thrust something thick and hard and sinewy into my mouth. It was his tongue. I fought to fling him off, but he was tenacious and strong for one so small. He was cling-ing to me like a limpet.

As we struggled I became aware of the feeling of being watched. And as I craned my neck to see around Signor Rivoli, who was blocking my view of the room, I glimpsed l'Inglese. He had come back. He was standing in the doorway watching. His face was a mask, frozen with shock, horror, anger. His eyes were glaring, shooting darts toward us.

'No, amore', I cried, and with a superhuman effort I flung Signor Rivoli off. He flew up into the air, hit the ceiling and dropped to the floor like a stone. He didn't move. Was he dead? I didn't care.

'It's not what you think', I cried, 'I can explain'.

But l'Inglese wouldn't listen. He said nothing. He just turned and went out of the room, and the sight of his disappearing back broke my heart. I leapt out of bed to run after him. First I tripped over the body of Signor Rivoli, and fell to the floor. There was a crunch as part of me landed on part of him. He made no sound and it confirmed my suspicion that he was dead. Good. That would save me from having to kill him myself for causing this trouble with my Inglese.

My hands hurt where I had put them out to save myself, but I scrambled up and dashed toward the door, only to trip again over the massive knapsack that nincompoop had left on the floor. This time I hit my head on the wall when I landed. I felt dazed but had to hurry on. I picked myself up a second time and raced out into the corridor. L'Inglese had got away. I ran down the stairs, my head swimming. I couldn't see him. How had he got away so fast? Through the corridor and into *la cucina* I ran. The outside door was shut. I opened it and went out. He had to still be in the yard. He couldn't have got further than that in the few seconds it had taken me to pursue him. Down the steps I flew. I realized I was naked, but I didn't care, I had to catch up with him. I had to explain. He had to believe me. I know how it must have looked to him, but he would have to understand. I would make him understand the way it really was. In the future we would laugh about it together, but not now. Now I must run and catch him and explain. Then as I was opening the gate someone caught hold of me. I struggled to escape. I had to get away. I had to find l'Inglese.

'Rosa', said a voice.

'It's not the way you think', I implored, 'Let me explain. It was a mistake. He got in while I was asleep. I thought it was you. I was dreaming. But then I realized it wasn't. You, I mean. It was him. Because his willy is very thin. That made me realize something was wrong. And then I woke up, and I saw that it was him, and I was trying to get him off when you came in. You've got to believe me. Please believe me'.

I was panting. I realized then it wasn't l'Inglese, it was Mauro.

'Where is he?' I cried, breaking free and looking all around in a panic.

'Who?'

'L'Inglese'.

'I don't know', he replied, 'I thought he'd gone. And good riddance to him, I say. I for one won't miss him. You've been dreaming. Sleepwalking. Sleep running, even. I just saw you charge down the steps, cross the yard, and unbolt the gate, and all the while you were fast asleep. Funnily enough they say I used to sleepwalk, when I was young. I thought I ought to stop you, though, before you got onto the open road. You might get yourself talked about, running around the district naked'.

I shrank back in mortification. Mauro had been peeling off his shirt and held it out for me. I leapt into it. The shame of it. It was good he is so big and the shirt covered up a lot of me. I noticed his chest was covered with a thick thatch of hair.

'Are you going to be all right?' He asked.

'Yes', I said, turning to come back inside, 'thanks'.

I left him. I came back inside. In *la cucina* I took a quick slug of almond wine to steady my nerves. I felt exhausted. What a night. What a ridiculous dream. I was pretty confident now that I had dreamed the whole thing, but I was still cautious going back into my bedroom. Suppose I did find Signor Rivoli there? But I didn't. He wasn't there and the knapsack wasn't there, and I had really dreamed the whole thing. I climbed back into bed weary beyond anything. I was too tired even to take off Mauro's shirt, and his smell surrounded me, and it was a good smell. Thankfully, without any agonizing and analysis, I fell into a deep, dreamless sleep and slept late into the morning, much later than usual.

I had lots of mosquito bites in unexpected places, and a red and angry gash across my forehead where I had collided with the wall, but it was a huge relief that it had only been a dream: that I had not shared intimate moments with Signor Rivoli; that l'Inglese had not been a witness to them; that I had not wandered naked around the region, and possibly been arrested on public indecency charges. Of course, I had humiliated myself in front of Mauro, but I had had so many embarrassing moments in front of him I had somehow got used to them. Whether that was a good thing or a bad thing I didn't know.

CHAPTER THIRTY ONE

In time Bruno Fissaggi was well enough to leave hospital. The thumb had grown back onto him. This, in fact, was said to be a miracle of medical science, because such a thing was unknown before now, and he had his photograph taken with the thumb in the forefront, and he was put in the newspapers.

Then the Church got involved, and said it was the will of God, and nothing to do with science at all. Padre Goffredo was instructed by the Bishop to hold a special mass for the recovery of the thumb, which he did, although it had to be conducted *in absentia* because Bruno Fissaggi, disliking the fuss, refused to participate, and the thumb could not come without him.

He was able to cut hair again (it was his right thumb), and business began to boom because there were always people who wanted to see the miraculous thumb, even when they didn't really need a haircut, but he made them pay in any case, because as he himself said, he was running a barbers, not a sideshow.

At the neighboring pastry cooks, the Pasticceria Tortino, they began to sell bloody thumbs made of *pasta reale* which caused trouble because Bruno Fissaggi said that he should have a share of the profits of the thumbs because it was all down to him. Manrico Tortino said that he was already paying *pizzo* (protection money to the mafia) and wasn't about to start paying Bruno Fissaggi also.

But the intriguing thing was this: Bruno Fissaggi always maintained that the thumb was not his thumb. And I suppose he should know whether it was his thumb or not. The other victim of the explosion, Selmo Archangelo had sustained terrible injuries: one of his legs was blown off, and was never found, and some of his teeth were embedded in his nose, but both his thumbs remained intact and attached. So it seemed then that a bit of Don Umberto was living on, on the hand of Bruno Fissaggi. And it was a strange thing to contemplate.

Anyway, all of that comes later. To return to the time I am talking of, immediately after I had given my blessing to the union, Biancamaria Ossobucco shed the heavy mourning it was the custom to wear, and plans for the wedding proceeded apace. Even I was to be a bridesmaid, which I thought quite ridiculous at my age, but Biancamaria Ossobucco was so set on the idea that I didn't have the heart to disappoint her. Mauro, of all people, was chosen to be the best man, and with no thought of the expense involved was, with Rosario the bridegroom, to have a suit made to measure by Banquo Cuniberto, the tailor, who, in recent years, had become ever so high and mighty.

Another person who shed their mourning was Sophia Bacci. That same day, the day that what remained of Don Umberto's exploded body was lowered into the ground, she wore a red dress. And after that she always dressed in bright colors, and she seemed to have come alive again after all these years when she had hidden herself away from color and from life. I hoped that she would go one step further along this path and take a suitor. In fact, sometimes I wondered if Mauro might suit her, for in spite of his defects he has some fine qualities. And while he is stout, she is very thin, and they do say that opposites attract. In short, when I was at leisure, and musing on the matter, I did think that the two of them might make a good couple.

In the midst of the endless discussions about the wedding, came the sound of a motor laboring, and we were surprised to see a bus pulling into the yard. A big and bossy woman stepped out of it, and it took me a few moments to realize who it was, but then I saw it was Aventina Valente, the barmaid of Linguaglossa, the widow of my brother Luigi. She looked very different to how she looked the last time I had seen her when she appeared in a whirlwind and a fur coat for Mamma's funeral. It was her hair. That was what it was that was different about her: it had gone blonde in color, and was enormous, teased up like a wiry bush. She could see my eyes were drawn to it. She patted it with her hand, and her podgy fingers sparkled with diamonds and other precious stones. I expected the hair to make a metallic noise, but it did not.

'It's a beehive', she said, 'They're all the rage right now in the States'.

So this was the new look also sported by Signora Bandiera. Call me old-fashioned, but I couldn't see the point of it.

Aventina Valente had brought with her her four enormous American daughters, Patty May, Sandra Ann, Betty Jean and Liza Lu, her son-in-law, Brad P. Freeway III, and her two grandchildren Nancy and Brad P. Freeway IV.

They had come, she said, for the wedding of Rosario and Biancamaria Ossobucco, although how they had found out and made the journey from Chicago so quickly I did not understand. All the girls and she were going to be bridesmaids, she said, and chubby little Brad, whom they called Ivy, was to be a pageboy. I wasn't entirely delighted about this, for instead of it being just me and the triplets, there would be now a huge herd of bridesmaids, and I had the feeling instead of a wedding it would become a circus.

Aventina Valente then conducted her brood on a tour of the place. None of them could speak our language, and even she, the barmaid, pretended to have forgotten some words of her own mother tongue. They were delighted to discover that Betty the parrot could speak English, and tried to teach him some new words.

They looked into everything, took photographs of themselves posing with some things, and shrieked with laughter at other things. I for one did not see what was screamingly funny about a line of washing, but

I did wish I had got in my underwear before it was captured on film. They were excited about the puffing of the volcano and stood together in front of it grinning and shouting 'cheese' at the top of their voices while Rosario held the camera and pressed the shutter. They violently hoped for a devastating eruption during the course of their visit.

I had to double the quantities of *Pasta alla Norma* I was preparing for lunch, and ran out to harvest another dozen eggplants, but even then there was insufficient to satisfy the Americans' mighty appetites. Aventina Valente translated for her son-in-law, Gargantuan Brad, and it appeared that although he found the old country interesting, he did miss a square meal of the type found back home, and could murder for a big, juicy steak. The children turned up their noses at the white pudding I served with grilled peaches, and began crying for ice-cream which I didn't have.

Although I was busy serving our guests (they seemed to believe they were in a restaurant and I was the waitress), I could see that Aventina Valente, who was seated next to Mauro, was very taken with him. I could tell this because she was sitting so close she was almost in his lap, and was thrusting her large chest up against him, and I think this must be an American custom, because our women don't tend to act in this way. She was quick to feel his biceps and even undid some of his shirt buttons in order to judge the hairiness of his chest, and it was hairy, as I already knew: it was like a full head of hair in there. And I have to say that Mauro seemed to be enjoying her attention. He was smiling and laughing and looking into her eyes with his black eyes sparkling, and in short I was shocked at the behavior of the both of them.

In the afternoon the seamstresses of Banquet Cuniberto were summoned and samples of stuffs got out and everybody measured, and they were even stripping off their clothes down to their underwear. Although it was the wedding of Biancamaria Ossobucco, she had very little say in what was decided, and no more did I, with the result that yellow was chosen, the yellow of a canary, which, I have to say, is a color that does not flatter me. The style was to be straight and short and shiny, and I said that I wanted the length of mine to be no higher than my knees, for I for one would not be wearing the miniskirt, and the seamstresses were to work without stopping until all of the dresses were got ready.

Finally, when the triplets had tired of little Brad and had submerged him in the water trough, though not enough to drown him, and Nancy had fallen off the fence into the muck in the pigsty, and Aventina Valente had been able to put Mauro down, they once more climbed back on board the bus, and finally swept away.

They were staying in a hotel in Taormina. Think of that! All that expense, and all that way to go. I had never met anyone who had been to Taormina. They said that was the only place where they could be sure of running water.   Well, we had running water here, but I was glad she wasn't going to stay with us.

CHAPTER THIRTY TWO

That night, I had fallen asleep, when I was awoken by someone creeping up under the bedclothes, kissing my feet, my legs, tiny whispered kisses, fringed by a moustache. He was back. I felt a gush of moist warmness surge inside me.

'Is that you?' I said.

'Suppose it isn't', he whispered, nibbling my inner thighs, 'suppose it's someone else entirely?'

His tongue crept inside me.

'In that case', I said, 'you'd better keep doing that, and I'll let you know'.

He did keep doing it, and my cries of ecstasy announced to the world, or at least to the valley, that he was back, and it was good to have him back.

When we lay panting and weak in each other's arms, we talked. So much had happened in the few days he had been away. First I told him the news of Don Umberto being blown up in the barber's shop. He didn't seem at all surprised at this.

'You see, I told you not to worry about him'.

'Did you know he was going to die?' I asked.

'Let's just say: I had a feeling about it'.

He wasn't amazed either by the news of Rosario and Biancamaria Ossobucco.

'I thought it would happen sooner or later', he said, 'anybody can see he's crazy about her, and she needs someone to take care of her after everything that's happened. Not everyone's as self–sufficient as you are'.

'Am I self–sufficient?'

'I think so'.

Then I told him how Signor Rivoli had brought my commemorative plate all the way from Palermo. I didn't tell him the bit about Signor Rivoli wanting to marry me though; it didn't seem the right time to mention it. Then I told him about the arrival of Aventina Valente and her Americans, and how they were staying in a fancy hotel in Taormina.

'So', I concluded, 'Where've you been?'

'Just seeing to a bit of business, I told you. Did you miss me?'

Yes. But I got a lot of things done when you weren't here, interfering with me all the time'.

'Me interfering with you. I like that'.

'So what were you doing?'

'Business. Nothing interesting. But necessary'.

I let the matter drop. I could tell he didn't really want to talk about it. And so we interfered with each other some more, and it was while I was on top of him and lunging backwards and forwards, gripping onto the iron bedstead for support, that everything began to quiver and to shake. The floor and the walls shuddered, and the picture of the Madonna and the baby Jesus hanging above the bed became dislodged and fell down. There was a tinkling of glass and a rattling of things on shelves. The clock began to strike, and, in the yard, the pigs began squealing and the dogs howled. Then, as soon as it began, it was over, and l'Inglese said:

'Steady, my Rosa, I know you're pleased to see me, but don't get too violent'.

With that he climbed on top of me and we finished what we had started. Then, almost immediately, he fell asleep. But I couldn't get back to sleep. I tossed and turned, thinking about things. Of course I was glad he was back. But why wouldn't he tell me where he had been? I don't like mysteries now, and I didn't like them any better then. After all, he knew everything about me; I had no secrets. I also knew the only thing that would soothe me. I threw on my robe and went down to *la cucina*.

My ceremonial plate had fallen off the dresser, and I picked it up and polished it and put it back. A jar of jam had fallen down also, and I cleared up the sticky mess. Apart from that the earth tremor had not caused much damage: in the larder just a few bruised peaches and broken eggs.

I crumbled some yeast into a bowl and added just the right quantity of water and mixed them together to form a smooth, lump-free batter. Then I tipped a sack of flour onto the table, and into a well in the center I poured my yeasty liquid and added several good handfuls of sea salt. I worked the dry flour into the liquid, until the mixture came together and then I began the kneading. I love the feel of the dough in my hands, the scent of the yeast, the physical act of kneading. Before long I was lost in my own world of pushing the dough over and over itself, pressing it away from me with the heels of my hands, working it rhythmically, almost hypnotically, feeling the texture of it change, and become silky, smooth and elastic. I put my whole body into my kneading, my sturdy legs that support me, my back and shoulders, my strong arms and hands. Then, when it had been kneaded until just right, not too much, not too little, I lifted it into my big rising pan, covered it with a damp cloth, and set it to rest by the warmth of the stove. While it rested, I sat down at the table, and idly traced patterns in the scattered flour with my finger. I was calm and the world, the real world, seemed far, far away. Then I heard the soft flap of bare feet on the flagstones. It was l'Inglese.

'Rosa, it's three o'clock in the morning. What are you doing?'

'Making bread'.

'I can see that. But you don't have to do it now, do you?'

'It soothes me, that's all'.

'God bless America'.

It was Betty, underneath the cloth covering his cage. L'Inglese looked baffled.

'It was the Americans', I explained, 'They've been teaching him some new words'.

'Now why do you need soothing, hmm? Come on, what's this all about?'

'Why won't you tell me where you've been? I haven't got any secrets from you'.

'It's not a secret. I've been to Napoli'.

'Napoli? What were you doing there?'

'I didn't want to tell you because I didn't think you'd understand, but there was a big card game...'

'A card game?' I said. 'You went to Napoli to play a game of cards?'

'Hot dogs', said Betty, 'Hold the onion'.

'Well, put like that it does sound a little silly, I admit'.

'So is that what you call 'business', playing cards?'

'Yes. That and a few other things'.

'Such as writing cookery books?'

He broke into a smile 'Well, that's more of a hobby, and a way of meeting sexy librarians'.

'I see. Well, it's better than being an assassin, I suppose'.

'You thought I was an assassin?'

'No, not really', I replied, 'A jewel thief, maybe, or a spy'.

'Sadly, the truth is a little less exotic'.

'And do you always win, at cards, I mean?'

'Not always, no. Nobody wins all the time'.

'Then what?'

'Then you find consolation in the arms of a beautiful woman', he said, pulling off my robe, 'you know the old cliché, unlucky at cards, lucky in love...'

'Chicago Bears', screamed Betty.

Insalata

Salad

CHAPTER THIRTY THREE

So I had discovered that l'Inglese plays cards for a living. It did seem strange to me. Not solid. Not dependable. But then we can't all be farmers I suppose. At least I knew the truth. He wasn't hiding things from me. I guess there's a certain glamour in being a gambler. But I would rather raise crops, and rear pigs, and knead bread.

As it was Sunday, I made a special breakfast. In addition to the usual bread, cheese and olives, I fried quantities of ricotta fritters and they were tasty, I have to say. To make the fritters mix flour, baking soda, sugar, fresh eggs, and ricotta together, adding a little milk if necessary to thin the mixture. Heat some oil until it is very hot, then drop spoonfuls of the batter in, being careful not to splash yourself with the boiling oil or you will burn. When the fritters are puffed and golden brown, scoop them out of the oil with a slotted spoon, drain them on a cloth, and roll them in sugar.

As they savored the fritters, some of the farmhands spoke of the earth tremor, but really, it is nothing out of the ordinary for us, we are used to such things, and don't pay them a lot of notice. What was more interesting to them was that l'Inglese was back.

'Every day they swaps over', muttered Gaddo, 'tomorrow runty will be back. You see if I'm not right'.

'This bigger one suits her better in size, rather than the tiddler', added Aulo, 'For she a big girl. Always has been'.

'I don't favor neither of 'em foreigners', chipped in Luciano, 'Young Mauro here, he'd be a perfect match for 'er, but she don't see it'.

Mauro said nothing, but immersed himself fully in the eating of his breakfast.

Luckily their country accents are so strong, l'Inglese didn't often understand them.

Later, when the tour bus arrived, the Americans were deeply disappointed not to have felt the earthquake in their luxury hotel in Taormina.

Aventina Valente was wearing a dress that was too small for her body, and the big girls were wearing shorts. Shorts! Well, we had certainly never seen anything like it, and the yard was soon full of farmhands, who, of course, were not working, it being Sunday, and were always ready to witness a spectacle.

It appeared they were going on a day trip to the volcano in the hope of seeing an eruption, even if it was only a small one. They were going to take Mauro with them. Mauro! Because he had grown up on the flanks of the volcano he was going to show them the lava flows and the craters, and, if possible, the summit itself. Because it was said there were some flank eruptions on the south side of the volcano, in the region of his family home, they were going to pay a visit to his mother. His mother! He said he loves me, and yet he has never suggested taking me to see his mother. I couldn't help but feel uncharacteristically cross. Anyway, as it was his day off, there was nothing I could really say against it.

When she fixed her eyes upon l'Inglese, Aventina Valente was quick to approach him, like a spider finding a juicy fly imprisoned in its web. She began to touch him with her hands and thrust her body against him and flutter her eyelashes at him, all the while talking to him in English. I, of course, couldn't understand any of it, but they did seem to know each other, which made me think of the time of Mamma's death, when Luigi was still alive, and he and the barmaid had swept in for the funeral. Lui had said that l'Inglese was no good and he had had him removed. I remembered that very well, and I had believed him, although, in my heart, I never gave up hope of seeing l'Inglese again.

'Have you met Aventina Valente before?' I asked l'Inglese later.

'I don't think so'. He replied, 'Dreadful isn't she?'

I'm sure that's what he said.

So the volcano viewing party were settling themselves into the bus, and as they were on the verge of going, I rushed into *la cucina* and quickly reappeared with a basket of what I had to hand: a bottle of wine, some slices of bread, a portion of a sausage, a few leftover fritters and some fruits: apricots and peaches and plums. I thrust it in at Mauro through the window.

Word came back that although they appreciated the gesture, the picnic was insufficient to feed everybody, and couldn't I provide something more?

'Picnic!' I said, furious, 'kindly tell them it is not a picnic'.

Of course it wasn't a picnic. It is the tradition in our region to make an offering of food to the hungry volcano and by doing so, we hope she will not have too devastating an eruption. O these Americans. Did they know nothing of our ways?

As the bus pulled out of the yard, l'Inglese said:

'I would have rather liked to go along. See the volcano close up. Sounds like fun'.

It was then that I felt very cross indeed.

Anyway, I had no time rage. I had so much to get ready before the nuptials. Biancamaria Ossobucco had sent a crate of chickens which I needed to slaughter for the big dish of Polo alla Messinese that it was traditional to serve at weddings. It was vast quantities of this dish that I prepared in those dark days after the murder of Bartolomeo. Nancy and Ivy had released the chickens, and I needed to catch them all and put them in the coop, before I could wring their necks and pluck them.

I had not discovered until now that l'Inglese was afraid of chickens. A phobia, he called it. When he saw them all running about willy nilly in the yard, clucking and squawking, he started to panic, and in his panic he began to leap around the yard making clucking noises, and he looked just like a chicken himself. I couldn't help but laugh at the sight, and so did the farmhands, who were still standing by, hoping for more entertainment.

'I'm all right with a few chickens', he said later, looking a bit shame-faced, 'it's just that I don't like to be surrounded by them'.

He had business to attend to in town, he told me, and so took himself away. When I had finished rounding up the chickens, I went back into *la cucina*, and began to prepare the wedding cake. It would be the biggest sponge I had ever made, and I had set apart the rest of the day to make it, and to prepare the *pasta reale* figures of the bride and groom. I am famous throughout the district for my marzipan likenesses, and I was looking forward to getting on with them without any interruptions.

Although I did not have human interruptions, I have to say that for the rest of the forenoon, and into the afternoon, the volcano began to behave very strangely. It must have been because Aventina Valente was paying a state visit, and the old volcano was acting up accordingly. There was a lot of belching of smoke, and we are used to that, but the smoke was green this time, which is not so usual. In addition there were strange and rhythmic shudders, like a giant with hiccoughs, and it did make me wonder whether there would be landslides again, which there often had been in the past when the volcano had been stirring.

Apart from this, it was relatively quiet. The silence in *la cucina* was only broken occasionally by the idle chatter of Betty. He had expanded his repertoire and could now say things like:

'Donuts'.

'French fries'.

And 'God bless America'.
I was concentrating on getting the face of Rosario just right, and as
we look so much alike I was able to look at my reflection in the mirror
to clarify any points I was uncertain about, when Gaddo limped in
with news. He said lava flows were now threatening Nicolosi, and
some parts of the town were being evacuated as they were directly in
the line of a fast moving lava flow. As anyone who is familiar with
the geography of the region will know, the village of Saluci is very
close to the town of Nicolosi, and it was possible the smallholding of
Mauro's mother would be affected. Well, the Americans wanted an
eruption, and it seemed they were getting one.

I was engrossed in my marzipan, and after I had finished Rosario,
and an extremely life-like copy of Biancamaria Ossobucco complete
with pock-marked complexion, I was reluctant to stop. Next I formed
the triplets, wearing their little dresses of garish yellow. I was tempted
then to make myself, but thought that I couldn't really include myself
without adding the big figures of Aventina Valente, her daughters,
and Nancy and Ivy too, and that would mean I would have to make
several more batches of marzipan. Then, as l'Inglese would say, I
thought: 'why not?' I had great fun recreating Aventina Valente.
You may be sure I made the enormous beehive, and I made her body
big and her clothes small, and I even added the spidery eyelashes that
she stuck onto herself with glue.

To make her daughters, I had to return to the larder for another sack of almonds and I could hear noises coming from within: bumping and thumping, moaning and groaning, and immediately I feared the nutria that had been in the store cupboard of my sister–in–law Pervinca. Had it got into my own pantry? But when I ripped the door open I did not find a nutria. No, instead I found Aventina Valente and l'Inglese.

Immediately they sprang apart but they had been in a close embrace in there, I'm sure they had, although it was dark, and difficult to see at first. My heart leapt up and did a somersault in shock, because I don't expect, when I am going to my larder, to find people in there, least of all my lover and Aventina Valente. They were in a state of undress: they had taken off some of their clothes. L'Inglese's pants were round his ankles, his shirt was open with all the buttons undone, and I'm sure I glimpsed his willy, upstanding and purple, before he hurried to cover it with his shirttails. She was practically naked. Her too–tight dress was missing and her big bosoms were loose. I didn't want to understand it.

'But you went into town', I murmured to him, 'and she went on the bus tour of the volcano. I saw her going. How did you both get back here and into the larder...?'

'Rosa, I can explain', he said, hurriedly.

She tittered.

'We got very hungry. That's it. Yes. We felt hungry, and we knew you had a lot of....sacks of almonds in here, and so we thought we'd just come in and eat some and that's the truth, I swear, that's all it was...'

'What's happened to your clothes?'

'Well, it was, it was hot, in here, yes, very hot, so we just took them off because of the heat'.

'Hot', screamed Betty, 'Hot. Very Hot'.

The squawking roused me from my reverie. It had been another of my ridiculous fantasies. Honestly. L'Inglese and Aventina Valente. Sometimes my mind acted very strangely, and I seemed to have no control over it. It was the heat, probably. Betty was right. Perhaps I was dehydrated. I had a long drink of cool water and then set to work with my pestle and mortar to crush more almonds into dust. It was hot work, and I was conscious in the stillness and the quiet of the strong aroma of my perspiring flesh and the little tears of sweat that oozed out of my pores and formed irritating trickles that ran down inside my clothes.

Once I had ground the almonds I mixed them with the sugar, egg yolks, and a little rosewater to stop the almonds becoming too oily, and brought the mixture together, into a smooth, soft, but not sticky, dough. Then I colored some pink for the flesh, some bright yellow, for the dresses, and left a little lump uncolored in the bowl, covered with a damp cloth, so that I could color it in small batches for details like hair and flowers and so on.

Although I had generalized ideas of how the big American girls looked, I didn't know the specifics, but I made them good and beefy in short yellow dresses, and I think it was obvious who they were. Of course, it's a time consuming job, and it was late afternoon before I had finished. I had just set all the figures on the cake: the bride and groom, myself and the triplets, Aventina Valente, the four big American girls, Nancy and Ivy, and of course I couldn't resist including Carciofio. I think I had captured his gray fur very well indeed. It even gave the impression that if you patted it, it would release a puff of dust. Although it was a big cake, the figures had nearly filled up all the available space. I was just musing on whether I should include Mauro, seeing as he was the best man, and I couldn't quite decide. Part of me was against the idea because he is so big I would have to crush a great many more almonds to form a likeness of him. Furthermore, if I included him, then should I also include l'Inglese? Although he didn't have an official role in the wedding, I didn't want him to feel left out. So I was wondering about these things, and I had just washed my hot and oily hands, and was drying them on my apron and admiring my handiwork, for I have to say that it was some of the best *pasta reale* I had ever produced, when I heard the sound of the rackety tour bus approaching.

When it pulled into the yard, the bus looked different. It was no longer white, but was blackened. It had some holes punctured in it, some of the windows were broken, and it seemed to be limping, being lower on one side than the other.

When the sightseeing party disembarked, what a sight met my eyes!

Aventina Valente stumbled down the steps of the bus and fell into my arms sobbing. She smelt strongly of being smoked, like a ham smells, when I have smoked it, and as well as being blackened from head to foot, the most remarkable thing was her hair. It was missing. She was almost completely bald, with just a few stray strands standing up on end like pipe cleaners. It had been burned off. Apparently a fireball had landed in it, and before anybody could smother the sparks, they combusted with the vast quantities of hairspray that had been used to construct that sticky structure, and burned its way through to her scalp. Her false eyelashes had also been singed, and now looked like dead spiders clustered around her eyes. Her clothes were ripped and she was altogether a sorry sight, and in spite of my dislike of her, even I felt the smallest bit sorry for her.

The others of the party were similarly disheveled. Gargantuan Brad had lost his camera down one of the craters into which he had been peering, and his big running shoes had been badly burned. His feet were scorched and the smell of burnt rubber coming off him was something dreadful and quite nauseating. Patty May had lost one of her big white front teeth, and looked very odd without it. Sandra Ann and Betty Jean were swathed in bandages, and Liza Lu was covered in a thick coating of ash that had stuck to her skin and hair and hardened like a crust. The children were wailing, and wanted to be taken straight back to Chicago this minute. Mauro was missing.

It seemed that they did get their wish of seeing an eruption, and at a closer range than perhaps was advisable. The farmhands were quick to gather and gawped at the group with their mouths open until I shooed them away.

I tried to do what I could for them, but they insisted they were not staying; their only thought was to get back to their hotel in Taormina for a shower, a change, and of course a big meal. Aventina Valente could think of nothing until she had acquired a wig, either at a theatrical costumiers or a fancy dress shop, or failing that, a hat. Patty May was wondering whether she could fly her dentist over from Chicago to fix her teeth before the wedding. They had simply stopped off to tell me they had become separated from Mauro, who, it seems, had become something of a hero in the drama.

He had been rescuing survivors from rooftops, constructing makeshift barriers to stop the lava flow, and carrying herds to safety: sheep, goats, pigs, even mules. Brad had got it all on film. But sadly the camera was now in the crater.

In the midst of this a wagon pulled by the prize-winning mule, Dolores, drew into the yard. It was being driven by l'Inglese, which was strange, because our people tend to be very attached to their mules. I didn't understand why Licurgo Pastone would have entrusted Dolores to l'Inglese, who he hardly knew.

The wagon was loaded up with goods of all kinds, but before I could look into that, Aventina Valente bolted onto the bus, ducked down under one of the seats, and began screaming for everybody to get back on board. She urged the driver with much unnecessary cursing to drive off, and I suspect it was because she was not fit to be seen.

CHAPTER THIRTY FOUR

'They seem to be in a hurry', l'Inglese said as the bus clanked past, making an ominous grinding noise and belching out horrible gusts of burning oil vapor.

'Yes', I replied, 'they've been burnt alive by the volcano. What is all of that?' I asked, pointing to the goods on the wagon, 'And why have you got Dolores?'

He began to hand things down to me. First there was an armful of beautiful red roses, wrapped in the paper of *Fiori Folli.*

'For you, my sweet', he said.

No one has ever, before, or since, given me flowers. I stood and looked at them there in the yard, and they were the darkest red gets before it becomes purple. The feel of them was like velvet, like peaches, like baby cheeks, and the petals were furled one perfectly inside the next. The scent of them was the absolute essence of rose, and I felt tears wetting my eyes. When I think about them now I can still picture those perfect roses that day, the day of the eruption.

There were, amongst many other things: a pink plush-covered arm-chair, and the plush was the bright pink color of candy, a hurdy-gurdy, a mariner's hammock, a ventriloquist's dummy, a glass dome displaying dead and dusty butterflies, a crate of medicine bottles, and a glossy brown wig.

'Isn't that the wig of Padre Buonaventura?' I asked. It looked very like it to me.

The items looked stranger still standing around in the scrubby yard.

Before l'Inglese stepped down he looked around carefully.

'I say, those chickens aren't still loose, are they?'

'No', I replied, 'Don't fear the chickens. We'll be eating them smothered in mayonnaise soon enough. Now what is this all for?'

'Just a little game of cards, signorina, that's all'.

'Not the mule', I replied, 'surely you're not going to keep Licurgo Pastone's mule?'

'Might do'.

'But it would break his heart'.

He gave her a sound pat on the flank and a cloud of blue dust rose up into the air, which made him cough, and he quickly began to toss his hair to get the dust out of it.

'No, you're right', he said, 'she's sweet, but very dusty. I shall give her back'.

So I carried the roses into *la cucina* to put them in water, though what to use as a vase troubled me, for we are not really given to displays of flowers. I had to put them in one of the stoneware water jars, as that was the only thing sufficiently large, and though it wasn't splendid and grand enough, the roses still looked beautiful.

L'Inglese labored up the steps under the armchair like a pink tortoise, and the only place to put it was the parlor. It was so bright and new it put the rest of our furnishings to shame, and seemed too fancy for the *fattoria*. In my lifetime nothing new had ever been bought. But Mamma's ghost took a liking to it and adopted it as her own. If anyone else ever sat in it, in the blink of an eye they found themselves bruised in the buttocks on the flagstone floor.

The butterflies, on their faded foliage, under their dome, went on top of the great oak chest that had been put there during the Inquisition. Soon, it seemed they belonged there, and had been there always.

L'Inglese was most pleased with the wig and the medicines, and with these he squirreled himself away.

I was back in *la cucina* after that, admiring my roses, and my cake in turns, and perhaps I was wondering what had happened to Mauro, or perhaps it wasn't then, but later, anyway, it was certainly at that time I heard braying outside. It was no ordinary braying, but a song, with the mules lifting up their voices in unison.

Looking over the top of the stable door I saw Carciofo and Dolores standing in the yard with soft mealy nose to soft mealy nose, and in the setting sun the bright rosette of the prize-winner was flashing scarlet on Dolores's halter. Those two mules were gazing into each other's eyes and were singing a duet.

Across the yard Rosario was watching too, and he said:

'It's in the air'.

I asked:

'What is?'

And he answered:

'Love. That's what it is. It's love'.

And I suppose he was right. I asked if he could return Dolores to Licurgo Pastone, and he could, and then, as he was going into town anyway, I asked him to transport the precious cake in his cart. He started to cry at the sight of it, for his heart was so full, and it was magnificent, although I say it about my own work. We had a quick cuddle, and then one of my copper pots hit him on the head. It must have been Mamma throwing it because she never let him touch me, and even though she was dead she wouldn't allow things such as that to go unnoticed. So we carried the cake down and set it in the cart, and packed the area around it with straw so that it wouldn't be damaged on the journey into town. Then the three of them set off together through the gate, and behind them I could see the angry glow in the sky from the volcano, and I felt a strange wistfulness that I couldn't explain.

Later, after dark, l'Inglese called to me from upstairs and when I opened the door to the bedroom, it was lit all around with candles. Beyond, where he was standing, waiting for me, I could see that the bed was covered in rose petals. The scent of them filled the room. It was so beautiful it made me gasp.

I said:

'O you haven't plucked the petals from my roses, have you?'

He was a bit deflated, and he said:

'You're always so practical, *signorina*. No, I haven't touched yours. I had some other ones which I kept back, and those I have plucked to make you a bed of roses'.

'I'm sorry' I said, realizing my mistake, 'I suppose I am a bit too practical sometimes. I'll try not to be'.

Then my clothes melted away, and l'Inglese lifted me up in order to lay me down on the bed of petals. But he couldn't manage it because I was too heavy, and he had to let me down clumsily, and clutching his back with both hands he said:

'Fuck. I've strained my back',

I said:

'Now who's being unromantic?'

And we both laughed because it never is like it is in the movies. So we climbed into the bed where the scent was so strong all around. I could feel the caress of the velvet petals against my skin, and l'Inglese climbed on top of me, and we were still laughing and began kissing and nibbling one another. Then he was covering my body with more of the petals, writing messages with them on my skin. Soon I was wet and aching and warbling so loudly that the whole of the valley might hear, but I didn't give that a thought, and if I had I wouldn't have cared.

Later we were lying hot and perfumed and sweaty and panting. The candles had burned down, the rose petals began to dry and fade to brown, and we must have fallen into a deep, thickly scented sleep. It was then that a noise tore me awake, and reluctantly I swam through the fragrant layers like a pearl-fisher rising to the surface of the sea. As I lay there I heard an engine droning and I feared bad news because it is not normal to hear a motor in the middle of the night. When I licked my lips I could taste the sulfur in the air. In the darkness I could hear the sound of l'Inglese's breathing, and not wanting to disturb him I felt around for my dress and pulled it on. Then I went outside to see what was going on.

CHAPTER THIRTY FIVE

The beam of headlights dazzled me, and lit up the thousand flying creatures of the night. It was Mauro driving a strange truck. He stuck his bandaged and blackened head out of the window.

'I've brought my Mamma here', he said nodding to the inside of the cab although I couldn't see anything, 'they've all been evacuated from the village, the lava flows are getting too close'. His voice sounded hoarse.

'Is she hurt? Do you want to bring her into the house?'

'No, she's all right. Tired out, but not hurt. Clinging on to the roof of the henhouse when I got there. The gasses were bad, and the smoke. I'll take her back with me, then I can look after her'.

'I'll come with you', I said and climbed up onto the steps of the truck for a ride, clinging on to the window opening as Mauro drove through the yard, past the pigsty, and along the track that leads to the cottages and converted stores where he and Rosario and others of the farmhands live. It was like a roller coaster ride, and I had wished I had taken the time to put on underwear. But there was no one to see. Through the window I could just make out a small curled up figure on the double seat beside Mauro. His hands were bandaged, his clothes were torn, and he smelled like a herd.

'They're dropping concrete blocks. Whether they'll manage to divert the worst of it I don't know', he said, 'it's bad over there. Worst one I've seen'.

'The Americans said you were a hero', I said.

'No', he said modestly, 'You've just got to try and help if you can. Were they all right?'

'I think they got more drama than they bargained for. Aventina Valente got her hair burnt off. But she's okay apart from that. Looking for a wig shop in Taormina. Big Brad lost his camera and scorched his running shoes. They're all right though'.

He pulled up in front of the grain store. I jumped down from my perch and nearly twisted my ankle. In my mind I'm just as nimble as I once was, but my body doesn't remember. Mauro jumped down and winced as he landed. His boots were blackened shreds and his feet were burnt.

He lifted his Mamma down and carried her carefully as an egg inside the house. She was tiny, with a mass of white candy floss hair, a brown face, and black dress and cardigan, much like my own Mamma. He laid her gently on the bed and she slept on and we stood and looked at her as you look on a sweet, sleeping child.

I hadn't been inside the old granary since Mauro had moved in, and I noticed how clean and neat and tidy everything was. He had got some bits and pieces of furniture in there and it was like the inside of a toy house.

He looked dead beat. His normally brown face was ash-colored and his body seemed smaller. Shrunken by the effort and the tiredness. I noticed a photograph of myself on a shelf. It wasn't one I remembered having taken. I looked quite good in it.

'Where did you get that?' I asked.

He shrugged shyly and wouldn't say.

'Shall I get you something to eat?' I asked, 'I can run over to the kitchen...'

'Thanks. I'm not hungry. Just thirsty' and he pored himself a big cup of water from a pitcher and drained it. Some of the water fell in drips down his chin and onto his dirty chest and the drops fell like glistening beads amongst the forest of hairs. He wiped his mouth with the back of his bandaged hand. 'You want some?'

I shook my head.

'What about your Mamma? Will she want something?'

'I don't think so. But I have some food, if she wakes up'.

We stood together in the middle of the floor. Quite close together.

'You smell gorgeous', he said, inhaling, 'I'm sorry I'm so filthy. After all that smoke and burning and sulfurous gasses and dust and herds of stinking goats. You smell like a rose'. Then he added, 'A rose that's had a lot of sex'.

I felt my face glowing hot. I was a bit shocked. That he could smell it. And that he would mention it. What he said hung there in the room like an awkward cloud.

'I'll be going then', I said quickly, 'let you get some rest. If there's anything I can do..'

He watched me go. I don't know why but I felt bad. Outside it was dark, the only light being the glow in the sky from the volcano, but that was enough to guide me back to the *fattoria*. As usual the mosquitoes were lying in wait for me, and bombarded my bare legs with their savage stings. Back in *la cucina* I had the urge to make a quick batch of aniseed cookies, and this is something I hadn't done for a long time.

CHAPTER THIRTY SIX

The day before the wedding.

The next morning as I roused myself from sleep I wondered if I had dreamed the whole thing, the bed of rose petals and the night–time conversation with Mauro, but the withered rose–petals were all around, so I hadn't dreamed that part of it at least. L'Inglese was still sleeping soundly. I had the feeling that I had stayed in bed later than I should have done on account of getting up in the night, and I had a lot to do today for it was the last day before the wedding.

So I left l'Inglese sleeping, dressed, and went down to *la cuci*na where I prepared a tray of breakfast for Mauro's mother. Somehow I felt drawn to the idea of her, believing she held the clues that could un–lock the secrets of the past. I didn't know then, that smoky morning, that she would become dearer to me than my own Mamma had been, but, once again, I am rushing on ahead of my story. As I walked past the pigsty the pigs were lined up expecting me to be bringing their breakfast. When I didn't have the steaming pail in my hands, or turn in at the gate, they were cross and began grunting in such a furious way they seemed each of them to be putting a curse on me.

As I approached the row of little cottages I came upon Rosario and I swear he was dancing and he had a smile on his face that stretched from one of his long ears to the other and he said:

'Only one more sleep, Rosa. One more sleep and she'll be mine forever'.

It did make me wonder whether he had been crazy all along, and had only been pretending to be sane. I hoped it wouldn't end badly after all.

When I got to the grain store I was too late, for Mauro and his Mamma were already eating their breakfast. There was a fresh loaf that smelled almost as good as one of my own, a honeycomb, a portion of ham, some peaches, and a pot of hot, fragrant coffee, and I felt a bit redundant.

Everything was clean and bright; even the two of them were freshly laundered, and it was a big change from how things were in the night.

Immediately the tiny Mamma got up and threw her arms around me and greeted me like a daughter. She was saying my name over and over and within a few moments it felt like we had known each other all our lives.

'Rosa', she said, pulling me towards her, 'I feel you are the daughter I never had. Filippo was always talking about you so I feel I know you. You know the way some men say their wives can't make a dish as well as their Mamma? Well, with your Papa it was the reverse. He would say 'Magnolia, you make the *polpettine* very well, but you should taste that made by my Rosa; that is a dish worth eating'.

'Why couldn't he just let me know he was still alive?' I blurted out, 'I've thought about it hundreds of times, and I just can't understand it. Why?'

She patted my cheek with her doll's hand.

'You know Rosa, I couldn't understand it either. It was about the only thing we didn't agree on. But the only reason I can think of is this. He was scared. The longer he left it, the harder it became. I just don't think he could face you, after all that time, and what he did. He couldn't bear you turning him away'.

'But I would never do that'.

I was crying by now, and she was holding my giant hands in hers.

'I know you wouldn't. You wouldn't do that. You don't have it in you to be hard-hearted',

'She does Mamma', interrupted Mauro, 'she has a heart like a stone.'

'Son', she silenced him, 'Pour the coffee. This is a time for us to talk, and you to make breakfast'.

Mauro did as he was told and pored me out a cup of the strong, steaming coffee and it was very good I have to say, for it is not everybody who can make good coffee.

Donna Magnolia turned back to me:

'Rosa, when you get old, you get frightened, and that is hard for you young people to understand'.

'I'm not young', I said, 'I'm forty seven'.

'That's young to me', she said, 'I didn't have Mauro here until I was fifty'.

When I had finished the coffee Donna Magnolia took the cup and turned it upside down on the saucer.

'I don't believe in fortunes', I said, while we waited for the grounds to settle.

'Neither do I', she said, 'Now let's see what we have here'.

She studied the grounds for some time with such concentration that, although I don't believe in it, I was certain it was bad news, and she was wondering how she was going to break it to me.

'I see a marriage, but a marriage broken off', she said at last.

'My father's getting married tomorrow', I said, 'my real father, that is, he's a half-wit, he's marrying my sister-in-law, but I don't think it will be broken off'.

'I see confusion', she continued.

'O he's confused, definitely', I said, 'His brain is as soft as white pudding, but when it comes to Biancamaria Ossobucco, he seems almost normal'.

'When the confusion clears, I see great happiness'.

'That's a relief. I do so want them to be happy. I feel responsible for them, in a way, like a couple of children, they are'.

'And a baby. A beautiful, chubby cherub of a baby. A baby with a full set of teeth'.

'They're sure to have a baby', I said, 'Biancamaria Ossobucco is young and strong although she has the pock-marks on her face. She has had triplets already. My nieces. All of them named after me. I delivered them you know'.

'Rosa', she said, putting down the cup, 'I'm not talking about your father'.

Like I said, I don't believe in fortunes.

I felt there were a great many things I wanted to ask Donna Magnolia, but there was no time; already they were about to leave. Word was in that the lava flow had, at the last moment, been diverted away from the village of Saluci, and the villagers were now able to return. Donna Magnolia was anxious to see her property again, having a great fear of looters, and as Mauro had to return the truck, the two of them were on the verge of setting off. I had only just caught them. Mauro would be back in time for the wedding the next morning.

'But I don't want to let you go', I said, walking alongside the truck and holding on to Donna Magnolia through the open window, 'I feel I want to keep you here'.

'I'll come back again', she said, 'I've got the feeling we're going to be together a lot in the future, Rosa'.

And with that they drove off and I felt flat and sad. As I passed the pigsty the pigs looked at me so sorrowfully I realized I still hadn't fed them and then I felt guilty as well as flat and sad. I hurried back to *la cucina* and prepared them a succulent breakfast to make up for their earlier disappointment.

Then I had to turn my attention toward the chickens. There were fifty of them to slaughter and pluck, so I put on my coarse butcher's apron, caught my hair up in a knot on top of my head, and let myself into the stable where I had them all cooped up. They immediately began to panic, for they knew the hour of their death had come, and squawking loud enough to raise the dead, they ran around in frenzied, feathery circles.

I am not as fast a runner as I used to be, and it took me several sallies before I grabbed the first one by the legs. To slaughter a chicken you hold the legs in your left hand (if you're right handed, that is) and then with your palm facing outward you hold the neck with your right hand so the head protrudes through your second and third fingers. Then you jolt your hand down so the chicken's head bends backward and you feel it's backbone break. It is important to stop then or you will pull its head off.

So then there was one down, forty-nine to go. You get quicker as you get into the swing of it, and the pile of dead birds was increasing, and the number of live ones rushing around was decreasing, but still it took me about an hour to dispatch the lot of them.

Then you have to begin the plucking, and it is important to do this while the bird is still warm, because then the feathers come out easily. If you leave your chicken to get cold, it is much more difficult to pluck, and of course, you must be careful not to tear the skin. Soon there were feathers floating in the air, sticking to my sweaty flesh, in my hair, up my nose, making me sneeze, and I did not look very glamorous when l'Inglese hurried by carrying the mariner's hammock and a book on ventriloquism.

'I'll just keep out of the way, shall I?' he said, his face as pale as ricotta.

'I don't understand why you're afraid of chickens', I said, 'They're birds, like Betty, and you're fond of him'.

'That's different', he said, 'Betty can talk'.

I went back to my plucking, and I was still up to my ears in feathers when I heard an engine, and it wasn't Mauro this time, it was the Americans in another tour bus. The previous one had been condemned.

The tuna man had got a ride with them from the coast, and he staggered off the bus first holding in his arms a massive bloody slab of tuna that was like a whale. It was lovely and fresh with a beautiful blue sheen on the flesh and scented by the sea. Just caught that morning, he said. The Americans, who followed him down at a safe distance, considered it 'gross', and vowed never to eat canned tuna again if that's what it looked like before it got into the can. I helped the man carry the tuna up the steps into *la cucina* and together we laid it gently on the table, and it looked like a flayed human body lying there, but bigger.

Aventina Valente had something strange on her head. She had found a wig after a great deal of searching, but it was not a good-looking one. It was yellow and nylon and fluffy, but it enabled her to face the world again in her brazen way. Brad was still limping. He had had to buy a new pair of normal shoes which pinched, as there were no running shoes available on the whole of the island that suited him. The dentist was on his way over from Chicago, but it was feared he would not arrive in time. The others were still bandaged, but they hoped they would be able to leave off the bandages for the big day. They all seemed quite cheerful, and now that the ordeal was over, they looked back on it as an exciting adventure, and themselves as heroes in the action.

Before long the cart carrying the seamstresses of Banquo Cuniberto drew into the yard, and with flurries of yellow stuff the group retreated into the parlor for fittings.

Finally I was able to finish my plucking, and then I had to carry all fifty of the fowl into *la cucina* for drawing and trussing. First I sharpened one of my knives on the steel until it was good and sharp, and then, taking each chicken in turn, I slipped the knife under the skin at the bottom of the neck, and cut up toward the head. Then, stretching the skin taut, I severed the neck bone at the bottom end. Next I removed the neck bone; to do this you insert the forefinger of your right hand in there, and move it around so that you sever all the innards. Then you cut between the vent and the tail, being careful not to sever the rectum. Cut right around the vent so that you separate it from the body and then you carefully draw the vent with the attached guts out of the tail end. The gizzard, lungs and heart will follow the guts, and if you like you can use these to make a stock or a stew, or you can feed them to the sheepdogs as a special treat. Finally you remove the crop from the neck end of the chicken.

You must repeat this with the other forty nine chickens, and I was working away at my own steady pace when I heard screaming and shouting, and the dress fitting party burst into *la cucina* in various states of undress. It transpired that several of them had been kicked out of the new armchair, and they refused to remain in a room that was haunted by poltergeists.

'It's no poltergeist', I tried to reassure them, 'it's only Mamma'.

But they wouldn't be comforted, and insisted on staying in *la cucina* with me. It was not convenient, because those that weren't being worked on kept getting in my way, and stood around me gaping in ghoulish horror, and it wasn't long before Betty Jean fainted, and I just wanted them to go away and leave me in peace.

Eventually I managed to truss the chickens. To do this you must thread a large bodkin with some twine, then force the chicken's legs forward and shove the bodkin through the body low down. Then you push the bodkin through the wing, and across the skin at the neck. Push it through the other wing, and tie the ends of the twine together. Rethread the bodkin, pass it over the leg, below the end of the breastbone, and around the other leg. Finally cross the thread behind the hocks and tie it around the parson's nose.

I soon built up speed, and worked away until I had trussed all fifty chickens, and when they were lined up in orderly rows on the table with their gray and puckered flesh I felt the satisfaction of a job well done.

Then I had to break off so that I could have my dress fitted. Of course I was smeared with blood and chicken guts, and had feathers in my hair, but I have my work to do and I can't spend all day primping and preening like some women do.

So I was standing there being pinned and poked and pummeled by Vittorina Palmira when l'Inglese came back from the olive grove where he had passed the morning reading in the hammock. I tried to pat my hair into shape, and rubbed my face with the back of my hand to clean it a little, but I don't think he even looked at me.

Aventina Valente seized the opportunity to take hold of him and soon they were chatting away in English in an animated way. Before I knew it she was stroking his hair and he was showing her his bottles of medication. Although I was supposed to be keeping still, and Vittorina Palmira, who had her mouth full of pins, was urging me by San Clarus, the patron saint of tailors, to stop wriggling, I felt myself swelling with fury and finally I burst all the stitches she had been struggling to put into my bodice.

It was then that the suggestion was made that the party should go on the bus into town and drink *apperativi* and eat snacks at the bar of the *Due Ladrone* and I was dismayed to see l'Inglese clambering onto the bus with the rest of them, without a backward glance at me, and they all of them disappeared. The seamstresses followed, and I was suddenly alone, and although I couldn't have gone with them for I had too much to do, I had the feeling that it is nice to be asked. I was now, of course, able to get on with my work uninterrupted, but nevertheless there was a part of me that felt like Cinderella.

Still, as always, it is not my way to wallow in self pity. So I sharpened another bigger knife, and set about filleting the tuna fish and then I grilled the portions over a charcoal brazier that I had lit out in the yard.

Then, when I had set my fowl to boil in several of my largest cauldrons, adding chopped celery and onions and parsley and basil, and the heat in *la cucina* was something dreadful, and there was a fug of flavored steam, at that moment the grinning bridegroom arrived with many trays of eggs, and more than ever did he remind me of the pickled shark. Finally I was able to whip up a vast vat of mayonnaise, and I got so hot and sweaty with the whipping that I had to take a break, and sponge myself down with cool water, and change into a different dress.

It was late in the evening when I was carving the boiled chickens, and the pile of assorted bones on the table was reminiscent of a massacre. More than once it exercised my mind how I would keep the finished dish sufficiently cool to stop it going off in the heat, for I did not wish to poison all the wedding guests. Such a thing has been known in the past, and the shame of that would be more than I could bear. So I finely grated the zest of twenty lemons and added this to the mayonnaise with some of their juice, but not all, for I did not want to make the mayonnaise too runny, and a good mound of chopped capers went in also, and a good many hairy anchovies, and it was then that l'Inglese came in and announced:

'I'm sorry, Rosa, but I've got to leave tonight'.

And I said: 'but it's the wedding. You can't miss the wedding'.

'I'm sorry but I have to'.

And there was a kind of awkwardness hanging in the air, and the thought occurred to me: Was this it? Was this goodbye? Was this the time when he would leave and not come back?

So I continued to stir the hairy anchovy parts into the mayonnaise, and some tears dripped into the mixture. And they were my tears.

Then l'Inglese's arms went round me, and I let go of the spoon in the mixture, and I put my arms around his neck, and I buried my face in him and I sobbed. He held me tight, and let me sob, and then he said gently:

'Come on. Things aren't as bad as all that. Suppose we have a drink, eh?'

So I fetched a bottle and two glasses and we sat down at the table. It was dusk and inside *la cucina* it was becoming brown, and it's the time of day when it is a little sad. L'Inglese said quietly:

'I haven't been entirely honest with you, Rosa', and my heart sank like a failed soufflé as I wondered what I was going to hear, and without meaning to I swallowed my whole glass of wine in one gulp in preparation.

'What I've told you, about what I do, isn't really true. Well, it is true, but it isn't the whole truth. The reason I didn't tell you was really for your own safety, and mine, too. But now I feel I owe you the truth'.

He paused, and then said quietly: 'I'm an agent with the FBI. We work to combat organized crime'.

'the *Mafia?*'

He nodded. Everything had gone very quiet.

'That's really why I had to disappear that time from Palermo. My cover was blown: you remember the doorman at the library?'

'Crocefisso, of course I remember him'.

'He was working for me. He was a member of the Corleonesi clan. But he was trying to help us bring the *capofamiglia* Don Indelicato Lupo to justice. They found out, and you know what happened...'

Good grief, Crocefisso an informer! I'd never have imagined it.

I was silent for a moment as I struggled to take it in. Then another thought suddenly occurred to me:

'My brother Luigi. He knew about you. He said he'd had you *rubbed out.'*

'Well, quite clearly he hadn't, because I'm still here. But we were certainly interested in him, and his associates. We know they are using those pizza parlors as fronts for money laundering operations. But that has nothing to do with us, with you and me, I swear to you'.

All of this was making my head spin.

'So what about Don Umberto? *Did* you have anything to do with that explosion?'

'Certainly not. You talk as though I was one of them. I don't kill people. My job is to gather information, here, and in America, to put it together like pieces of a jigsaw puzzle, and build a case which will hold up in court. Of course we've been interested in Umberto Sogno's activities for years. There has long been trouble between his organization and the Greco clan; and our information was that the feud was escalating. It could only be a matter of time before something happened to him'.

'So the card games, the writing of cookery books?'

'Are really just covers. They are real passions of mine, hobbies, if you will. A pretext like that is invaluable: gives you a reason for being somewhere, makes it easy to pass through border controls, helps you blend in if you need to, or helps you get talking to someone. Everybody wants to write a book, including me. And I'll do it too, one day, when I retire from all this. Tell anybody you're an author and they're always interested, ready to help...'

I was. I remembered well enough.

'So are you really Randolph Hunt, like you told me?'

'No. It is, was, an alias. I stopped using it after that. I have several others now'.

So I had never even known his name. Not that I ever thought of him as anything other than l'Inglese. But it was strange to love someone without knowing his name.

'So what is your real name?'

'It's a bit of a mouthful: Pomfrey Farquarson–Fortiscue'

'I see. So are you really English?'

'I was educated in England, obviously. My father was Scottish. My mother was Russian. But I was born in America, and raised in France'.

So my Inglese was really my Americano! But it didn't matter. To me, in my heart, he would always remain my Inglese.

'So, now you know everything about me. Does it put you off?'

I thought about it.

'No'.

It didn't put me off. It was interesting. Exciting. Better than being a gambler. More worthwhile, definitely. But idealistic. I couldn't imagine a time when our island would free of the mafia. It's impossible to bring them to justice. There's never any evidence. Nobody is prepared to testify. In the unlikely event of a boss going to jail, there will always be another one ready to take his place. But I didn't want to go into all that just now.

L'Inglese went on:

'My work is unpredictable, and can be dangerous. It can mean I have to go away at short notice, sometimes without any notice, like now, for indefinite periods. It means you miss things, like weddings, birthdays, anniversaries. And I can never tell you anything about what I'm doing, for your own safety and for mine. You must never talk about it to anyone, even to members of your family, people you've known all your life. If someone asks you, you'll have to lie, and that won't be easy for someone as honest as you are. We'll have to come up with a story, and rehearse it, so that you don't even have to think about it. I shouldn't be telling you any of this. The people I work with, their wives and families don't know what they do, but I think you have the right to know the truth. So that's why I have to go, and I don't know when I'll be able to come back. But I will come back. That is, if you still want me to?'

'Of course I do', I said, 'I thought you were going to say you were leaving, for good, I mean, but you're not, you'll come back, so that's all right. I can cope with that', and I started to cry again because it was like I had been teetering on the edge of a high cliff, and now I didn't have to jump off, and it was all right. He would come back. He would come back.

Then I covered over the mayonnaise, and the chicken, and the tuna, and together we went up to bed, quiet, and a little subdued. We loved each other in a tender, almost sad, but beautiful way, and when I woke up early the next morning, it was as though I had dreamed him, for he was gone.

Contorni

Side dishes

CHAPTER THIRTY SEVEN

It was the day of the wedding. I remember feeling sad that Guera and Pace wouldn't be here to share it with us, for they loved family celebrations. Then I scolded myself for being foolish: for if they were still alive, their wife wouldn't be marrying my father. Then I thought of l'Inglese. He too would be missing the wedding. Where was he now? On a plane? On a ship? When would I see him again? Would it be years? Or just weeks? Would I live my life waiting for him to come back?

I asked myself these questions, and many more as I scrubbed and scalded an old tin bath, for it was the only thing that was big enough for the quantity of *Polo alla Messinese* I had prepared. Then, when it was clean and sparkling, I tumbled in the chunks of tuna and the pieces of chicken, stirring them together so that each spoonful would have some chicken and some tuna in it, being careful not to make it into a sloppy mush, and my mind ran on l'Inglese and I missed him, and he had only just gone.

I gently poured on the lemon mayonnaise and turned the meats in it to make sure they were all coated. Then I decorated the top of the dish with slices of lemon, olives and capers. It tasted wonderful, and looked magnificent. Finally I covered the top with clean cloths to keep out the flies, and just then Gaddo and Luciano came, and you can be sure I made them give their hands a thorough wash. They could barely lift the trough between them, but they managed it, and with my help we got it down the steps, and onto the truck for the journey into town. I stood and watched it bump away into the distance, and I hoped it wouldn't come to grief.

Although Biancamaria Ossobucco had claimed she wanted a quiet affair out of respect for her not–long dead husbands, of course, in our region, there is no such thing as a small wedding. It was to take place at her house in town, for Biancamaria Ossobucco, out of consideration for me, did not want to burden me with the whole weight of a wedding to provide refreshment for. But in addition to the *Pollo alla Messinese,* and the cake, I had offered to make *cannoli,* for no wedding can really take place without them, and although other people can make them, nobody makes them as well as I do.

I had three hours before the ceremony, and, naturally, I would have to make a great many of them, for it is not possible to eat only one, and there would be a great many guests there, and I would also have to get myself ready, but that shouldn't take too long.

First I made the special pastry. I tipped the flour on to the table, sprinkled it with some sea salt, then added some sugar and some cocoa, and, forming a well in the center, added softened butter, some egg yolks, and some Marsala wine. Gently you must bring the dough together into a ball, but you mustn't knead it too much and make it hot with the heat of your hands or it will become tough like leather. Then you must cover the dough and let it rest. While the dough is resting you should make the filling. Take your fresh ricotta, and beat it with sugar until it is light and fluffy as a little cloud. Then add finely chopped chocolate and the grated zest of a citrine, a lemon, and an orange. Those zingy peels do smell lovely. Then keep the filling in a cool place until you are ready to use it. The final step is to roll out your pastry very thinly, in the same way that you roll dough to make pasta, and cut it into squares. Roll the squares diagonally around your *cannoli* cylinders, and glue the join with a little egg white, pinching together with your fingers so they don't come apart. Heat a pan of oil until it is hot and fry batches of the *cannoli* until they are golden brown. Drain them well, and while they are still warm, slide out the mold. You can see this takes a long time, especially when you are trying to make several hundred. As the hour of the wedding approached, I was still frying away, and I was sweaty and hot and seemed to smell of frying. I wished then that I hadn't offered to make the *cannoli,* but it is not my way to give up on something once I have started. Quickly I spooned quantities of the ricotta mixture into my large piping bag and set to filling the fried pastry tubes, and had just got them all finished, and dusted with icing sugar, and packed into a crate when it was time to leave.

I gave myself a speedy wash, threw on the dreadful yellow gown, and thrust my feet into the white shoes that were too small. They had been ordered as a job lot and were all the wrong sizes. I knew that I would be hobbling about all day in the heat and that I would get blisters which would take a long time to heal. Finally I pulled a comb through my hair, and was ready to accompany Rosario the half-witted bridegroom into town.

CHAPTER THIRTY EIGHT

And so it was the wedding. Of course, Rosario was entitled to his turn at happiness. He was beside himself with joy. I almost didn't recognize him as he came into the yard wearing his first ever smart suit. Close shaven, hair cut, perfumed with cologne. He looked like a normal person for the first time in his life, and, weirdly, I felt in some sense maternal.

He had painted the little cart that Carciofo drew, and decorated it with flowers, and I got in, because I couldn't walk all the way into town in the shoes. As I was spreading out the layers of the dress so it didn't get creased, Mauro came up, and he too looked like a different person. Mamma always said that fine feathers make fine birds and she was right. Mauro looked almost handsome in his fine dark suit, and he was clean, and close shaven, and he too had had his hair cut, for his face looked larger and neatly shaped, and he was even a little bit shy, it seemed to me, as I looked at him admiringly. The three of us were filled with the happy spirits of those who are involved in a wedding, and while I rode in the cart, Rosario and Mauro walked alongside on either side of Carciofo.

As we went along the road into town people came out of their houses to look at us, for a wedding is always an excitement here where not much happens. Little children ran alongside and Carciofo thought about kicking them, for he did not seem inspired by the spirit of the wedding, and does not like to be interfered with. People were waving, shouting out their congratulations, and Rosario was like the cat that had got the fish. The bells were ringing out once more (Biancamaria Ossobucco had herself paid for the repairs to the *campanile*) and the streets were crowded, and even I felt fluttery and excited.

We drew up at the steps to the church of San Antonio Abate where every wedding of the Fiores is celebrated, and already my feet were painful. Parmenio Folli, the florist, approached with the buttonholes for the bridegroom and the best man and I pinned them on as a photographer appeared and began taking photographs. With surreptitious glances all around Rosario unharnessed Carciofo and led him up the steps. He was insistent that the mule who had been his lifelong friend would be a guest at his wedding, and although Padre Goffredo was against the idea, the mule was definitely going to church. Like many people who do not have a full load of brains, Rosario can be as stubborn as a mule, and once he takes an idea into his head nothing can shift it. The plan was to secrete Carciofo in the confessional on the basis that the priest probably wouldn't look in there until the ceremony was over.

'You look beautiful, Rosa', Mauro said, although I thought the yellow made me look jaundiced like Marinangela Brolese looked before she died, and I said,

'You don't look bad yourself', and I meant it. He didn't look bad.

So Mauro joined Rosario in encouraging the mule to go up the steps, which he was not keen to do, there being a great many of them. No sooner had the three of them gone through the doors, than Biancamaria Ossobucco was driven up in an open carriage with the triplets, and Aventina Valente, and I was annoyed because I felt that I should be the one to go in with them. There was a second carriage behind containing Patty May, Sandra Ann, Betty Jean, Liza Lu and Nancy and Ivy and it was a squash in there with all of them.

I have to say that Biancamaria Ossobucco did look lovely. Her pock-marks did not notice much, and the dress was very fine. The team of seamstresses appeared from nowhere, like bees buzzing around a full white rose, flapping and smoothing, and pulling at her skirts. The triplets were squealing with excitement, and although Rosita did have an accident in the carriage, the resulting puddle was small. There was a lot of milling about on the steps while Parmenio Folli handed out the bouquets and arranged us in cohorts, for it was ridiculous to have so many bridesmaids, and finally, on the stroke of eleven, we filed up the steps and through the doors.

Shortly afterward Biancamaria Ossobucco and my father Rosario were joined together in holy matrimony by Padre Goffredo. I always cry at weddings. I can't help it. Tears streamed down my face as I thought of Guera and Pace, and Carciofo brayed from his hiding place in the confessional, and Padre Goffredo realized he was beaten, but took his defeat in good part.

Afterward there was more confusion on the steps as the photographer tried to organize us and it seemed to me that Aventina Valente was never far from Mauro's side. This irked me for I was supposed to be the Matron of Honor, that is, the chief bridesmaid. I had been asked by Biancamaria Ossobucco. Aventina Valente had not been asked at all, and was only included because she had invited herself.

We spent so long smiling that our faces were aching. Our eyes were dazzled by the full force of the midday sun. The noxious odor of mothballs rising from the wedding guests, and the sulfurous gases that were still seeping out of the angry volcano, caused many to suffer asthma attacks. It was a relief when the photographer finally allowed us to leave the steps and follow in a procession back to the house.

CHAPTER THIRTY NINE

My first concern was to see to the refreshments which had been laid out in the big saloon, but I found everything was well arranged so that I only had to make a few minor adjustments. The cake looked magnificent, and had been set up on a round table to itself. I made a mental note to keep a watch on the little ones to stop them nibbling the marzipan figures, and I would be keeping a careful eye on Carciofo too, for I have never known a mule with such a sweet tooth.

Biancamaria Ossobucco had hired in waiting staff, so I did not have to go around handing out the eats and drinks. I must say it was a novelty for me to be a guest at a wedding, and not have to do the work. The *Pollo alla Messinese* was delicious, and soon the Americans were helping themselves to plateful after plateful, without realizing that this was the dish they had seen me making, and were disgusted at the puckered chickens and the bloody tuna.

After lunch there was a lot of chatting to do, as there always is at weddings, for it is an opportunity for everyone to get together. I believe I was the only one who gave a thought to the fact that it was scarcely a month since many of us were gathered here for the dreadful deathbed drama of my poor darling twins.

Just as the lunch was cleared away, the tea was served, and the *cannoli* were the best I have ever tasted, although I suppose I shouldn't say that as I made them. Soon a queue was forming for seconds and thirds. At one stage, through the thick crowd of guests, I did catch sight of Aventina Valente feeding one of my *cannoli* to Mauro and she took hold of the other end of it in her mouth and they both nibbled away towards the center until their noses touched and it was quite disgraceful.

Other than this, I was quite satisfied with the refreshments and felt that we had provided a good spread which is important. I hoped the wedding food would be remembered in the region for a long time to come, both in terms of quality and quantity, but later something happened which totally eclipsed everybody's memory of the food, and the wedding was remembered forever, but for something else entirely. Anyway, although I like to eat, I certainly felt that I could not eat anything more for several days, and I'm sure that many of the other guests felt the same.

Through it all, Rosario was dancing around with a blissful look upon his face, and I did hope that it wouldn't end badly, for although I am not a pessimistic woman, we are as a people cautious, and it is well and widely known that the price of happiness is death.

After tea it was time for the cake to be cut by the happy couple, and I was slightly concerned about Rosario having the big knife in his hand, but my fears proved groundless, nobody was stabbed through, and the cake was so praised by everybody it warmed my heart. Of course I still have the photograph the photographer made of it in my box of treasures, although it is slightly ripped and crumpled after the passage of the years. Immediately the children fell upon the marzipan figures, and I could almost feel the new big teeth of little Alberto Fiore biting into my marzipan flesh, and it was a strange feeling.

Then it was time for the entertainment to begin, and a stage had been set up in the courtyard, with tables and chairs arranged around it. Once again Biancamaria Ossobucco had spared no expense, I have to say. She had not only booked Selma Maccarone, but had also managed to get the famous *castrato* Martino Volta, and the two of them sang together such tender duets that the notes rose up like doves to the heavens, and I don't know what came over me for I just couldn't stop sobbing. As a result, my cousin, the spinster Betsabea Calzino, the daughter of Zio Pietro, who perished in the landslide at the twins' funeral, went around telling everybody that the menopause had struck me down in the middle of the wedding, and people kept coming to stare at me to see if it was true.

Then there was a fire eater, on account of the triplets so enjoying the one at the *festa*, and a fire broke out when one of the burning torches caught light to one of the hired tablecloths. A spark fell into the wig of Aventina Valente and it was like history repeating itself, but thanks to the quick-thinking of Gargantuan Brad, who upended a pitcher of water over her, the wig was saved, although Aventina Valente was somewhat damp and furious.

Then, after that little interlude, Privato's band began to play. By now the sun had gone down, and the lanterns were lit. The sky was the color of lavender, and the guests started to pair off for the dancing. I began to busy myself clearing away some of the finished−with glasses and plates, for I did not expect to dance, but then, from behind, hands seized me around the waist. It was Mauro and I was quickly maneuvered onto the dance floor.

Now I do love to dance, although I haven't danced in years. It was a waltz, and I was surprised to discover that Mauro is a fine dancer, for although he is wide, he is light on his feet, and he moved me around with such skill I too was dancing well, although I was out of practice.

People were saying:

'Why, look at Zia Rosa'.

'Who'd have thought she could dance like that?'

'Good couple they make, those two'.

'Thank God that oddball foreigner has finally gone'.

Mauro didn't once tread on my toes, which was a mercy, because I was dancing in bare feet (the wedding shoes were so very uncomfortable that I had taken them off, earlier on, and now couldn't find them). We swooped and glided. Sometimes he held me close and his body was hot and strong. His buttery odor mixed with the biscuity scent of new cloth, and little gusts of citrus cologne came and went. I liked being led around the dance floor by him, and I was enjoying myself whereas I hadn't expected to. That waltz ended, but joined seamlessly with another one, and without a word we continued. I was conscious of whirling faces watching us go by. I was glowing with warmth for dancing is hot work, and it was then that Mauro staggered me by saying:

'You didn't believe any of that stuff did you – about him being a secret agent?'

I was so shocked, I stopped dancing for a second until those muscular arms moved me on again. How could Mauro know about that? It was supposed to be top secret.

'I don't know what you're talking about', I lied.

'It's no secret. Everybody in the region knows'.

'They do?'

'Oh yes. He's been telling everybody. Fausto Pustolino heard it from Manlio Estivo who was telling it to everyone who was waiting for the bus',

He broke off as he dipped me over backwards and took my full weight on his brawny forearm. The onlookers gasped, expecting me to hit the floor, but then I surged up again, and we sashayed on.

'and when the bus came Lupo Calderone, who was getting off, had already heard it in Randazzo from the man who plays the mouth organ outside the ecclesiastical outfitters'.

I didn't know what to say. The number finished. Everybody clapped. Mauro let me go and said, finally:

'I wouldn't believe a word of it, myself. Like Padre Buonaventura, the guy's a fake'.

I busied myself about, gathering up the dishes and the glasses, and carried them into the kitchen, for the hired waiting staff had disappeared. I filled the sink with hot water and detergent and began to wash up. As I scrubbed away with the little mop on a stick I did not know what to think. Was Mauro right? Did everyone in the region know l'Inglese was a secret agent? If they did, and he was, he could be in big danger. If he wasn't a secret agent, then why tell me he was? If I began to doubt that, should I doubt the other things? How did Mauro know what l'Inglese had told me? Had he been listening? Soon my arms and hands were red and puckered, water was dripping from my elbows, my layers of tulle were damp, my bare feet were standing in a puddle, and the stack of clean dishes was like a tower, but I had not unraveled this knotty problem. I was just thinking of getting my hands into a sack of flour when Biancamaria Ossobucco and Rosario came in, for wherever she goes, he must follow, and she led me back to the patio, saying:

'Rosa, you mustn't be in the kitchen doing the dishes, I want you to enjoy yourself'.

I submitted, although in truth I was better left alone in the kitchen. But it was Biancamaria Ossobucco's big day, and I wanted her to be happy.

Aventina Valente had managed to dry out her wig, and although it now resembled a cat that had fallen down a well, nevertheless, once again, she was everywhere at once. As Biancamaria Ossobucco and Rosario led me back to their table, the band began to play a tango, and Aventina Valente dragged Mauro to his feet.

Although other couples like Petronilla and Paolo, and Selma Maccarone and the castrato Martino Volta, Berenice and Didimo, and Innocente and Concettina Capone, and Parmenio Folli and Betsabea Calzone, and Patty May and Gargantuan Brad and others besides began the dance, they soon left off feeling they had no place on that dance floor. With everybody else present they had their eyes fixed on Aventina Valente and Mauro as they strutted backwards and forwards with the jerky and dramatic motions of the dance, clutching one another's bodies shamelessly, and gyrating their hips. Aventina Valente was quick to pull up her already short skirt to reveal her doughy legs and provocatively thrashed them around in the air before winding them around Mauro's in a display which had everybody spellbound. I have to say that here, in this region, we had never seen anything like it. Even the frustrated mule of Ippolito Brolese left off its incessant braying and watched with its head stuck through the laurel hedge.

When it was over there was a pause, then a burst of wild applause. Mauro, at least, seemed to feel a little self conscious, for he blushed a vivid crimson, and tried to disappear from the public gaze. But Aventina Valente was reveling in her moment of glory, preening and posing, wiggling her body, and flashing her diamonds. She kept a tight grip on Mauro's hand, and they seemed to be a couple.

Later I saw her sitting on his lap feeding him trifle from a spoon, and Betsabea Calzone leaned across to me and said:

'They'll be next to the altar. You see if I'm not right'.

I did not reply because I did not know what to say, and it was at that moment that the rabid dog burst into the courtyard through the open doors and everybody began screaming. It was one of the giant yellow sheepdogs of Nebore La Marca, and for days past it had been staggering around the region with a wild look in its eyes, and now it was foaming a green foam and snarling.

The dog was quick to approach Aventina Valente, and why it was drawn to her in particular I cannot say, and she vaulted onto one of the tables and began a frenzied braying which matched that of the mule of Ippolito Brolese, and of Carciofo who had got into one of the bedrooms, and was peering over the little balcony, his head framed by purple petunias.

Padre Goffredo held up his crucifix and asked that we join him in prayer, but we were too busy panicking. Instinctively I grabbed hold of the triplets and held them high above my head while I kicked my legs in the air to repel the advance of the dog. Rosario had snatched up the bride and she was clinging on to the triplets also, so that we were like one of those formations of acrobats who stand in tiers on each others' shoulders.

Gargantuan Brad smashed one of the hired chairs onto the dance floor to break it, and with the splintered prongs was approaching the dog with menacing motions and it was then that the dog reared up and with a savage snarl sank its fangs into the well—upholstered but—

tocks of Betsabea Calzone. While the dog's attention was engaged in this assault, we noticed a streak of blue serge flying across the courtyard, and with a crash Mauro landed on the back of the dog, seized it by the head, and with one deft movement snapped it's neck. Then the dog lay on its back with its legs in the air, the legs twitched once or twice, and then it was still.

After the shock of this event, many of us were crying, including me. My sister-in-law Vereconda was quick to start screaming:

'It's an omen. It's an omen'.

But she has been saying this for so long that nobody takes much notice. Biancamaria Ossobucco collapsed in tears, for no bride wishes her wedding to end in this way. Betsabea Calzone was carried away to Dr Leobino's surgery, the stiffening dog was removed in a sack, and I began to brew strong, hot coffee which was what we needed to calm our nerves. The plucky band of Privato began to play tentatively again, but nobody felt like dancing, except the children who were now prancing on the tables, snarling, rearing up, playing mad dogs. The wedding was over, and it was certainly one that wouldn't quickly be forgotten.

CHAPTER FOURTY

Aventina Valente had decided to treat the newlyweds to two nights in her hotel in Taormina as a wedding gift, so they were unexpectedly going on a honeymoon after all. At the end of the wedding we waved them off on the tour bus with the Americans, but strangely, Aventina Valente herself was missing from the party.

Biancamaria Ossobucco tossed her bouquet out of the window above the crowd, and I'm sure she aimed to throw it at me. I did catch it, but, of course, we all know that I will never marry, and some of the girls muttered that it was a waste for me have it.

Although Rosario was reluctant to leave Carciofo behind, he accepted the separation as inevitable, for he knew in his heart the hotel would not allow a mule into the rooms. With a great deal of cajoling the aged beast was led up the ramp into the back of the truck. Into the front seat I loaded the triplets, and they were so exhausted they were asleep before I had pulled away from the house. It was an odd sensation driving in bare feet, but there was no help for it.

Back at the *fattoria* all was quiet and dark for it was now the early hours of the morning, and one by one I carried my nieces up the stairs. Each time I passed through *la cucina* a voice said:

'I'm with the FBI'.

And

'Top secret'.

It was Betty.

When I pulled down his night-time cover said:

'We work to combat organized crime'.

He sounded just like a comic book hero.

Later the four of us were cuddled up together in my bed, for the girls do like to sleep in with their Zia Rosa, although it is something of a squash, and I am always being kicked by six little feet, and pummeled by six tiny fists. Naturally I found it hard to sleep, because of the steaming wriggly bodies surrounding me, and because the day had been too long, too hot, too exciting and too full of incident and I had done too much chatting and couldn't wind down. My blistered feet were murdering me, a slow and sadistic death, and I was seriously thinking about getting up again and soaking them in a mustard bath. Most of all I was thinking about l'Inglese.

Even the senseless chatter of the parrot unnerved me. Was it a joke to everybody but me? If I started to doubt l'Inglese, where would that route take me? I had doubted him once before, in Palermo, when I had followed him that time through the streets close to the docks, and of course, it wasn't him at all, only the back of someone else entirely, and my mischievous mind playing tricks on me. What reason did I have to doubt him this time? None. And yet, there was always this itching there, like a mosquito bite you can't stop yourself scratching. There was an air of mystery about l'Inglese. He wasn't like one of us. We are born and grow up in a place where everybody has always known us, and everything about us, our families, and our ancestors, and they always will, and there's no escaping that. He was different, and there were mysteries about him, but it was the danger in him that had first attracted me to him.

I began to wonder if I should get up and start making the bread for breakfast, for there is no point in lying in bed if you cannot sleep, and it was at just this time that the disturbance started. Cries cut across the stillness of the night air, slicing through my worried thoughts. Shrieks, they were, and they grew louder, and more frequent. As I stretched my ears to work out where they were coming from and who was making them, the valley began to echo with screaming and whooping and laughing. They were cries of rapture, lovers' cries, and they were loud, and grew louder still, became high-pitched and more frenzied, and ebbed and flowed like a tide. After a while I worked out where they were coming from: from the row of cottages where the farmhands lived. I realized that raucous and indecent laughter could only come from the mouth of one person: Aventina Valente. And who the man was, I could guess also.

The slumbering animals were unsettled by these unexpected noises. Down in *la cucina* Betty set forth with an ear–splitting squawking, and it was like it must be in the jungle, his natural home. Outside, the other animals joined in this strange chorus: the pigs, the chickens, the cats, the rats, the birds, the dogs, the mules, the goats, the sheep, and in the far distance there was even the low, deep reverberating bellow of the bull of Indelicato Paternostro. This eerie cacophony roused Little Rosa from sleep, and she asked,

'Zia Rosa, what is that noise?'

And I replied, 'It is just the night sounds of the animals, *cara,* now go back to sleep'.

But I knew it was the clamor of Aventina Valente roused to the heights of passion by Mauro and I was cross and could not sleep all over again. He said he loved me, and yet here he was enjoying a night of unbridled passion with the barmaid of Linguaglossa. There is something in men that I just do not understand.

CHAPTER FOURTY ONE

The following morning the baby Rosas and I were making *sfincione* for lunch. I explained to them that their grandmother was making this very dish at the moment of my birth, and that I had been born on the table amongst the anchovies. Rosina said:

'You already told us that four hundred times'.

I had forgotten that when you are three you know everything.

It was then that the tour bus of the Americans trundled into the yard once more; this seemed to be a daily fixture now of our lives. Quickly I added another sackful of flour and some more yeast to the dough, for I knew what we had already prepared would not be enough.

It is strange that I cannot communicate directly with these huge nieces of mine. They rolled off the bus, began waving their weighty arms around, making whirring noises with their lips, and it was fascinating.

The bus driver, whose name was Natale, and who didn't speak their language either, stood with me and the triplets and Carciofo and watched their display, and when they paused he clapped enthusiastically, for he was hoping for a generous tip when the time came.

Nevertheless none of us could understand the meaning of it. Then, when we were beginning to wonder what would happen next, Aventina Valente and Mauro strolled up, looking as nonchalant as it was possible to look. Both of them were limping. Both had savage bites on their necks, as though vampires, or bats, had drained their blood in the night.

It appeared that the trip was over, and they were bound for Palermo, from where an aeroplane would take them back to Chicago. So, after many hugs and kisses, Aventina Valente finally parted from Mauro, saying,

'Let's not say 'goodbye', just 'au revoir'.

She took her place in the back of the bus from where she rapped on the glass with her diamonds, and waved with tears in her eyes, until the bus pulled out of the yard and disappeared from sight in the clouds of dust that rose up from the road beyond.

I for one was relieved to see them go. Mauro didn't seem distraught either, although a smug sort of smile was playing on his lips.

Once we had stopped waving and come back into the yard, I gave Mauro one of my looks, which I believe said all I wanted to say.

'What's eating you?' he asked.

'Me?' I said, 'Nothing. But something's been eating you – there are bite marks all over your neck. You should be ashamed of yourself'.

'Why?'

'Well, if you don't know I'm not going to tell you'.

'I do believe you're jealous'

'I am not. But you are dishonest. You said you loved me'.

'I do love you. More than ever'.

'How can you say that when you've been sleeping with Aventina Valente?'

'I haven't had any sleep, as it happens'.

'Please', I held my hand up. 'Spare me the details. Everybody in the valley could hear the rumpus. And you know very well what I mean'.

'I'm no worse than you, sleeping with *James Bond.* It didn't mean anything, with her. Just exercise. She came after me with her big laugh and her big chest and her big eyes and her big hair which comes off and her touching and feeling, wanting a good time. What am I supposed to say: 'No thanks, I'm staying celibate until Rosa comes to her senses?'   Or should I enjoy myself while I'm waiting, if there's no harm in it?'

'It's not the same thing at all', I said, archly, going back up the steps into *la cucina* where the triplets had gone ominously quiet.   No.   It wasn't the same.   What l'Inglese and I have is something special; we love each other — well I love him.   It certainly isn't just 'exercise'.

CHAPTER FOURTY THREE

That day, the day after the wedding, I felt rather flat. I suppose it was inevitable; there had been all the excitement and the preparation, and now it was over. The beautiful red roses had withered and died, suddenly, and that episode seemed a long time ago now. The bouquet of Biancamaria Ossobucco, too, was already wilted and brown. I piled the dead flowers onto my compost heap; they remind me too much of cemeteries.

Betty kept up a steady stream of chatter:

'The pizza connection'.

'Fidelity. Bravery. Integrity'.

'A dry sherry'.

In the end, although it was day, I pulled down his night cover to muffle him. He was getting on my nerves.

The girls were more than usually busy. I do have to keep watch on them constantly. During the course of the early morning, when my back was turned for only a few seconds, they had lowered Rosina in the bucket down the well shaft. Shortly after that they had tried to slaughter one of the piglets (they are all three of them very like me in that respect: all of them want to be butchers when they grow up). While I was putting away the cleaver, the big knife, and the saw, they had found a tin of whitewash in the old chicken shed, and had begun to paint Carciofo. Rosario would have a fit when he came home.

It was then that I had the idea of visiting Betsabea Calzone, who had been put into the Infirmary. Although she could be an irritating ninny, it was a dreadful thing that had happened to her, and seeing the tiny girls would be sure to raise her spirits. So I gave their hands and faces a good wash and combed their hair, and there was a good deal of squealing because it will get so tangled, and I redid their plaits and then we all piled into the truck and drove into town.

I had never once been in the town Infirmary, but as we went inside it reminded me so much of the Infirmary in Palermo, it was like stepping back in time. The smell was identical: disinfectant, medicine, floor polish, lingering and stale odors of food. The corridors were the same, lined with the blue–gray vinyl that makes the soles of your shoes squeak, and the tightly made beds with the regulation bedspreads the color of sand.

We found Betsabea Calzone, in the bed next to Selmo Archangelo, and I have to say she looked better than she had in years. She was in high spirits and had already had visits from Padre Goffredo, the castrato Martino Volta, a very nice man who had taken a wrong turn on his way to the post office, and to top it all, even the mayoress Donna Rea Reparata Gusto had dropped by and had her photograph taken for the newspapers.

Betsabea Calzone was relishing the attention her injury gave her, and she insisted on raising herself off the bed and turning so that I could see her bandaged buttocks. Luckily she could not display the actual wounds, for I didn't want the sight to upset the girls and give them nightmares.

I soon realized that taking three three-year olds in there had not been such a good idea after all. They were quickly all involved in hoisting the pulleys of the machine which had the leg of Old Man Domani in traction, and then they had run off with Betsabea's false teeth which were in a glass of foamy cleaner on the bedside locker. There was certainly a trend in having false teeth amongst our people at this time. In the spring there was not a set of dentures in the region, and yet now, it seemed, everybody had them.

Once we had gone in, though, it was difficult to get away, for Betsabea can talk for hours without pausing for breath. It was only when the triplets discovered a corpse behind a screen, and were playing happily with it, that I had to leave her in mid-sentence, and picking the three of them up in my arms, I hurried toward the exit.

When we got to the doors, there was a flurry of activity. A gurney was being wheeled in, surrounded by people, one of whom was Indelicato Paternostro, and he was crying. Padre Goffredo was administering the last rites, a photographer was taking photographs and the flashbulb kept exploding like a rocket, and the nursing sisters were trying to restore order for it was like a riot. Little Rosa, who was sitting on the top of my head, and thus had a bird's eye view of what was going on said:

'Is Etna dead?'

And although I didn't know it at the time, the tot was right. Poor Etna was dead.

Later that day, the dreadful truth emerged.

It was almost as though the gods thought we had enjoyed ourselves too much at the wedding with the feasting, dancing, and merrymaking; they threw at us news which reminded us yet again that the price of happiness is death.

Every day someone died, it seemed to me. And this time it was Etna. Poor little Etna, who was only sixteen. It appears that it was not only her sister, Amoretta, who had fallen for the charms of the bogus priest. Ever since her sister's disappearance with him, Etna had suffered the agonies of a young love not returned, coupled with a jealous rage that had turned her mind. I myself had seen her lying on the floor of the house when I had taken the cheesecake, and now, of course, with the benefit of hindsight, I wish I had done something to stop her taking the terrible action that she did.

What happened was this: she went deliberately to the choral at the far end of the town where Indelicato Paternostro keeps his white bull. The bull we heard roaring in the night. The terrible bull that takes ten men with clubs to subdue it when it is time to mate it with the heifers. The same bull that, when I was a girl, gored the sweetheart of Pasquala Tredici, and in her grief she entered the *Convento degli Angeli,* where she still is.

It seemed Etna had planned it all in horrible detail, even wearing a red dress to enrage the bull, she climbed over the fence, and walked straight toward it. Of course the animal was infuriated by this intrusion, and he pawed the ground, and breathed great puffs through his pierced nostrils, puffs that caused the dust on the ground of the choral to rise up in clouds, and still the poor girl walked towards him with the utmost bravery. Finally the bull lowered his huge head and charged. He galloped toward her and speared her on his great crooked horn. It went right through her, and her blood poured down over the bull's white face, and he galloped around blindly for ages, tossing her body like a rag, because once she was impaled on the horn, he couldn't get her off.

Indelicato Paternostro had to call in men to help him, and the poor child was a terrible sight to see when they finally did release her, and got her to the Infirmary, which is where we saw her. But of course, it was too late, and there was nothing anybody could do. They tried to prevent Pervinca from seeing her, but she would look, and it was dreadful. And so my brother had lost two of his daughters to the same bogus priest and none of us knew how to comfort him.

CHAPTER FOURTY FOUR

The following morning was the funeral of poor Etna. As usual I busied myself with the refreshments, because while I was doing that I could avoid thinking.

It was an unbearably somber gathering in the best parlor; a room we hardly ever used, except for funerals. Of course I remembered all the other funerals, the other buffets, the other heartaches, as I handed round the coffee and the plates of pastries: those filled with almonds, cinnamon and rosewater, the fennel seed fritters, and the little pistachio cakes. Nobody knew what to say to Giuseppe and Pervinca. What could we say? So nobody said anything.

In the midst of this, once again there rolled into the yard the tour bus, and the newlyweds spilled out of it full of joy, for they did not know about the death of Etna, and, fresh from their wedding, they had arrived back in the middle of a funeral, and it was awkward, I have to say.

When she heard the terrible news, Biancamaria Ossobucco, being an emotional sort of person, collapsed on the floor and had to be brought round with smelling salts. The triplets were loudly demanding to know if there were presents for them from Taormina. Doda Rospo was brandishing the meat cleaver, in case she happened across the bogus priest while attending the funeral. Carciofo got in, and, while our backs were turned, was gobbling the pastries. It was another time when things went wrong and were not as they should be.

The following day there were two more deaths, and it seemed to me that we were being tested to see how much we could take.

First of all, news came from the Infirmary that Betsabea Calzone had died of rabies. This was shocking because when we had seen her last, only two days before, she felt fine and had never looked better. But since then, when we were all immersed in the tragedy of little Etna's death, the disease had seized hold of her, and, in a horribly aggressive form, had laid waste to her. She became paranoid, suffered hallucinations, began an incessant dribbling and crying, and finally started to panic at the sight of water. After this she became delirious, went into a coma, and died. Padre Goffredo was with her at the end, and although he has seen a lot of deaths, he was shocked.

Sad though this was, at least Betsabea Calzone was a single woman. The second person to die that day was poor Pervinca, and she left Giuseppe with five children to raise alone. It was a strange thing that happened, because after the tragedy of one daughter running away with the priest who wasn't a priest and another one deliberately goring herself to death on the horn of a bull, it seemed Pervinca could not bear it. So the ground opened and swallowed her up. It was as simple as that.

At first nobody could believe it. Giuseppe himself was there and saw it happen, and as the earth closed over her, he began to dig madly with his hands to free her. Other witnesses ran to get spades and hoes and whatever other implements they could grab in the moment, and they all started to dig in a frantic attempt to unearth her. Later they got the tractor and ploughed up the land all around. But it was no use: no trace of her was ever found.

It was on that same site where the *festa* is always held, the place where there is the annual rain of toads, and some say that the ground is bewitched. Although that may be true, I don't believe it. Later Giuseppe had a monument put up, and it is still there, and every year when it is the *festa* we think of poor Pervinca.

After that, not long after, it is true, but this is the place to mention it, Giuseppe married Sophia Bacci. When they came to tell me about this, I was astonished, because I would never have put those two together. She had spent so much of her life devoted to the memory of Bartolomeo, I never thought she would give it up. There had been a time when I thought she and Mauro might make a match, but nothing had come of it. I would have considered Giuseppe too rough and ready for her, for she is more ladylike, it's true, but before he was forced to marry Pervinca, he was said to be very keen on Sophia Bacci.

So Sophia became my sister-in-law, and I where I had always admired her, I grew to love her. She took on those five children, and she loved them like her own. She fed them well, kept a good larder and kitchen, and made all sorts of other improvements. Then she added a child of her own to the number in the house, and I was surprised at this too, for I would have thought she was too old for babies. She is the same age as me, and I am too old for babies, and it just goes to show the truth of what I always say, no matter how much you have seen in your life, you can always be surprised.

Pesce

Fish

CHAPTER FORTY FIVE

Anyway, all of this comes later than the time I am talking about. It was the end of the summer, and the rains came early that year. Although it shames me to say it, I felt a sense of melancholy that fall, a lowness of spirits that I couldn't raise.

I knew it was serious, because I couldn't even feel enthusiastic about the time of the wild mushrooms, and usually this is one of the high spots of my year. Normally I spend nearly all the fall slithering on my belly in the hidden places, or climbing the trees, where the choicest of the *fungi* are to be found. This year, I could only make myself go out hunting once or twice, and although I came back with my basket laden with beauties, they brought me no real joy.

Sometimes I heard Mamma murmuring, on the rare occasions when she vacated the plush armchair in the parlor and came into *la cucina*, yes, at those times I heard her muttering that I was feeling sorry for myself, and that wasn't the way I had been raised.

Biancamaria Ossobucco wondered whether it was the menopause as Betsabea Calzone had mentioned before her sudden and agonizing death, and I supposed she could be right.

Naturally, Biancamaria Ossobucco was pregnant by now, and so, at the age of forty-eight, I was to have a new sister or brother, or new sisters and or brothers, because Biancamaria Ossobucco was already an enormous size and there were, of course, some months yet to go. As she stroked the bulge that was bigger than she was, she confided to me her ever-present fear: that her babies would be joined together like her first husbands, and however many times I tried to reassure her, she would always come back to the same theme.

Although I tried to put on a show of being cheerful, even the news of these babies couldn't lighten my heart. There was something weighing it down. And I knew what that something was: it was l'Inglese.

I thought back to those times over the summer. That time just after he had come, when there was a sudden shower of warm summer rain, and he pulled me outside into it, to feel it on my skin. We danced around in the yard feeling the shock of the fat, heavy drops, and we made love standing up, against the wall under the vine, the rainwater pouring down our faces and penetrating our hair and clothes. How strong that love had felt. Thinking about it even now made my body clench inside.

Now the rain was coming down outside. But it was a different rain. It was cold. It was dark. And he was gone. I was alone, making hot, buttered toast that I kept putting in my mouth and chewing and swallowing, but it didn't make it better.

He was gone again. That was the problem. We had had a fine time while he was here. But now I was alone again. And this was my life.

He had said he would come back. And I believed he would. If he didn't get killed. (I didn't even want to consider that possibility). So, yes, he would come back. Some time. Last time it had been nearly four years. So would it be like this for four years? Would I feel so melancholy as this for four years? Then he would come back. And we would love each other again, and, hopefully, have fine, amazing, giddy, joy-filled happy times, again. And then he would leave. Again.

Is that what I wanted? Is that the way I wanted to live my life?

In my heart I knew the answer was no. I wanted more than that. But what I wanted I didn't know.

CHAPTER FORTY SIX

But I had my work, and I was never busier than I was that fall. I always was involved with the outside work at harvesting. When it was the *vendemmia*, we would all be out in the vineyards, gathering in the grapes. A few weeks after that, the olive harvest is our busiest time of the year. All of us are in the olive groves from dawn until dusk, shaking the olives from the trees with rakes, gathering them from the canvas sheets we place on the ground underneath. The cold, misty nights are spent working the press. I don't have time to cook, so supper is usually no more than a hunk or two of rustic bread drizzled with the new oil just squeezed fresh from the press. Delicious.

More than this, at that time, I became a farmhand myself. I worked harder than ever, pushing myself on, so that I was so tired, physically tired, that I had no time or energy to brood.

Of course, I couldn't avoid Mauro, but I tried not to be alone with him if I could help it. Since the time of the wedding, when he had slept with Aventina Valente, an awkwardness had come between us like a fungus and now we were strangers to one another.

I was sad about this because I did not want to be on bad terms with him. Before that, I thought we were friends, and I enjoyed his gossip and his jokes. I wanted to ask him about his mother; I missed her, too, but something hampered me. Sometimes I caught him looking at me with his black eyes, and there was something in his look that I didn't understand.

So, in this way, the days passed, and the weeks passed, since l'Inglese had gone, and I came to accept my life the way it was now, again. I remembered how I had mourned for him the first time he had gone away, when I hadn't known why, and he had just disappeared, and I started the fire that nearly killed me. I felt my life was just going round in circles. Stupid circles. And I didn't want it to be that way.

When the cold, wet days of the olive harvest were over, and we had gathered in all the olives and had pressed our oil, we had many lovely bottles of the grassy green liquid, both to sell, for our oil is highly prized, and brings us in a good amount of money, and to keep for ourselves. It felt good after all the hard work to know that the harvest was in, and that it could not suddenly be spoiled.

Then there follows the day of *i Murticieddi,* the dear little dead ones, or All Souls' Day, on November second. As usual, I had been busy making the fruits of *pasta reale* for the children to find under their pillows in the morning.

Mauro had gone to Saluci to visit the full grave of Filippo, with his Mamma, and I did not know he was going until after he had gone. Naturally, I visited our cemetery to honor our dead. The stark new graves of Guera and Pace, Etna, Pervinca, and Betsabea Calzone were startling and brutal and dark from the rain. Five dead since the last *i Murticieddi.* Too many. In addition I visited the old graves, among them Mamma's, and the empty grave of Filippo, and I envied Mauro his full up grave, for an empty grave is not good.

It is not supposed to be a sad day. It should be a cheerful day when we remember fondly those who have died, and give thanks for having known them, but the rain continued to fall, in fact, it poured down, causing the customary fear of landslides, and in my heart, it was raining too. November is such a bleak month. It was cold and dark and I could not get warm, and though it was still early when I returned from the cemetery, I decided to go to bed. And this was the way my life was.

CHAPTER FORTY SEVEN

That night, the night of *i Murticieddi* I had a bizarre dream. In the dream was Mauro, and he was sleepwalking. He had once said he sleepwalks, and in my subconscious mind I must have remembered this, for he came walking into my bedroom.

In the dream Mauro had come back from Saluci and he came into my bedroom and climbed into my bed. I was asleep and I felt him climb in beside me, and, because it was only a dream, I snuggled into him. It is, as you know, a small bed, and Mauro is a big man. In the dream he did not want to be alone, for he had come from visiting the grave of Filippo and I understood, for I had been visiting many graves, and I did not want to be alone either, with the dead, I wanted to be with the living.

So Mauro came, and in the dream, when I rootled under his arm, his arm went around me and held me. I snuggled into his chest and it was bare and thickly hairy. I, too, was naked which was unusual, because in the wintertime I always wear a flannel nightgown. His smell was strong, and, as you know, it is a smell that I like. In the dream his body was warm, and padded, for he is not a man only of skin and sinew; there is flesh on his bones, although he is not fat. It was good feel the warmth of our two bodies close up under the covers, knowing that outside of the bed the air was cold, so that you would see the vapor of your breath, if you let your nose poke out. It was like being on a summer island far away from the cold and from the dead.

In the dream we did not talk, for it was not a time for talking, and I felt small tucked under his arm, but the little iron bed was groaning under the weight of the two of us, and at each and every movement it shuddered.

It came about that he began to caress my body with his large and sensitive hands. And because it was only a dream, I allowed his hands to rove over the hills and the valleys of my body, and I could feel at the same time the movements on the inside of my body. I felt puckers, like a tender skin on the surface of a *bianco mangiare,* when you gather it in perfect pleats with your fingertip. That is how the inside of my body felt then, in that dream.

And because it was only a dream I let myself go, for I knew that I would only wince at my foolishness in the mauve light of the morning. So I allowed my body to answer the call of his body, and my hands felt his large and solid body and it was warm and soft and sweet-smelling and I felt it with my fingers. Along it. Around it. All over it. And I was amazed at the information my fingertips were relaying to my brain in the dark.

At a certain point I stopped thinking and began only feeling and there were the whispers of names and breathings and murmurs. There was a sudden plunge like a dive into deep and crystal waters on a hot day. I, deep down under the water, like a bubble rising up to the sun-dazzled surface, unstoppable, unpoppable, whoosh, I rose, and then there was a starburst, and a simultaneous sudden jolt, and that was the moment when the bed broke.

There was screaming, obviously. I screamed. And someone else screamed. A man. And when you have a dream and you wake up, the dream ends. If you went to bed alone, there shouldn't be anybody else there. But there was, and it was Mauro, and he groaned:

'What's happening? Is it an earthquake?'

Mortifying thoughts rushed into my mind like a flood. I said:

'But it was only a dream. It can't really be real, can it?'

He, more awake now, said:

'Rosa? Is it really you? Where am I? I don't understand'.

A part of me didn't want to turn the lamp on, because I didn't want to face real life, and him, and myself also. But I scrambled to the place where I thought the lamp should be and I did turn it on. The glare illuminated Mauro, naked, sitting on the buckled remains of the bed. I, too, was naked and I snatched the covers and pulled them up to shield myself from him, and I was angry.

I stood over him, and said:

'What do you mean by this?'

'I don't know'.

He did look genuinely bewildered as he peered around the room, and his eyes were squinting because they were unused to the bright light.

'I was dreaming. I don't know how I got here. I don't remember'.

'Have you been drinking?'

'No. Have you?'

'Me? Of course not. I was dreaming. If I'd thought for a minute it was real...'

'Then what?'

He was shivering now because I had the only covers and he was bare and millions of goose bumps were tracing blue points over his enor-

mous body. I wasn't conscious of feeling cold yet. Rage and em-
barrassment were keeping me hot and painful as a burn.

'It would never have happened'.

'Wouldn't it?'

'No. Of course not'.

'But it did happen. There's no going back'.

'I love another man'.

'Forget about him. Listen. It's incredible, I tell you. It's fate, bringing us together. I must have been sleepwalking. I've no idea how I
got here. They say I sleepwalk. You do it too, I've seen you. You
can't deny it. So I sleepwalk here, to your room, all the way across the
farm. I dream of making love to you. At that same moment, you
dream of making love to me. And it's real. It's not a dream. It's a
dream come true'.

'No. It's not a dream. It's a nightmare'.

'A nightmare? He was offended. 'You're telling me it was a
nightmare? It wasn't beautiful? You hated it?'

'It was a dream, I tell you. You do things in dreams you would never do in real life. I'm always having crazy dreams. It doesn't mean I want those things to really happen. It was a mistake, okay?'

'It wasn't a mistake to me. It was one of the most amazing things that has ever happened to me'.

'Don't be ridiculous. It was just a dream. Snap out of it. Go away'.

'It's so cold. Won't you come back to bed?

'Will you get out of here?'

Part of me felt like climbing back into his arms and the broken bed, and part of me felt like beating him with my fists. Finally my words sunk in, and he got up and looked for his clothes and began putting them on. Neither of us said anything more. And then he had gone and there was a hole like a wound left behind.

Then I too got dressed, because there was no way I was going to get back to sleep. After I felt certain he must have left the house I went down to *la cucina* and Betty turned to me and said:

'Who's a naughty girl then?' and he began screaming: 'Naughty girl. Naughty girl. Naughty girl.'

One day I knew I would release Betty into the wild. But that time had not yet come. I made haste to light the fire for it was so cold my teeth were chattering, and brewed some tea. I knew what was coming, and I couldn't really face the conversation I knew I was going to have with myself.

Of course, after I had burned my tongue on the tea, I tipped out a whole sack of flour onto the table, and added the yeast and water and began to knead.

To recap I had had sex with my brother (that Don Juan with loose morals) while I was fast asleep, and I had cheated on l'Inglese while he was away on a top secret assignment for the FBI. It was a mess.

'Shame on you', said Betty, and it was as though he could read my mind. I had seldom been more ashamed of myself in my whole life.

CHAPTER FORTY EIGHT

It was awkward, after that. It was a cold time and a lonely time. More than ever I kept a distance from Mauro and tried to pretend that what had happened between us had not happened. Instead I turned my thoughts toward l'Inglese and missed him and wondered where he was and when he would return. I felt that when I least expected him, he would appear.

The day after *i Murticieddi* is the birthday of Vincenzo Bellini, when we celebrate the composer's birth. By tradition I prepare huge quantities of Pasta alla Norma for the whole family, but I did not feel like celebrating, and I could not meet Mauro's eye.

That morning, I moved my broken bed from my room. I didn't want to be reminded of that episode. In its place I moved in the bigger bed that Mamma had shared with Filippo and later Antonino Calabrese, and the suitors that had come after him. This bed has been in the family since the time of Garibaldi.

In the cold month of December we have many festivals. The first is the *Immacolata Concezione* with its parade of maidens. This year I did not join the parade. In my heart was the guilt that sucked my blood like a leech.

The following week is the *festa* of *Santa Lucia* when we make the *cuccia*, the wheat berry pudding, to thank the saint for saving our ancestors from famine.

You must begin the preparations three days in advance, for it is important to soak the berries in water for three days, changing the water every twelve hours otherwise it stagnates and smells bad and the berries taste sour. Then, after the three days of soaking, you must drain the berries and boil them up on the stove in a large pan of salted water. You must boil them until they are soft, and it takes a good two hours, sometimes more. When they are cooked, drain the berries and leave them to cool, and while they are cooling, you prepare the white cream.

Mix some wheat starch with a little milk, gradually adding more and more milk, whisking well to prevent lumps from forming, then you add some sugar. Cook this mixture on the stove, stirring all the time to prevent the milk from burning onto the bottom of the pan, until it thickens and coats the back of the spoon. Then you remove the custard from the heat, and put in the zest of the lemon, and allow the flavor to infuse and the custard to cool.

When it is cool there may be a skin on the surface, a tender, rubbery little skin, and I love to pull my finger across it, and gather it up into little wrinkled pleats. Sometimes I feel like this inside, when I am thinking about l'Inglese sweeping me up in his arms when he comes back, and the two of us falling backward onto the table, scattering the wheat berries, becoming smeared with the lemon custard in our haste to join ourselves up again.

Would I tell him about the mistake with Mauro? No. Of course not. I would take that particular nugget with me to my grave. Would I spend my life waiting for l'Inglese to come back, or would something change? On this question, I was less certain.

As I thought about it, I mixed the cooled wheat berries with the white cream, and spooned the mixture into glass dishes, before decorating the surface with powdered cinnamon, and some little gratings of chocolate.

Biancamaria Ossobucco, who was so huge she had difficulty now in coming through the door, loves to eat a great many of these puddings, and as she finished one, her puffy hand reached out for another one, and she said to me:

'Rosa, *cara*, you want to talk about it?'

And I replied, wearily, '*Cara, non*'.

For it never was my way to talk about it.

CHAPTER FORTY NINE

Almost immediately after *Santa Lucia* is the time of *nucatoli,* the special Christmas cookies with their filling of almonds and honey. It is our way to offer these cookies as gifts to our friends and neighbors. Every year I make them in huge quantities, for everybody in the valley expects a package of them, or it cannot be *natale.*

It is a little secret of mine to prepare the dough the night before, so that it can rest, and I believe this is one of the reasons why my cookies are so delicious, for it is not good to rush them; a rushed cookie is not good.

So you take your flour, and the lard you have saved from the last pig you have slaughtered, and some sugar and a little baking soda, and you mix these together, lightly, for if you labor with this dough it will be heavy. Then put it aside and cover it while you find yourself thinking about which is the next pig you will slaughter with your big knife. Will it be big Roberta? Or will it be Felice, with his chubby haunches, and sweet, bristly cheeks?

You must then shell your almonds, and the triplets have become skilled at this job, for they love to help. Once shelled, toast the almonds in a pan, and the scent of the almonds toasting is one of those smells that always makes me think of Christmas. Then grind the almonds in your pestle and mortar. Grind and grind away until you become quite sweaty, even though it is the middle of winter. Grind until your hand and arm begins to ache, and do not stop until your almonds become as fluffy and powdery as fresh breadcrumbs.

Then you must melt a good quantity of honey with a little water, and bring it to the boil. When it is boiling, add your almonds, and keep stirring until the mixture forms a paste that does not stick to the sides of the pan. It is important that this mixture is fairly dry, otherwise it will seep out of the cookies during the cooking. Leave the honey and almond paste to cool, and let it rest overnight.

The following day, roll out your pastry into a thin sheet and cut it into even sized rectangles. Make a thin sausage out of some of the almond paste, put it lengthways along one edge of a pastry rectangle, and roll the pastry around the paste. Be sure to seal the edge well with water, pressing it down firmly, so that the seam won't open up in the oven. Then cut lengths of this sausage and form them into 's' shapes on a baking sheet. Using a sharp knife, cut little snips into the 's' to make the shape which traditionally we call 'the dog with eight legs'.

Then the cookies go into the oven, and you may find yourself gazing through the window pane, wet with condensation, while you wonder just where your life is heading. But don't let your cookies burn, they must be no darker than golden brown.

The next step is to make the glaze, and again you must take your time over this: the perfect glaze can take up to half a day to get right. Mix egg white with icing sugar and grind them together in your pestle and mortar. Once more grind away slowly until you make a thick glaze which is sticky and which you can hold between your thumb and forefinger.

Then, when your cookies have cooled sufficiently, use your finger to lay a light coating of glaze over each biscuit, following the shape carefully so that each of the dog's legs is coated, but so there is a margin of cookie showing and you don't get the glaze over the edge because this would look messy and unprofessional.

Finally, when the glaze is on the point of drying, add a light sprinkling of powdered cinnamon, and a sliver of pistachio.

These, then, are your *nucatoli*, which you make into little packages and give as presents. The triplets love to go around with these packages, telling everybody that they made them themselves with very little help from their Zia Rosa.

Carne

Meat

CHAPTER FIFTY

Natale is a bittersweet time for me, for it is the anniversary of Mamma's death, the time when my brothers thought I had murdered our own mother. I will never forget that. Few people would, in my position.

New Years passed, and *Befana*, when the good witch brings gifts to the little ones, flying through the air on her broomstick. These are quiet times on the farm, for apart from pruning the trees and the vines, there is not much work to be done when the days are at their shortest and coldest.

Then, in the depths of winter, it is time to slaughter a pig or two, when the cold weather will not turn the meat, and it can be salted, and smoked and cured to preserve it. One morning, when the sky was the color of violets, I let myself into the sty and my friends the pigs greeted me with many a good natured nuzzle and grunt, and the fresh dung deposited among the straw underfoot steamed in the frosty air, giving off a pungent aroma. I scratched the pigs, and tickled them, pinching here and slapping there, all the while sizing them up with the eye of a butcher, and it was obvious to me that the time had come for Roberta to grace our table.

In preparation, I set up the gambrel in the yard, sharpened my knives, and got ready my big saw, scraper, hook, the scalded buckets in which I would collect the blood to make into my famous sausages, and various other basins in which to put the fat, catch the guts, and the pluck and so on.

The following morning, after a hearty breakfast, for I knew I would be working all day out in the cold, I put plenty of water on the stove to boil, dressed in my rubber boots and apron, and tied up my hair. You may be sure that underneath I had on my thick winter underwear, with the long legs, the very same underwear I had once revealed by accident to that cat Costanza as I removed my boots at the Library with an over-vigorous motion of the legs. My breath, and Roberta's, formed a cloud of vapor, as she trotted happily along by my side, lured on by the sweet promise of a cookie all to herself.

Then, as I stuck in the knife in her throat and killed her, a voice said:

'Buon giorno, Signorina',

I thought it was Betty; that he had escaped from *la cucina*, and I looked through my legs because I was bending over with the knife in the pig, and it was l'Inglese. He had come back. Again. It was so good to see him. He was upside down, his beautiful shoes were in the muck, and his sparkling blue eyes were laughing. I was conscious that I did not look my best, for I had felt the warm blood splatter onto my face, and I knew the rubber apron and boots were not glamorous, but that could not be helped. I said:

'You're just in time. Quick, come and hold this bucket for me, will you?'

He stepped gingerly through the mucky straw to where Roberta lay. I was squatting with the knife in my hand, and I stuck it in, just in front of the breastbone. I pushed the knife in a little further and sliced forward, severing the artery, and the blood began to gush out in a spurt. But l'Inglese did not hold out the bucket. He slumped down onto the straw. He had fainted, and I was terrified that the blood would be wasted. There was a moment of fear in my heart before other hands seized the bucket and held it out under the gushing surge. It was Mauro and he said:

'Heaven help us, the Nancy boy is back'.

He was back. But the timing was not so good, because once you have killed the pig, you have much work to do, and it cannot wait. Once we had drained the blood into the buckets, we broke off briefly in order to carry l'Inglese up the steps into *la cucina*, and it was inevitable that he got somewhat smeared with blood on his clothes. We sat him by the stove, and I gave him some grappa to restore him, and he was weak, and a little confused. Mauro was tutting and muttering, and took out some jugs of boiling water to begin the scraping. Betty was ecstatic and began to sing 'God Save the Queen', and reluctantly I had to leave l'Inglese to himself while I returned to the yard.

It appeared that Mauro was an expert with the scraping hook, and was already scalding and scraping away to remove the bristles from the skin, and we worked on together, without even needing to talk, for each of us knew instinctively what to do. This is a fiddly, time-consuming job, and Roberta was a big animal, and it was some hours before we had finished the scraping. Finally, when there were no more bristles left, and Roberta was white and bald, Mauro dipped the trotters in a can of boiling water and, using the hook, pulled off the toenails one by one.

While he was doing this I dashed back inside to see if l'Inglese was all right. I think he was feeling a bit embarrassed that he had fainted, for he was deep in conversation with Betty, and waved me away with a gesture of his aristocratic hand.

Outside, Mauro had finished the trotters, and was cutting slits in the tendons of the hind legs for the gambrel to go through. I took up the big saw and split the breast-bone. Then, together, we pulled Roberta up on the gambrel. He cut off her head and put it into brine, while I cut round the anus and tied it up with string to stop it leaking. Then, taking the big knife I slit right down the front, holding back the guts with my left hand, and positioning a big basin beneath, I hauled the innards out.

Mauro began to throw buckets of cold water inside the carcass to clean it, and then we propped it open with some sticks to allow it to stiffen, and as we did this, the light began to fail, and I realized how stiff I was from bending and stooping and stretching and working all day in the cold. Only then did I begin to think about l'Inglese, and began to grow warm inside at the thought of the night that was to come.

CHAPTER FIFTY ONE

I was lying in a hot bath and l'Inglese was sitting at the far end massaging my toes. He had lit candles around the room, and the light from them flickered and danced casting strange, fluid shadows.

The pig blood and gore had even got into my hair, and bristles were floating on the surface of the water. It was good to feel clean, but my body ached like the body of an old woman.

'Did you miss me?' He asked.

'Of course', I answered, 'It has been very dull here without you'.

'Good'.

'Good? Why is it good?'

'It means you're pleased when I come back'.

'O I'm pleased', I said and I felt myself open, and the warm water enter my body.

I stood up and the water ran down my body in rivulets, cascading back into the tub.

'I love your body when it's wet', he said, 'there's something incredibly sensuous about it'.

And soon his tongue was tracing the path of the rivulets over my glistening body and I felt the thaw for the first time that winter in my body and in my mind.

In the bedroom, as we hurried to the bed, he noticed it had grown. I felt my face flush with shame.

'I thought it was time we had a grown up bed', I said, trying not to remember the night when my little bed had died under the combined weight of Mauro and myself.

And so we made love again and again throughout the night and I loved the things his body did to my body.

At some point during that night, my voice said:

'Where do we go from here?'

I wished it hadn't. I really didn't want it to ask that question. Because I didn't want to know the answer.

And his voice answered:

'We get married'.

And this was not the answer I was expecting. It was not the answer I was expecting at all.

'We do?'

'Yes'.

He rolled out of the bed and crashed onto the floor.

'Fuck', he said, 'I think I've just broken my leg. But never mind that for the moment. I want to ask you properly. On bended knee: Rosa Evangelina Fiore. Will you marry me? Will you be my wife?'

'Yes', I heard my voice saying. 'Yes, Pompe Funebri ...what was it again?'

'Never mind, go on'.

'Yes, Pompe Funebri whatever it is, I will marry you. I will be your wife'.

And that, reader, is how we became engaged to be married.

CHAPTER FIFTY TWO

The next morning, when I woke up, but before I opened my eyes, I wondered if I had dreamed the whole thing: him coming back, and asking me to marry him. I didn't want to open my eyes just in case, because I couldn't bear the disappointment if it wasn't real. But I hadn't dreamed it. He was there. Lying next to me in the big bed, asleep. As I looked at him I felt an overwhelming burst of tenderness: I loved his nose. I loved his breathing. I loved his closed eyes. I loved his lips, pink and parted slightly. I loved his little moustache. I loved his silky hair. I didn't mind it was falling out. I loved his body, pink and plump where it protruded from the covers. We were going to be married.

And as I gazed at him he began to stir and woke up and I said:

'Did you mean it?'

And he said:

'Almost certainly. Mean what?'

'About us getting married?'

'Of course. I never make a joke of getting married'.

And so I was going to be a bride. And I dressed once more as a butcher and spent the day jointing Roberta.

I salted the two lovely hams and the bacon, and I would smoke some parts of these too, after they had salted for the necessary time.

Then there were some joints which we would roast as fresh meat.

I made my special sausage mixture out of the blood and the lard, and of course I did not forget to flavor it liberally with fennel seeds, and I made other sausages out of some finely minced lean meat and more pork fat.

I made brawn out of the trotters and the head and all the scraps of skin and bones. You must boil these up for a long, long time, and of course the kitchen becomes foggy with steam but that can't be helped, and you must add salt, pepper, garlic and spices: some cloves and nutmeg, and a leaf or two of bay. Then you strain the mixture through a muslin cloth into your pudding basins, and as it cools, the fat rises up to the surface, forming a seal. This brawn will keep a long time and you cut it into slices and serve it with pickled or fresh vegetables and a generous hunk of bread and it is tasty as well as nutritious.

I don't know how it came about, although of course as a people we do like to gossip, and our gossip has the tendency to spread with the speed of a forest fire in August; neither l'Inglese nor I had mentioned the news of us getting married to a single soul, yet, while I was butchering the pig, people kept coming, first in ones and twos, and then in larger groups, to congratulate me and wish me joy.

Biancamaria Ossobucco, Rosario and the triplets made haste to embrace me and I couldn't work out how they had heard the news so fast. Biancamaria Ossobucco said,

'*Cara*, I must speak the truth, and say that he was not our first choice for you. But you have got the biggest, most sensible, and cleverest brain of any woman I have ever known, and you must know best what is the right man for you. Heartily I wish you joy, and hope that your marriage will be fruitful with babies. I can only speak for myself and say that both my marriages have made me very happy...'.

Of course, at this she began to cry, for she is a tender hearted soul, and her condition also, I think, makes her more than ever emotional.

At this point l'Inglese came in, and she embraced him, and wished him joy as her son-in-law and her brother-in-law combined, and Rosario wiped his hand clean on the seat of his pants and held it out shyly. The triplets began to cry and said they didn't want me to marry the funny man with the falling out hair because they wanted me to marry Zio Mauro, and I said,

'Don't worry, my ducklings, I'm not going anywhere, nothing will change, your Zia Rosa will always be here'.

Then l'Inglese disappeared again, and when he reappeared some time later he had put a lot of greasy stuff on his scalp which was glistening.

Although I was up to my elbows in pigs guts which I was cleaning out to make skins for my sausages, we opened a bottle of the new wine and drank to our happiness.

The farmhands came in next to congratulate us, and there was some confusion amongst the less clever ones as to which of the three suitors I was marrying.

My brothers and their families came too, although many of them seemed a little awkward, and I could tell they thought I was making a mistake.

Giuseppe clapped me on the back and said:

'Well, who'd have thought it, eh? Rosa a bride. At her age'.

And Sophia, who was by now pregnant and glowing and the same age as me, gave her husband a look and he said no more.

The only one of my family who did not offer me congratulations was Mauro. When I saw him in the yard he said, simply:

'Don't do it, Rosa'.

After that I didn't see him for a couple of days, then someone said he had gone back to Saluci, and I knew I would never see him again.

Anyway, I was a bride. I had a wedding to arrange. And I didn't have time to fret about my relatives who couldn't be happy for me.

Time passed in a whirl, and looking back on it now it was like the time I was driving the truck when the brakes failed. We saw Padre Goffredo, and arranged the date, and it was 1st February 1963, only ten days away, and although I had agreed to it, I didn't feel there was enough time.

What was I going to wear? I thought I would have something sensible that I could wear again — for example, the pink two- piece I had made for the mayor's visit to the Library back in the spring of 1955. Or perhaps a smart navy blue, which I would be sure to wear when I had important business to attend to in town.

But Biancamaria Ossobucco could not be happy with me in a two-piece. She worried at me like an itch until I agreed to drive her and the triplets in the truck to Randazzo where a bridal salon had recently opened. Honestly, the place was becoming so sophisticated these days I hardly recognized it. So we went in and before I knew it the pushy *signora* in charge had frog marched me to the rear and stripped off my housedress and as usual I felt ashamed of my underwear but there was nothing I could do about it.

'I've heard all about it', she said, 'Madame is marrying with a foreigner, isn't that right?'

I nodded and stood there feeling like an awkward schoolgirl while the triplets ran amok, playing among the rows of full skirts wrapped in tissue paper. The *signora* and her henpecked assistant dressed me up like a mannequin, in a pearl-encrusted gown and a diamond tiara and a frothy veil, and when I looked at myself in the mirror tears welled up in my eyes and I felt like a princess in a fairy tale, not plain old Rosa Fiore.

L'Inglese insisted on making the wedding cake, in the English manner, a cake of dried fruits, not sponges, as we generally have. He spent a lot of time making the cake, and wouldn't let me see it because it was to be a surprise.

I asked him when his family would be arriving for the wedding, and he said he had no family, they had all died, and I thought that was strange because in the whole of our region there isn't a single person who doesn't have any family. And I began to worry about it.

CHAPTER FIFTY THREE

It was the night before the wedding, and everything was ready and I still couldn't really believe it was happening to me. L'Inglese was going to spend the night in town at the house of Biancamaria Ossobucco, for it is believed to bring bad luck for the spouses to see one another on the morning of the wedding. Biancamaria Ossobucco and Rosario and the triplets were going to spend the last night with me at the *fattoria.* It was late and I had gone to bed but I could not sleep because I was excited, I suppose, and, in truth, a little nervous.

As I lay in the bed I tossed and turned a hundred times trying to get to sleep, for I did not wish my face to look puffy for my wedding. My wedding. Would it really happen?

Then, in the middle of the night, I was conscious of the window being opened from the outside and someone climbing in. My heart stopped for it was a bandit on the loose, desperate, and cunning, a bandit who would stop at nothing to carry out his evil schemes. Instantly I was awake, and looking around in the dark for something with which to arm myself, but there was nothing to hand. Often in my dreams I was searching for a weapon, and really I should hide one in my room, so that I would have it when needed.

The figure of the bandit dropped down onto the floor from the window ledge, and I didn't know whether to scream out, or to pretend to be asleep and hope he would creep past and go on his way. But then he called me by name:

'Rosa, are you awake?'

I recognized that voice. It was Mauro.

'What are you doing?' I asked, reaching out and turning on the lamp, 'Climbing through people's windows. Why not come through the door like a normal person?'

'I wasn't sure if *he* would be here', he said,

'My *fiancé?* No. He's spending the night in town. What do you want?'

'I just had to talk to you'.

'Well, hurry up, I need to get some sleep'.

'Don't do it Rosa'.

'Please don't start that again. I'm marrying him. It's all arranged. The refreshments are ready downstairs'.

'There's more to marriage than a buffet', he said.

'I'm perfectly well aware of that'.

'I just wanted to say this: I love you. Don't marry him. Marry me'.

'I'm marrying him', I said, finally, 'Now please just go away and leave me alone. Forever'.

'Don't do this to us. We are meant to be together. You're making a big mistake'.

I closed my eyes again and feigned sleep, and when I opened them again he was gone. Then I knew it was just a silly dream. Mauro had not really come in through the window. So, with relief, I went back to sleep, a thick lemon scented sleep, the consistency of *zabaglione*, and when I woke up on the big day I was rested and fresh and leapt out of bed ready to be a bride.

CHAPTER FIFTY FOUR

It was the day of the wedding. My wedding. The day I thought would never be for me. I dressed in my beautiful gown that was hanging on the thickly padded hanger on the door of the guard robe. I pinned up my hair and put on the veil and the tiara and Biancamaria Ossobucco couldn't stop crying when she saw me, and I was worried she would go into labor, for I didn't want to have to deliver another set of triplets before my wedding.

Thankfully she did not go into labor, and everything passed in a whirl because I was so nervous. Before I knew it I was standing at the door of the *chiesa* and the wedding march was playing. I was holding the arm of Rosario, and behind me the triplets were holding onto my train, and I was so proud I wished Guera and Pace could be with me to make my happiness complete.

At the end of the aisle stood l'Inglese in his suit with a long jacket and even at this distance I could see a lot more of his hair had fallen out in the night. He turned and looked back at me and smiled. Padre Goffredo was dressed in his beautiful wedding vestments with the golden headdress, and he nodded and beckoned me to come forward.

Rosario and I started on that long walk together. On either side were the dense crowds of my relatives, looking, smiling, nodding, chattering, waving, and I felt my cheeks glowing hot under the scrutiny of everybody.

Finally we reached the altar, and I stood next to my l'Inglese. It was like a dream, and soon we would take the vows that would join us together forever. Padre Goffredo began to read out the words and I remember feeling very hot then. I was prickly and feverish, and began to think quite seriously about fainting. I had to will myself not to faint now. I could faint later, when it was all over. Not now.

Padre Goffredo joined our hands together and l'Inglese began to repeat after the priest the solemn words:

'Ego Pompe accipio te Rosa Evangelina in uxorem meam...'

when suddenly there was a noise at the back of the *chiesa*, the doors were thrown open and when we turned around it was Mauro coming in, riding on the back of Carciofo, and he called out:

'Wait. I have something to say'.

Because Mauro is so big, Carciofo could hardly bear the weight of him, and yet the mule walked steadily down the aisle, pointing proudly his tiny hooves, aware of his importance in this moment of history. I could tell from the air around Rosario that he was worried about his beloved mule, and Padre Goffredo was bristling at having the mule in his church once again. I was furious because Mauro had interrupted my wedding. I wondered what on earth he was going to say. I looked at l'Inglese and he was puce and dumbfounded and it seemed that the passage of Mauro and the mule along the aisle took forever. Time stopped and it felt as though we had all been bewitched, for we could not move and could not make a sound and the air was taut with tension. Finally the decrepit mule staggered up the steps before the high altar and Mauro clambered off. Clearing his throat he proceeded as though addressing a jury in a court of law:

'I have something to say about this marriage. Padre, Rosa, here, Rosa Evangelina Fiore, the bride, met this man, this Pompe Funebri, him (here he gestured toward l'Inglese with a contemptuous nod of the head) in Palermo. In the library, the Biblioteca Nationale, where she worked, as assistant junior librarian, under the direction of one Signor Bandiera. She has a silver plate with her name engraved on it. Awarded for twenty-five years service. You can see it displayed on the shelf of the dresser in the kitchen. He said he was a chef, research-ing into the ancient manuscripts, in order to write a cookbook. Turns out that wasn't true. Like a lot of the other things he told her. He didn't even tell her his real name. But let me go on. So, she agreed to give him cookery lessons. And, of course, one thing led to another, in the heat of the kitchen, and they began an affair with each other: stripping off, smearing each other with food and so on, you get the idea. Sorry, Padre, I didn't mean to make you blush. Anyway, one day, Rosa has it in mind to make a *braciolettine*. She has all the ingredients: the beef, salami, *caciocavallo* and *pecorino*, tomatoes, raisins, pine nuts, onions et cetera. Carries them over there in her basket. Finds he's disappeared. Vanished. Not so much as a good-bye. Nothing. Gone. Like he's never really existed. Distraught, she is. Starts a fire in her apartment and nearly dies. But she doesn't die. She survives. Her Siamese twin brothers, the ones that were murdered before you came among us, went and fetched her back. Soon after, her mother also dies. Her brothers, yes, they're all sitting here, think she murdered her mother, and she will never forget that. So she takes over the running of the farm. Over time she begins to see that this affair with this Pompe Funebri was just a sort of summer fling. You know the sort of thing, we've all done it, well, not you Padre, obviously, but the rest of us sinners, for sure. She knows it wouldn't work out between them, in real life. She used to ask herself 'could our love have lasted beyond that glorious summer?' And of course the answer has to be: no. So, anyway, she's okay. She's over it. And then, in the spring, in the time of the wild asparagus, I come to find her. I know as soon as I lay eyes on her that she is my destiny. I love her. And she loves me. She does. She tries to deny it. But it's bubbling up in-side her, like the sap rising in the spring. And just then, just as we were poised on the brink of coming together, this Inglese, this Pompe Funebri turns up, out of the blue, after four years of silence'.

Here Mauro paused, and some of the members of the congregation seized the opportunity to shake their heads woefully, to clear their throats, or shift their positions in their seats. A few of the babies let out cries which were quickly muffled, and Carciofo began to tap with a dainty hoof on the marble pavement.

'Yes, he comes back', Mauro continued, 'like a bad penny, he turns up again. And Guera and Pace were murdered that same night. Does he have a plausible explanation for why he disappeared? Where he's been for four years? No, of course not. There were *complications* he said. So he hangs around. Tells her he's not really a chef. This time he's a gambler. And so he idles around on the farm, but the ways of the farm don't suit him; he's got a phobia of chickens, for one thing, he faints at the sight of a pig being slaughtered, and he's in a state of perpetual agitation about his hair falling out: he thinks it's the water. He doesn't do any work, doesn't even lend a hand at harvest time, just spends his time oiling his hair, teaching a parrot to speak English, and fleecing people at cards. Then he comes out with a story about him being a spy, a secret agent with the FBI, something of that sort. And she believes it. Nobody else in the region believes it. But she does. She is a bit gullible. But that's part of her charm. Her landlady in Palermo had the measure of her, and him, the poor old woman who got burned alive in the inferno. She said there were men out there who would take advantage of a girl of such naiveté and such big bosoms. And he has done. Next week he'll probably tell her he's a Martian. And she'll believe him. Look around you. Has he invited one single solitary person to this wedding? No. He must be the only person in the world who doesn't know a single other person in the world to invite to his wedding. What's he hiding, eh? Answer me that. We've already had one conman come amongst us, with disastrous consequences for the family'.

Here Giuseppe began to sob, and many in the congregation crossed themselves.

Mauro continued:

'Anyway, all that is just the background. What I really want to say is this: this marriage cannot go ahead. Rosa does not love this man. She just feels bad about letting him go. In her heart she loves me. But she's just too stubborn to admit it'.

Padre Goffredo said gently:

'Is this true, Rosa? Do you have doubts about Signor Funebri? Do you really love Mauro here?'

I felt all eyes burning into me and I could not look at l'Inglese.

'Yes', I said, 'I do love him. But also I love Signor Funebri. I love both of them'. And I realized it was true. I did.

'You can't marry both of them, Rosa', said Padre Goffredo.

'I know', I said, quietly, and in the *chiesa* there was complete silence, and I felt everybody hanging on the weight of my words.

'When I'm with Signor Funebri I love him. But when he's not here I... I...have doubts'.

Padre Goffredo nodded. 'But, my child, if you have doubts, you are not ready to take these sacred vows. Could it be that you are confusing lust with love? If it is only when you are in the bed with him that you love him, then that is not a solid basis for a marriage'.

'I know it, Padre', I said.

'Rosa, you need to think about this very carefully. I cannot conduct the sacrament of marriage if you are in doubts as to your true feelings. Holy matrimony is the union of one man with one woman. There isn't room for three'.

'I know it, Padre', I said, feeling like a child, 'I'm sorry'. I turned to l'Inglese, 'I'm so sorry'.

His face looked like a piece of paper crumpled up. Then, in that moment of awkwardness, there was a shout at the back of the *chiesa*, and stampeding up the aisle was none other than Aventina Valente, and she was shrieking:

'If he's free, I'll marry him'.

And Padre Goffredo said:

'Which?'

And Aventina Valente said:

'I don't mind. Either one will do for me. I'll have the one she doesn't want'.

And Padre Goffredo said:

'This is disgraceful. The levity with which all of you are treating this sacred sacrament. The one she doesn't want, indeed! Like a husband is some kind of booby prize. I suggest all of you go away and reflect on what you really do want'.

Then I felt myself being picked up. It was Mauro's hands that were lifting me and he put me in front of him on the mule's back and Carciofo took off. He started to fly. It was incredible. He flew through the *chiesa*. Admittedly, he did not fly high off the ground, but went low along the aisle and through the double doors at the far end, and then, from the top of the steps, he soared upward, high into the sky. I had a great fear of falling, and suddenly the strong hands were

no longer holding me, and I slipped from the mule's back. I plum-
meted down to earth, and it was then that I woke up.

I felt a huge surge of relief that it had been a dream. That it hadn't
really happened. That my marriage had not really been such a farce.
It was just a dream. A stupid dream. Of course there are some people
who say that dreams are the expressions of your real true feelings. But
I don't believe that. With me they're usually only embarrassing nonsense, and the last thing that I would really want to happen.

It was my wedding day and it was supposed to be the happiest day of
my life. But I felt uncertain. I'm sure it's natural to feel a little nervous. That's all it was. Nerves. Anyway, wedding or no wedding, it
was time to get up and feed the pigs.

CHAPTER FIFTY FIVE

The morning of my wedding.

I was dressed in the fairy princess bridal gown, really dressed this time, I wasn't dreaming. It had the crinoline skirt, the low cut bodice embroidered with thousands of tiny seed pearls, and the long, tight sleeves that ended with little points on the backs of my hands.

I had put up my hair the best I could and Biancamaria Ossobucco helped me to put on the veil and the diamond tiara; underneath I had on the flimsy new underwear we had bought at the *festa*, and the dainty shoes (naturally, they pinched).

The triplets were beautiful in their little white dresses. Biancamaria Ossobucco was sobbing heartily and I did hope once again that she would not go into labor. At least not until after the ceremony.

I took one final around. I was leaving the *fattoria* as myself for the last time. When I came back, I would be someone else: the mysterious stranger, Signora Funebri. It would be odd. I had been Rosa Fiore all my life.

In the parlor, everything was arranged for the feast. The platters were piled high, lined up and covered over: there were the lovely hams which Roberta had provided the day l'Inglese came back, and which had been salted and smoked. There was the rich, dark blood sausage also. There were the stuffed artichokes, the winter greens, and the salads of lemons and oranges flavored with fennel and black olives. In the centre was l'Inglese's magnificent wedding cake. There were two cakes, one large, and above it, supported on stilts like a road to nowhere, was a baby cake, and both of them were covered with smooth white icing which he had decorated with swirls and stars and flowers.

I went down the steps into the yard. It was cold. Of course it was. But I couldn't wear an old coat over the top of the dress. I felt I wanted to say goodbye to the pigs. They thought I had come with a second breakfast for them and were disappointed that I hadn't. The dogs and the cats were watching too for they had sensed there was something unusual going on in the life of the farm.

A car came into the yard. A big car. Very shiny and clean. With a driver. Biancamaria Ossobucco had arranged it. I would have been happy to go in the cart, but she said it was too cold. We got in, the triplets, Biancamaria Ossobucco, Rosario, and me. And we drove into town for what felt like the last time.

When we got there the bells were ringing out and seemed very loud, as though the volume had been turned up, and everybody was looking.

Rosario propelled Biancamaria Ossobucco up the steps, and they disappeared inside. A cold wind blew, making my veil billow out like a sail, and there was the threat of rain in the air. The triplets held their little posies in their hands, following close behind me, and we went up the steps and through the open doors.

Dolci

Desert

CHAPTER FIFTY SIX

I realized I had been sitting in the pink, plush armchair for some time, because the winter afternoon was growing dark around me. The feast was congealing on the table. I had never liked to see food go to waste. I suppose the guests felt bad about coming to eat, in the light of what had happened. Well, the hams and the sausage would keep. The salads and the potatoes could be made into something, or if not, they could be fed to the pigs. The cake too, would keep. It had brandy in it, so that would preserve it. But who would eat it, now?

It was hard to move around in the big dress. I should take it off. I would do soon. Then I would stop being the bride. I wasn't a bride. I was in a bride's dress. But a bride is someone who is getting married. I wasn't getting married. I was a bogus bride.

In *la cucina* I was greeted by Betty:

'Here comes the bride, big, fat and wide'.

I picked up his cage.

'Don't shoot', he squawked, 'I'm an agent with the FBI'.

Gently I carried him to the door and out into the yard. The time had come. I opened the little door to the cage, but he didn't want to come out into the cold. I had to reach in, and take him in my hand. I was surprised how small he was; his personality was too big for that scrawny body.

'Good bye, my love', he screamed, and I launched him into the air.

As I watched him fly away a taxi drew up to the gate. A taxi. It had driven all the way from Palermo. I feared the return of Signor Rivoli, but it was not him. It was Doctor Carmine Luni, the missing dentist of big Patty May Freeway. He was responding to the cable urging him to come straight over with a false front tooth to replace the one she had lost in the eruption. He had a huge growth of beard, was thin and pale, and his clothes were ragged and hung off his body, but he clutched his bag of instruments proudly, and had in the trunk a rather battered cylinder of laughing gas. He was American, but his parents were from Agrigento, and he could speak a little of our language. I told him that Patty May had returned to Chicago months ago with the gap still in her teeth. He apologized for the delay, saying that he had been shipwrecked just west of the Azores, and had spent one hundred and fifty days marooned on a rocky outcrop with only toothpaste for sustenance. I felt sorry for him, but there was nothing I could do. Sadly he directed the taxi driver to take the Palermo road once again, and, with a wave, he was gone.

I was still sitting lost in thought in *la cucina* when Mauro came in. He picked me up like a doll and threw me over his shoulder.

'You won't regret it', he said, 'I won't ever give you a moment's cause to regret it', and with that he carried me up the stairs and into the bedroom.

CHAPTER FIFTY SEVEN

That day was two years ago now. Mauro was right, he has never given me any reason to regret what I did. But I did feel bad about it, nevertheless. L'Inglese deserved better treatment than I had given him: announcing in front of a packed congregation that in my heart I loved another man.

In the time between then and now, Biancamaria Ossobucco did go in to labor, not straight away, as I feared she would, but later, not until nearly a year after the tragedy of the murder of the twins and her new marriage, which stopped the clacking tongues that would have liked to insinuate some impropriety. I did help to deliver the babies, assisted this time by Ombretta Gengiva, and they were not joined, as Biancamaria Ossobucco feared. This time they were boy triplets, and, according to tradition, they were named after me, and their father also, and they were called Rosario, Rosio, and Rosalmo, and they were the sweetest, most angelic cherubs you could imagine, apart from my nieces, of course.

Following that happy time, Sophia Bacci gave birth to another baby boy, only one, but a good big one, and his name was Geronimo. When I visited the mother and baby shortly after the birth, Sophia was lit up from inside with a bright light of joy and I think she was truly happy for the first time in her life, and I was glad, and could not stop myself from weeping.

So now I worked with Mauro to run the farm, and we worked together side by side, and we lived together, and we loved together, and we cooked together, and what we had together was solid and good and real. There were not the highs and lows of my brief times with l'Inglese. I felt almost always happy, and almost always had a smile on my face, and often used to burst into song for no reason at all except that I just felt like singing.

Mauro wanted us to be married, for he wanted our love to be celebrated in the church, and known to everyone, and not be thought second best, but I didn't agree. I had tried being a bride before, and it hadn't worked. We were happy as we were, and I didn't think the benediction of Padre Goffredo would make any difference. I hoped that Donna Magnolia would come and live at the *fattoria*, but she wanted to stay on her own little farm on the other side of the volcano. I hoped one day she would change her mind, and Mauro, in turn, hoped one day I would change my mind also.

In truth, I did not think about l'Inglese very much at all, but, in the fleeting moments when he did cross my mind, I secretly wondered if he had been simply the creation of one of my vivid dreams. Had I just dreamed it all?

But then a flock of little green parrots would flutter down, for Betty had found a mate, and had bred a fine, large family, and they would chatter together in English, so he must have been real after all, and they would say in a chorus: 'I'm with the FBI', and Mauro threatened to shoot them.

Then, quite suddenly, in the midst of my happiness, I became ill, and I knew, in my heart, I was dying.

How could I leave my Mauro, now that we had found each other at last? My heart contracted at the prospect of parting from him. He was like a warm cloud around me. He made everything in my life good. I loved him totally; there were no doubts. I loved his mind, his kindness, his warmth, his way of looking at the world, his humor, his intelligence, his way of talking, his practicality and industry, his generosity, his cooking, the way everybody liked him — nobody in the region had a bad word to say about him. Physically, I loved him passionately: his body, the way his body made my body feel, his face, his smile, his big, honest hands, even his ears were beautiful to me. I had thought we would be together forever. That we would grow into old people together, and though we might be crooked and rickety then, we would still go everywhere together holding hands. We would still have endless, interesting conversations, still make one another laugh, still cook each other delicious meals, still make love in the night, and I knew, even if I lived to be a hundred, I would still feel a sense of joy and wonder at finding his sweet face next to mine when I woke up each morning. Now that wasn't going to be. I wasn't going to live. I was going to die and leave him alone, and when I had a sudden vision of his black figure visiting my rain lashed grave the next *i Murticieddi* I felt my heart would break.

My nieces, who were now five, were another burden on my dying heart. The thought that I wouldn't live to see them grow up into fine, strong women gave me a physical pain that stopped my breath.

When I looked around me at the farm, I felt a very great sorrow that the times and the seasons of the year would pass without me. Next year I wouldn't smell the orange blossom borne on the breeze. My kitchen garden would revert to being a scrubby patch without my tender care. I wouldn't feel the sun on my skin, or be here for the peach harvest or the making of the '*strattu* or the pressing of the olives. The happy chatter of the pigs would go on without my hearing it, and, when the time came, I would not be the one to slaughter them, and salt them, and make them into hams. I would miss plunging my hands into the cool, creamy curds of the fresh ricotta during the cheese making. I would miss so many things, and I didn't want to let them go. And so, from being happy, I became sad.

Of course, Mauro was worried about me, particularly when I lost my appetite, and my interest in food. He tried to tempt me with succulent morsels: the calves brains which he knew I particularly loved; the fresh grilled sardines; the zucchini flowers stuffed with ricotta which had previously been one of my favorite dishes; the salad of dandelions which are good for the liver; even the chicken broth with *pastina*, the food of invalids, but that also I could not stomach. I grew thin for the second time in my life (the first time was in the Infirmary after the fire), and I grew gray. Sometimes my body just wanted to stay in bed, and I had never felt like this before.

When his culinary cures failed, Mauro urged me to consult Dr Leobino. But I would not. I am ashamed to say that I am afraid of doctors. I have never in my life consulted Dr Leobino on my own account. I knew that he would only confirm the horrible truth that I was dying, and couldn't face hearing that from him, not yet. That time would come later.

But one day, when I was carrying the pail of breakfast for the pigs down the steps, I felt my legs buckle beneath me and everything went black. It was then that Dr Leobino was called in, in spite of my determination that he should not.

CHAPTER FIFTY EIGHT

When I opened my eyes Dr Leobino swam into view like a shark and quickly I shut my eyes again and feigned sleep. That way he wouldn't be able to tell me the awful truth.

'Rosa', he said, 'can you hear me?'

'No', I lied.

'Come on, Rosa, it's not as bad as you think'.

I opened one eye, and looked at him through it.

'It isn't?'

'No. You're not dying. You're going to have a baby'.

'But I can't be', I gasped, 'I'm fifty years old'.

'Believe me, you are', he said, 'I've seen many a pregnancy in my time, and you have all the symptoms'.

So I wasn't going to die, after all. I was going to have a baby. I lay back in my bed thinking about it. And I felt more astonished than I have ever felt about anything.

CHAPTER FIFTY NINE

Shortly after this Mauro and I did get married. Although I had said
that getting married did not work out for me, we both felt that our
baby should be born inside a marriage, and I was so glad not to be
dying, I felt reborn, and was prepared to do anything I could to confirm my grip on life.

It was a small wedding, although I did once say there is no such thing
as a small wedding in our region. Neither of us wanted the big fuss
of a big one. I had the navy two-piece – very smart it was, and I
had a pair of red high heels. Red! Think of that. There were eats
and drinks in plenty. Mauro saw to the buffet, for the smell of certain
foods made me feel peculiar, and I could not stomach anything other
than *cassateddi di ceci*, the sweet chickpea fritters we eat only in
March to celebrate the feast of San Giuseppe.

Everybody was happy for us, and said we belonged together. They
had always thought it, and it was only my own obstinacy that didn't
see it. It's a sobering thought that you can reach the age of fifty, and
still everybody knows what is better for you than you know yourself.

Finally Donna Magnolia did move in to the little cottage that Rosario had vacated. She would not live in the *fattoria* because she said
two women cannot share a kitchen, and I suppose she was right. She

said she wanted to make the most of her grandchild in the time that was left to her, for she had predicted that her own death would come on 27th January, but she didn't know what year. I hoped it would be a 27th January far in the future, and I was overjoyed at her coming. I remembered when, at the time of the eruption, she had predicted the birth of a baby, but I never imagined it would be mine.

Shortly after she came, the baby also started to come. It was a night early in the spring when the air was filled with the plump, sweet scent of almond blossom, and the newly married doves were cooing in their nests. Biancamaria Ossobucco was at my side (she was now Biancamaria Bufalino, but I could never call her anything other than Biancamaria Ossobucco), and Ombretta Gengiva came, it would have been impossible to keep her out, and, like her mother before her, she was crop–full of news:

'You know, Rosa, yesterday a woman in Malvagna gave birth to a monkey'.

Neither I nor Biancamaria Ossobucco said a word.

'Yes', she continued, without needing any encouragement. 'I heard it from Isotta Tripotto who heard it from Monima Botta who saw it herself with her own eyes. She was in Malvagna helping her married sister Galena prepare pastries. They were grinding the almonds when they heard the screams of the poor woman coming from across the street, and abandoning everything they ran into the house. They were the first to arrive and they saw everything. Yes, they saw the monkey swinging from the bedstead by the long tail. It had the thick brown fur, the long arms, the horrible fingers, the ears, the ugly muzzle. Everything, in short, belonging to the monkey. The mother immediately lost her wits. She went into a fit and bit through her tongue. The husband, he too was crazy. When he saw the beast that had sprung from his loins he took up his shotgun and prepared to blast off his own head. If Monima Botta had not wrestled it from his grasp he would be lying dead this minute'.

Of course I didn't believe a word of this nonsense, but at least listening to Ombretta Gengiva's prattle was a welcome distraction from the pain. But Biancamaria Ossobucco who, as I have mentioned before, is a gullible soul, crossed herself surreptitiously as she listened to Ombretta Gengiva's words.

'You do well to cross yourself, sister', Ombretta Gengiva continued. 'Sure enough it is an omen. My mamma often used to tell the tale of when she delivered your first husbands in this very house. 'Two heads joined to one body', she used to say to me, 'the look on Isabella Fiore's face when she beheld them'. I know that look myself, I saw it on the face of Angela Forbicina when I delivered those joined up babies of hers'.

Without pausing for breath, Ombretta Gengiva continued:

'Of course, Isabella was not the only one of the Fiores to give birth to a freak of nature. Carmela Fiore, your great grandmother, was delivered of a creature that had the gills and scales of a fish. It was dead of course. Such a thing could not survive, and in the midst of the hullaballoo the cat that had got in through the open window snatched it up and carried it off for his supper'.

'Ombretta Gengiva', I said, appalled, 'How can you spout such rubbish?'

'It's not rubbish at all', she said, offended, 'My Nonna told it to me. She was the one that pulled it out by its scaly tail. Why, Rosa Fiore, I could tell you things that would make your hair fall out in clumps'.

'I'd rather keep my hair on my head', I told her firmly, but nevertheless she went on with her tall stories late into the night, her voice mixing with the footsteps of Mauro pacing up and down the corridor, the barking of a distant dog, and, when the pain became too much, my own half-smothered screams.

When morning finally came, it found me the mother of a normal, single, beautiful, big baby boy. He had a full set of teeth, just as I had, and which is believed among our people to be a sign of good fortune. He was as wide as he was long, almost square, with big black eyes, the image of his father, and we called him Maurito.

I have never felt happier, or more proud of any dish that I have made, than I did when I looked at little Maurito, and I could not stop looking at him, and marveling how I could have grown such a perfect little thing: the tiny fingers and toes and lips and nose and cheeks and eyelashes, and the scent of him, that sweet baby scent that I could not stop myself inhaling. Big Mauro could not stop crying, he was like a spigot, and he would not put Maurito down, but carried him everywhere showing him his little world. Donna Magnolia could not stop clucking like a mother hen, and claimed, to anybody who would listen, that all had come about just as she had predicted. The baby Rosas were the only ones not entirely happy. They were, in truth, a little bit jealous, for they didn't want to share Zia Rosa with the big baby that had come in the night. They had enough of babies with their new brothers, and thought that all of them should be put together into the pigsty to live with the pigs. Of course, Biancamaria Ossobucco, that good-hearted soul, was weeping and fainting by turns, my father Rosario the half-wit swelled with pride, and even Carciofo could not stop braying, but whether it was with joy, or because he had the toothache, I cannot say.

The last thing I have to say is this: that same morning, the morning when the first of the wild asparagus was blooming, three years since Mauro had come amongst us, a Friday, it was, the postman brought me a letter, postmarked Chicago. Inside there was no writing, just a cutting from a newspaper announcements column and it said: 'Mrs Aventina Valente Fiore of Near North Side, Chicago, widow of Mr

Luigi Fiore, and Sir Pomfrey Farquarson–Fortiscue, Baronet, of Cragievar Castle, Aberdeenshire, Scotland, announce their intention to marry on March 20th'.

So l'Inglese and Aventina Valente had become a couple, and were, that very same day, the day of Maurito's birth, getting married on the far side of the ocean. It is strange how things work out, isn't it? So that was the end of the story, the story of l'Inglese. I pasted the slip of newspaper into my scrapbook, shut it up, and put it away.

The End

CPSIA information can be obtained at www.ICGtesting.com
Printed in the USA
LVOW10s0454100616

491939LV00028BA/965/P